WILD SCOTTISH GOLD
THE ENCHANTED HIGHLANDS
BOOK SEVEN

TRICIA O'MALLEY

LOVEWRITE PUBLISHING

WILD SCOTTISH GOLD
THE ENCHANTED HIGHLANDS SERIES
Book 7

Copyright © 2025 by Lovewrite Publishing
All Rights Reserved

Editors: Marion Archer, David Burness, Julia Griffis

All rights reserved. No part of this book may be reproduced in any form by any means without express permission of the author. This includes reprints, excerpts, photocopying, recording, or any future means of reproducing text.

If you would like to do any of the above, please seek permission first by contacting the author at: info@triciaomalley.com

"Love is the only gold." — *Alfred Lord Tennyson*

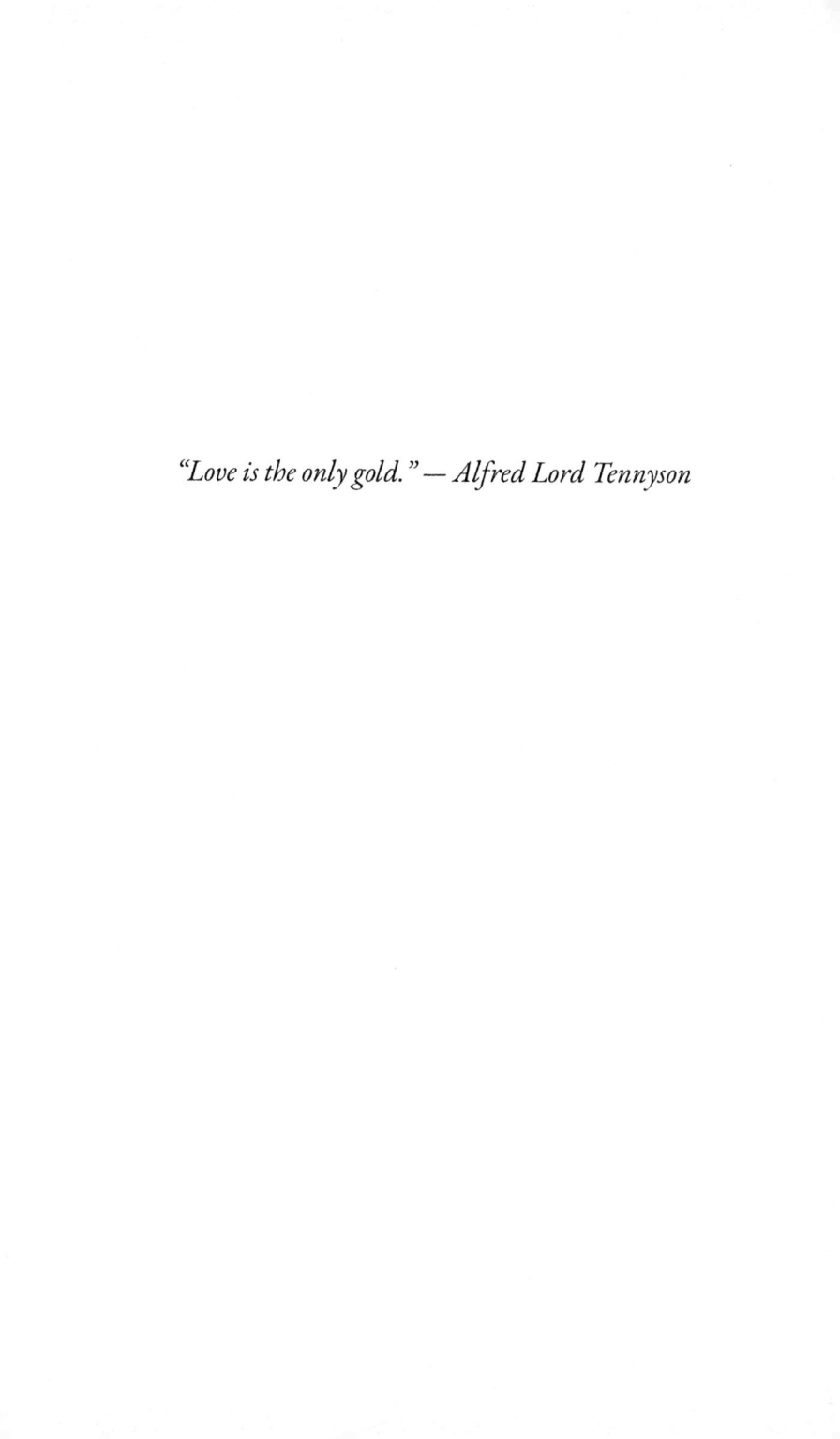

GLOSSARY OF SCOTTISH WORDS/SLANG

- Bloody – a word used to add emphasis; expletive
- Bonnie – pretty
- Hen – woman, female
- "It's a dreich day" – cold; damp; miserable
- Lorry – work truck
- Och – used to express many emotions, typically surprise, regret, or disbelief
- Scran – food
- Shoogly – unsteady; wobbly
- Tatties – potatoes
- Tetchy – crabby, cranky, moody
- Tea – in Scotland, having tea is often used to refer to the dinnertime meal
- Wee – small, little
- Wheesht (haud your wheesht) – be quiet, hush, shut up

PROLOGUE

Kaia

"What is this place? I thought we were going to Cartier."

I bit back my suggestion that they, indeed, should go to Cartier and instead angled the tray of gold rings to better catch the light.

"No, baby. This is *better* than Cartier. An original artist. Don't you want something unique that nobody else has?"

The woman, who wore every brand name under the sun, so many logos on her outfit that I gave up trying to read them all, glared at the man beside her. She towered over him, likely from the spikey heels she wore, and he grinned up at her. Tanned, reeking of wealth, and likely dating more than one such arm candy, the man slid me a quick glance.

I pasted a polite smile on my face.

I didn't feel like being polite. I wanted to take my tray of rings and boot the people out of the shop that I was showcasing my jewelry in this weekend. It was a trial run, to see if there were clientele for my pieces, and I was hating every moment of it.

I'd even dressed up for this, but apparently not well enough, based on the look of derision in Arm Candy's eyes. Even so, I kind of wanted to ask her what she used to get her hair so shiny. When she stuck out her lower lip and pouted, I knew I wasn't getting a sale. But at least I could get some intel.

"Sorry to ask, but your hair is just so pretty. What product do you use that gets it so shiny?"

Instantly the woman transformed from annoyed and petulant to engaged. Swinging her glossy mane over her shoulder, she leaned forward, nudging the tray of rings aside.

"Listen, I'll tell you this because you probably can't afford the product that I tell people I'm using ..." She tapped one manicured nail on my arm, her eyes earnest. "But the secret is a touch of castor oil—not too much—while your hair's still wet."

"Is that so?" Hmm, maybe I'd give it a try.

"Good for the dark circles under your eyes too." The woman gave me a pointed look and I internally winced. Right, so I hadn't been sleeping well these days.

Who could blame me when my life was falling apart?

If this woman looked close enough, she'd see where I'd hastily filled the scuff marks on my only pair of black heels with a permanent marker this morning. She didn't need to, though, having sized me up and dismissed me as not one of her ilk the instant she walked in the door and scanned my outfit. That being said, she'd warmed up marginally, and at least conversation would make the time pass. Any conversation.

To say business was slow was an understatement. Why the jewelry store owners had insisted on a Fourth of July sale *on* the actual holiday, I did not know. My luck had only worsened when they'd also picked that same day to allow me to showcase some of my new work. *Finally.*

Now I couldn't help but wonder if they'd just been looking for someone to run the store while they got sunburned at the beach with a cooler full of cold Corona beers. I couldn't say I blamed them. If someone was stupid enough, in other words, *me*, to say they'd work on a national holiday, well, I'd probably be at the beach too.

Sighing, I waited while the brunette nudged the tray of rings, finally giving them a quick glance. Only then did her eyes widen slightly.

"Hey, these aren't so bad."

Gee, thanks.

"See, baby? I'm telling you, sometimes it pays to be the person who starts the trends." Sweat glistened on the man's brow and I suspected he might be struggling with money issues. My prices were considerably cheaper than

Cartier's, so if he could convince his special lady friend to buy a piece from me, he might be off the hook—for whatever it was he was atoning for.

I just needed to sell one more ring. Two would be ideal.

It would be enough to cover my plane ticket out of hell to Scotland.

Dramatic, much?

Why yes, *yes*, I was. That being said, my current life situation had degraded to the point of barely tolerable and was lackluster on a good day. My bags were packed. My tools were ready to ship. The rest I'd sold or was in storage.

I just needed a few more sales and one extremely awkward conversation before I'd be on my way to Scotland, where I'd been promised a new beginning.

One *meager* inheritance of a tiny cottage, a barely running car, or so I was told, and a pillow to lay my head on. Furnished was the key word I'd heard from the solicitor who'd called me when a distant auntie had died. With no kin of her own, the cottage had somehow worked its way down to me, and frankly, I was happy for it. The pictures made it look charming, if 1970s pea-green carpeting and faded cabbage rose wallpaper was your thing.

It could be my thing if it got me away from Stan. Boring, dull, ever so patient Stan. Somehow, he'd worked himself into my life, rescuing me when my apartment building had flooded, and the relief I'd felt at not having to worry about rent for a few weeks had turned into a much longer roommate situation. One where Stan was convinced I was meant for him. I slept fully clothed on the couch, waking before he rose so I could shower and disappear to avoid the gross conversation that, no, I wouldn't put on a Princess Leia bikini and role-play while he laughed like Jabba the Hutt.

"You know ... this one is quite pretty actually."

I snapped back from daydreams of sleeping in a real bed again and beamed as the woman picked up one of my rings. I'd had a lot of fun with that one, hammering the gold and melding it so it twisted and coiled around the finger like a snake, and had dotted it with pavé diamonds down the back.

"Even better? You can stack it with this band, like so."

I showed her how she could interlock it with another band, making it seem like two sparkly snakes twirled around her finger, and she gasped.

"Oh, I love the mixed metals. White and rose gold. This is like Bvlgari, but cooler."

"See, baby? I told you this stuff was neat." The man dabbed at his brow with a handkerchief.

"We'll take it." The woman nodded to me, and I beamed at my new best friend. Unbeknownst to her, she'd just secured my ticket to a new life. I just prayed the man's credit card wouldn't be declined. The woman stepped away to wander around the room, looking at the other cases, while the man turned to me.

"How much?"

"Four thousand for the pair."

He blanched and pulled out his wallet. I saw a wad of cash and worry kicked up.

"Discount for cash."

The man opened his money clip and counted his bills.

"Can you do three hundred off?"

"Yup, no problem."

No problem at all, *sir*. Cash was king and I would be more than happy to take his money. He handed it over, and I quickly tucked it away. Out of sight, out of mind. Wrapping up the packages in pretty navy-blue boxes with gold etching on the outside, I handed the woman a bag with a bow knotted at the top.

"I hope you enjoy it as much as I enjoyed making them."

"Thanks." The woman breezed to the door, the man following one step behind her. Just before they left, she bent her head to his, and I caught her words.

"But we're still going to Cartier, right, baby?"

I shook my head, walking over to lock the doors after them, seeing the guy pleading with the woman in the parking lot.

I didn't care that the day was only half done.

I had what I'd come here for.

Picking up the phone, I dialed the owners.

"Hey, Debra? So sorry to do this to you, but I'm sick. Yes, horrible stomach cramps. I have to go."

I didn't like to lie, but Debra didn't seem to mind. Seeing as they'd only had one customer in four hours, I couldn't blame her. Instructing me to lock up for the day, I followed her orders and then hightailed it out of the store, already looking up flights on my phone. The good thing about last-minute Fourth of July sales?

I scored myself a killer deal on a ticket to Scotland.

Now to discover this so-called family of mine and just what kind of inheritance I'd really been granted.

CHAPTER ONE

Kaia

The clock struck the top of the hour, sending the kinetic mechanisms into a flurry of motion, and I craned my neck to take in the full glory of the thirty-foot Millennium Clock at Edinburgh's National Museum.

An Egyptian monkey statue sat on a large iron wheel and moved back and forth as the wheel spun, sending spirals twirling out from its center, cogs flying into motion, which in turn kicked off a flurry of activity inside the clock.

Glass eyes gleamed from burned wood crevices on the side.

Requiem figures twirled in a rainbow of color beaming through tinted glass panes.

Bells chimed.

A warning or a promise, I couldn't be certain, but the fine hairs at the back of my neck lifted.

I stepped back, craning my neck to see the spire, my thoughts consumed with the level of craftsmanship necessary to create such a large-scale and intricate piece. Consumed, I didn't track my surroundings well and slammed into what felt like a rock-hard statue.

Turning, I gasped, putting my hands out to catch what I thought was my blunder at tripping over priceless artwork.

Instead my hands met a *very* warm, *very* muscular, *very* male chest.

Shit.

This man was imposing, and I was not someone who typically allowed myself to be imposed upon. I wasn't a small woman by any means and prided myself on muscles honed by long hours of working as a metalsmith. Somehow, this man managed to make me feel ... almost dainty. An unusual feeling, to be sure, and one I'd file away to think about later.

In the meantime, I needed to make my apologies and step back from this towering brute of a man.

"I'm *so* sorry," I said, waving a hand in the air as I subtly slid a step backward. Off balance, I stumbled, and his hands came out to steady me.

At my waist.

It was such an intimate touch from a stranger, one whom I hadn't even gotten a clear look at yet, that a shiver danced across my skin. His hands felt like iron just pulled from the forge, heating through my shirt and searing the skin at my sides.

"Nae bother, lass." His voice, rough around the edges as though unused, was tinged with the music of the Highlands. "Are you all right, then?"

I forced myself to look up from where I stared at the intricate metal necklace he wore, the thick silver medallion hung on a leather cord shaped in a complicated design featuring a thistle and sword, and blinked up at one of the most handsome men I'd ever seen in real life.

My mouth went dry.

My pulse sped up.

I immediately threw out all plans of trying to see Greyfriar's Bobby. A new plan formed.

One which involved me, this mouthwatering Scotsman, and a gift to myself for finally starting a new chapter. And what better way to kick it off than with a proper hookup with what I dearly hoped was one very *improper* Scotsman.

My flirting skills were rusty at best, as I'd largely checked out of the dating game two years ago after I decided that I couldn't be trusted to pick good men for myself. I'd been on a hiatus of sorts since, but this wasn't about dating.

Oh no. This was about fulfilling a very unrealized need, one that I'd buried for too long.

Dark brown hair, just long enough to curl, a thread of gold running through it, capped a craggy face that was all sharp edges and commanding features. A short beard edged his jawline, and his eyes, God, *his eyes*.

They were the color of calm water just after a storm had blown through.

I smiled up at him, tilting my head, and shot him a flirtatious look from beneath my eyelashes.

A corner of his mouth quirked up, the valleys of his face dipping and rearranging, the sun peeking out over the mountains as he smiled.

His eyes shifted color, deepening slightly, and I caught my breath.

Still waters run deep, and all that.

"I'm not entirely sure if I'm all right," I answered, wetting my lips. "But I'm sure a drink at a local pub with a handsome tour guide such as yourself would help settle me."

Well, hell. It looked like it didn't take much to jump back into the flirting game. But even so, this was probably the most forward I'd ever been in my life, and nerves kicked low in my stomach as I waited to see if he'd be receptive to my invite.

"Och, an American lass, is it? New to town or just on holiday?"

"Just on holiday." It was partly true, as I *was* just on holiday, in Edinburgh at least. I had no need to tell him that I'd be here any longer than that. At least not for now. I gestured to the clock behind me. "I couldn't help but come to see the clock when I heard about it."

"Is that right?" The man's gaze sharpened, and he glanced over my shoulder to where the massive clock still whizzed and buzzed away. "I come to see it every time I'm in Edinburgh, as well. Incredible work."

"It is, isn't it?" Turning, I noted the clock's interior mechanisms slowly whirling to a stop, and admired how the iron had been forged to form so many moving parts. It would have been a fun project, a labor of love, and if I didn't have to make money to live on, I'd likely try to make similar art pieces myself. However, as much as I loved the more detailed work of jewelry design, blacksmithing was where I made the bulk of my income.

But first I'd need my own forge and workshop.

Something I hoped to have remedied soon, based on a few leads I had uncovered in Loren Brae, the town where I'd inherited a small cottage and a bit of land.

"It has a darkness to it, yet I find it to be hopeful."

At that, I glanced over my shoulder, my eyes locking on the stranger's face as he gazed up at the clock. Turning back, I examined all the intricate figures tucked away on the inside of the clock, death and chaos and light, and realized that this piece was both a reflection on our chaotic history and a hope for better tomorrows yet to come.

"Ever onward?" I suggested.

"Exactly that." Approval warmed in the stranger's tone.

"I'd love to get inside there, to see how it runs." I couldn't help that part of my brain that loved to dismantle things and put them back together just so I understood how they worked.

"Same, lass. Same."

A flutter of longing shifted across me, the word *lass*

bringing to light hidden fantasies brought on by one too many nights of binge-watching *Outlander*.

"Well." I cleared my throat and pursed my lips, checking the slim watch I wore at my wrist. "I should be getting on."

"I'd certainly be remiss in my duties of welcoming you to Scotland if I didn't take you for that drink at the pub. Just to make sure you were ... settled ... and all that."

His words held a promise, one that I'd hold him to, if he let me.

"I'm Kaia," I said, offering my hand.

"Thane."

Neither of us offered last names. Instead, Thane offered me his arm, and I threaded my hand through it, marveling at how this man dwarfed me. I wasn't one for needing someone to ride to my aid in times of distress, but if I was, Thane would be perfect for the job.

He led me down the curve of a pretty cobblestoned street, colorful mismatched buildings clambering over each other as much as the people clogging the sidewalks. Window boxes held cheerful flowers, and music lilted from open windows capturing an unseasonably warm evening air. Thane stopped in front of a pub with a sign on the window that proclaimed: "No bairns. Dugs welcome."

I smiled.

"Dugs."

"Aye, lass." Thane hunched his shoulders and growled a bit, mimicking a bigger dog. "Dugs."

Charmed, I swung inside, delighted to find there

were, indeed, a few *dugs* among the mix of patrons gathered at low tables scattered through the room.

"What can I get you?" I opened my mouth to protest, as I was technically the one who had propositioned him, but let it slide. If the man wanted to buy me a drink, he certainly could.

"Guinness, please."

Approval lit in his eyes, and my insides warmed. I wanted to see him looking at me that way in the bedroom, hopefully while on his knees. Rubbing my thighs together at the burst of desire I felt, I distracted myself by admiring a cute bulldog with a tartan bowtie.

Several drinks and a shared pizza later, I tumbled onto the mattress with Thane, both of us knowing this was where we'd been leading all along.

Our conversation had been interesting, but surface level. The only question I desperately needed an answer to—if he was married or involved with someone—had been answered with the evidence of no wedding ring and a promise from him that he was much too busy with work for a relationship. Instead, we'd stuck to light topics through the night—music, Scotland's favorite tourist spots, and favorite sports teams. Nothing too deep.

Nothing that would dig our hooks into the other's soul.

No, tonight was for playing, and I'd found a willing and able partner, and when his mouth slanted over mine, his kiss igniting my desire, I was pleased with my bold decision to flirt with this man.

Friction met me, work-roughened hands sliding over

the soft skin of my stomach, lifting, lifting, until my shirt dragged over my head, and he reached around to unhook my bra with one hand. My breasts fell, full and heavy at my stomach, and he groaned, burying his face between them.

Thane licked, and I arched backward as his hands came to my sensitive breasts, molding them in his rough palms. I gasped out a breath as his thumb slid across a nipple, the scrape as rough as the rusty edge of his voice, and when his lips followed, his teeth tugging lightly, I moaned. Threading my hands through his hair, I angled my hips upward, rubbing against the thick muscles of his thigh.

The man was seriously built.

Needing to touch, I ran my hands down his strong back and tugged at his shirt, pulling it over his head and gaping at the display of muscles that greeted my eyes. Thane was big in the way of men that worked with heavy equipment for a living, no slender and well-honed gym muscles here. No, this man resembled more of a Viking, with his wicked jawline, unruly hair, and broad, strong shoulders.

He was just missing his war braids.

But it didn't stop him from treating my body like land to be conquered, exploring every inch of me with a single-minded focus that had me dangerously tense, but every time I gusted close to an orgasm, he seemed to know, and eased back, leaving me dangling precariously on the edge.

Two could play that game, so I reached between us, clasping his hard length, and he groaned, sinking his teeth into the soft skin at the side of my breast.

"Do you take joy in leaving me unsatisfied, sir?" I asked, squeezing more tightly, and he moaned, his breath hot on my skin.

"Och, the first time you come it will be when I'm buried deep inside ye, lass."

My eyes almost rolled back in my head at the soft burr of his words, and I waited, all but panting in lust, as he sheathed himself with a condom before ranging himself over me.

"Och, and lass?"

"Yes?" I arched my back as he positioned himself between my legs, his body settling on mine, his broad shoulders cocooning me in our own little world.

"Welcome to Scotland."

With that, Thane slid deep, and I shattered around him, pleasure consuming me until dots of light danced behind my eyelids.

And when I woke, hours later, the dim light from the bathroom slanting across his memorable face, I slid from the bed. Pressing my lips together, I dressed quietly, before stopping just at the door of his hotel room.

Though I barely knew the man, I felt reluctant to leave him.

Indecision whirled, but finally, deciding against leaving a note, I slipped quietly from the room, closing the door with a soft click behind me. My body felt loose and satisfied, twinges of soreness in muscles long unused, and despite myself, I grinned.

Welcome to Scotland, *indeed*.

CHAPTER TWO

Thane

It had been six weeks since I'd been home.

And three weeks and three days since my night with the American woman who had flitted in and out of my life, disappearing as quickly as a flame in the wind.

I'd cursed myself more than once for being a deep sleeper, for not asking for her number, a last name—*something*. The taste of her kiss had consumed me, keeping me awake many a night since, while I reminded myself this was why I didn't do casual hookups.

Nothing about my night with Kaia had been casual, and my fingers clenched as I thought about sinking into her softness once more. She'd entranced me from the moment she'd stumbled into me as the clock had chimed its warning bells in the background.

She was a walking contradiction. Glossy dark curls, the color just on the edge of midnight, were piled on her head, tendrils escaping left and right from her bun. Nothing about her face seemed to match, and at the same time, it all worked perfectly together. A large mouth, lips the color of fresh plucked raspberries, seemed at odds with a pert nose. Azure wide-set eyes, blue with flecks of gold and gray, were turned up at the corners and shrouded in inky black lashes. Her body was strong, her stance confident, and yet she was soft and round and irresistibly touchable. Watching her had been like watching a colt first learning to walk, as she spoke in bouts of breezy confidence mixed with an almost strange hesitancy.

It was almost as if someone had told her to quiet down often in her life.

Was she back home now or still traveling in Scotland? We hadn't spoken of our plans, our work, or anything too deep. At the time, it was a simple understanding, a mutual attraction, a silent game we'd both agreed to. We'd both understood the score.

What I hadn't expected was for the scent of her hair to be embedded in my brain.

For six long weeks, I'd been working to repair and upgrade some iron work at Holyrood Palace, one of the most prestigious commissions I'd received to date. I'd been away from my smithy for too long now, but luckily, my second-in-command, Ian, had taken over most of our large projects, as well as the hiring of new crew. He'd even rented out a corner of our warehouse to another blacksmith new to the area who was looking for space to work but hadn't wanted to join our team.

A woman, I was told, who wanted the freedom to also work on jewelry and fine metals when she wasn't taking on grander projects. It was fine by me, as we had more than enough space, and I was always keen for extra streams of income.

Not that I necessarily needed it.

But once a poor lad, always a poor lad, I supposed. It was a hard habit to break, always wanting to know where my next meal was coming from, even though I'd far surpassed even my most grandiose dreams pertaining to my personal wealth. Still, a penny saved is a penny earned and all that, so I'd been happy enough to have a fellow blacksmith in tenancy at our workshop.

Grabbing my thermos of coffee, I left my wee cottage tucked in the hills overlooking Loch Mirren, just shy of a wee town called Loren Brae. I'd drifted that way after I'd completed an internship, having left secondary school early, and knowing I wasn't one for university. No, it had been straight into the trades for me, and I'd been lucky to find a mentor who'd not just taught me how to work with metal, but also how to love the craft. Anyone could weld or fabricate metal in a forge, with enough training, but the ones who looked for the beauty in the craft itself? Those were the ones who could meld art with function.

And those were the ones who scored great commissions—like the project I'd just finished in Edinburgh.

Aye, I was proud of my work, my reputation, and the business I'd built for myself and my employees. Settling in wee Loren Brae had proved to be bountiful for me, as the land for my shop had been cheap, and I had negligible competition in the surrounding area. I'd quickly built a name for myself and was happy to catch some scran at the wee pub in town every week or so.

The morning air was crisp, rain threatening as moody clouds clung low to the horizon as I crested the hill, Loch Mirren spreading before me. An expansive loch, her waters were still today, reflecting the colorful buildings of Loren Brae like someone had tossed a handful of confetti on a puddle. Towering above the village was the grand dame herself, MacAlpine Castle, and she looked as stately and important as ever. My eyes scanned the surface of the loch, looking for any disturbance ... a ripple of ... *anything*, really.

There'd been rumors over the past year or so.

Enough rumors that most of the lads at work were convinced the town was haunted, and I'd even lost two of my best employees when their families had insisted on moving away.

Kelpies, they said.

I wasn't much for mystical stuff and whatnot, but I'd be hard-pressed to explain away a few of the otherworldly shrieks I'd heard in the wee hours of the morning over the past year. The sound was enough to make your blood run cold, and each time, I'd lain in bed wondering when I'd work up the courage to go outside to investigate.

I'd not yet cracked the door open and strode outside. Some might call that weak, but I just called it self-preservation. No need to go borrowing trouble, as they say.

The best I could do was put my nose to the grindstone, keep the jobs coming in for those I did employ, and hope the folks at the castle would sort things out soon enough.

Whatever that entailed.

Turning down a gravel road that ran away from the town, my lorry bumped along the lane until my warehouse came into sight.

Blackwood Forge.

A building and business bearing my own name, with twisted intricate wrought iron gates, and a large sign arching over the drive.

Whistling, I pulled to a stop and grabbed my lunch cool box and thermos, before crossing the lot to where Ian stood in the door, a smile on his face.

"Was fairly certain you'd abandoned us for those posh twats up in Edinburgh." Ian grinned, holding out a hand. Clasping it, I laughed.

"Och, just because I like those wee finger sandwiches with my tea now, doesn't mean I'm posh."

"I knew they'd get to you. It's always those wee sandwiches that take a lad down." Ian shook his head sadly and followed me into the office space built into the front part of the warehouse.

My desk was clear, papers stacked neatly, each pile with notes and labels on top. Turning, I nodded to Ian as he took a seat across from my desk.

"Looks good in here. Thanks for holding it down for me."

"Aye, nae bother." Ian waved a hand, though his face held strain. I knew that look.

"What's up?" I sat and opened my thermos, taking a swig of my black coffee.

"Och, I've been waiting to tell you this. But it's about the distillery."

Common Gin was opening a new distillery on MacAlpine Castle property, and I'd been excited to bid on the project, knowing the owner, Munroe, liked to use local workers where he could.

"Did they not like the bid? I'm happy to go over it with them if there are any questions."

Disappointment filled me as Ian winced. *We've lost out to another company*. I had to admit, this one burned. It wasn't exactly how I wanted to return to work, particularly after such a prestigious job in Edinburgh, and find out that I'd lost out on a project in my own town.

"They've, uh, gone with another." Ian cleared his throat, his eyes drifting to the door. A prickle of unease shot up my back.

"Who won it?" I tapped one finger on the desk, trying to hold down my irritation. Maybe there was still a chance to have a wee chat with Munroe, or perhaps I could partner with the company he'd gone with.

"Och, that's the problem. It's our new tenant." At that, guilt flashed across Ian's face as my mouth dropped open.

"Wait ... what? Our new ...?" I half stood and then slumped back in my seat, dragging a hand through my hair. Lowering my voice, I narrowed my eyes at Ian. He gulped. "The woman?"

"Aye. That's the way of it. Seems Clarke Construction is the contractor, and Orla liked the idea of working with another woman on the project."

"Surely Orla knows we're well suited to the task." I'd worked with Clarke Construction a time or two in the past and had found Orla to be an efficient leader.

Ian just shrugged one shoulder, his lips pressed in a tight line.

"Damn it." I pushed back from the desk.

I'd *really* wanted that bid. It would likely be a fun one, since there would be more artistry involved, and Munroe had a substantial budget. Frustrated, I paced my office.

"How in the world did this woman get a bid in already?"

"Seems she heard talk of it at the pub. She's established herself fairly quickly. Eager to work, that one is." A hint of admiration peeked through, and I turned, glowering at Ian.

"Is she in today?"

Ian shrugged. "Most days she's here by now. As I said, eager to work."

A car door slammed outside and then another, likely my employees showing up for the day.

Taking a deep breath, I worked to tame my frustration—Ian didn't need my shite—knowing it wasn't helpful when we had a newcomer in our midst.

A laugh caught me. My skin prickled with awareness.

I knew that laugh.

I'd *dreamt* of that laugh.

My blood heated, desire unfurling inside me, and I

strode to the door, wondering if one too many sleepless nights had me hallucinating the American woman at my very doorstep.

But no, it wasn't a memory that drifted through the door, chuckling at something one of my workers said.

It was Kaia.

Her laugh died on her lips as her eyes locked with mine, and she froze mid step, the others continuing past her. Only when they saw her stop did they turn and see me in the office doorway.

Their greetings paused as everyone watched me and Kaia locked in a stare.

A throat cleared behind me.

"Um, Thane, this is Kaia Bisset, our new tenant." Ian walked forward, his head swiveling between the two of us. "Kaia, this is Thane Blackwood, the owner of Blackwood Forge."

"Thane." Kaia's voice was a whisper. Hardly the confident, booming laugh I'd heard from before. "I thought that was just a common name in Scotland."

"Um ..." Ian looked back and forth between us, confused.

I waited, wondering how she'd handle this, as I tried to disregard the emotions that burned in my core. Excitement to see her, desire to touch her once more, frustration that she'd taken a job from me. And finally, the rising dread of realization that she was now my tenant, and basically a co-worker, which meant she was off limits to me.

I never, *ever*, mixed work and pleasure. I'd learned

that the hard way and had vowed to never make that mistake again.

"It's lovely to meet you," Kaia said, making the decision for me, as she walked forward and held out her hand. "You've got a great team here, and the workspace has been perfect. I'm lucky to have found this spot."

I took her hand, a lightning bolt of lust surging through me at the smooth touch of her palm against mine, and held those moody blue eyes with my own.

"Aye, we're proud of what we've built here. Welcome to Loren Brae, Kaia."

Heat flashed in her eyes as we both remembered the last time I'd welcomed her to Scotland, buried to the hilt inside her. I dropped her hand, realizing I'd been holding it a moment too long, and took a step back.

My day had just gone from bad to worse, and my frustration was ready to boil over. Turning, I whistled to the lads.

"On you go, lads. We've got a project to finish. Ian? My office."

With that, I left Kaia behind me and closed my office door, needing an actual physical barrier between us, lest I throw her over my shoulder and carry her to my lorry to have my way with her.

Bloody hell, but how was I going to manage this?

"So, uh, that's Kaia." Ian sat gingerly across from me, aware of my tension, but likely still thinking it was about the Common Gin project.

"Enough about Kaia. We need to go over the budget for the Kinross farm."

With that, I bent myself to work. I'd been gone long enough that I didn't need to leave this office anytime soon, and hopefully, that would give me enough time to get my head on straight when it came to the gorgeous American with a bawdy laugh that was apparently sent to make my life a living hell.

"And after that, I'll pop up to the distillery and have a wee chat with Munroe."

Ian gave me a sharp look.

"You'll take the job from Kaia?"

"I didn't say that. I just want to see if there's an opportunity for both of us to work on the project."

"Careful there," Ian said, and then his mouth closed when I glared at him.

"It's my town, Ian. I'll damn well fight for what's mine."

"Right. Whatever you say, boss."

I knew when he called me boss, he was annoyed with me, but I didn't care. What I needed to do was figure out how to reclaim what was mine.

And keep my hands off what would never *be mine. Bloody hell.*

CHAPTER THREE

Kaia

I hadn't expected to start my day with a full-frontal of my past choices, and yet, here we were. Just when I'd started to find my groove, feeling confident in my routine, growing some carefully managed bonds with the others at Blackwood Forge, Thane had to show up and throw everything into a tailspin.

Sure, I'd *known* the boss was called Thane. Enough people spoke of him that I'd been aware, in a vague sense, that the big bossman was off on a huge project and would return at some point. And every time someone said Thane's name, a tiny burst of desire would detonate in my core, reminding me of one of the hottest nights of my life.

I'd told myself, repeatedly, that the chances of my

new landlord being one and the same man that I'd met in Edinburgh were slim to none. In fact, I'd convinced myself so completely that I'd never see Thane again that I'd done a good job of burying the memory of him and had instead focused on starting my life over.

I could still feel the imprint of his hands on me, his lips at my throat, whispering words of desire.

My cheeks flamed and I busied myself with unpacking my bag at my workbench, my back turned to the bustling workshop, as I drew in one shaky breath, and then another.

Leave it to me to be impulsive for the first time in years and get slapped in the face with it weeks later. *Well played, Universe. Thanks for the reminder that I make ridiculous choices.*

It was true, too.

Historically, I collected red flags like prizes when it came to the men in my life.

I'd fallen fast and furious for my first boss outside of my apprenticeship, and had been convinced, down to the very tips of my sparkly painted toenails, that my life was finally falling into place. I'd been able to afford my own studio apartment, was gainfully employed in a job that I'd loved, and falling for the boss had seemed like icing on the cake. At the time, I'd been too blindsided by love to notice the gazillion red flags that I should have paid attention to.

He never took me to his place.

He never held my hand in public.

He never spoke to me in more than a professional manner in the workplace.

He never took me on vacations.

He never stayed overnight at my apartment.

He never wanted to meet any of my friends or family.

It had been my father, in fact, who had finally, *gently*, but *firmly*, called attention to all these issues about the guy I kept raving about that they'd never met.

My sweet parents had always been supportive of me, even when I'd followed a less traditional path into a career that neither of them identified with. Both academics, they'd initially been befuddled by my choice of metalwork, but once they'd seen my commitment and happiness, they'd been on board.

Until my first real job and my subsequent love affair, that is.

And that's what it had been.

An affair.

Even now, four years later, the embarrassment and anger at finding out that my boss had been married still lingered. I'd been so blinded by his attention, by my attraction to him, that I'd missed even the most obvious warning signs. After I'd left that job, I'd gone on a string of rebound dates, increasingly more catastrophic in nature, that had concluded with an intervention from my best friend, Marisa, who'd insisted I take a forced sabbatical from dating until I could get my head on straight. Or as she'd so directly put it: "Get your shit together, Kaia."

Since that time, I'd remained focused on my work,

eschewing dating for late nights at my workbench, crafting jewelry, or working on intricate ironwork designs for my portfolio.

When the chance to move to Scotland had fallen in my lap, well, I'd jumped at it.

And apparently, into the arms of a delectable Scot. This could possibly be considered jumping right back into old poor decision-making patterns. However, there had been no one since Thane—*so, technically, not a habit*—and let's be honest here, would anyone pass up one night with Thane Blackwood? Not only was the man sinfully gorgeous, but he knew what to do with those strong hands … *not to mention his mouth.*

Sighing, I stood, staring down at my workbook containing mock-ups for the Common Gin project, and tried to steady myself against the anxiety that almost had me running for the door.

It wasn't the first of my uncomfortable experiences since moving to Scotland, and it likely wouldn't be my last. As my parents reminded me on our calls, the entire point of moving was to experience change, and with change came discomfort. It was why people so often stayed rooted in one spot, picking the familiar over the unusual, unwilling to navigate the unease that came with new beginnings.

Despite my commitment to stay focused on my designs for Common Gin, when the office door opened, and then slammed, I glanced over my shoulder to see Thane's retreating back. A truck engine revved, gravel spat, and he tore away from the workshop.

I guess I'm not the only one prone to dramatics.

Annoyed with men and their insufferable egos, I gave my worktable a small nod. *This*, I knew. My craft. My first love. Metal could be hard and stubborn, but much like a man, it softened under the right conditions. I needed to keep my head down and stay focused on work, and hope that I could make enough money to cement my stay in Scotland.

I hadn't been here long, but hell, I'd fallen for this country hard.

How could I not?

The cottage I'd inherited, well, it would be a stretch to say it was charming. It was certainly cozy, with only two rooms to the place, and dearly worn around the edges. But it was endearing, it was mine, and I could take my time pulling out the green shag carpeting and peeling back the faded wallpaper. The fact that it had come with a pint-sized Ford Fiesta was a small blessing for me, though I was still in strong negotiations with the gearbox about shifting smoothly. It was a bit rough and tumble, much like the cottage, and frankly, much like me. I figured we'd sort it out together, and slowly I'd make a place for myself here, so long as I kept my head down and did a good job for my clients.

Client, that is.

Just one client at the moment.

But it was a significant one, and if I could just ignore the weird things I was seeing out of the corner of my eye on the worksite, I'd be just fine.

Just fine indeed. Closing my eyes, I took a steadying breath.

Ghosts aren't real. You're just jet-lagged.

Except I'd been here long enough that *that* excuse was wearing thin. I'd had a few, mmm, *episodes*, I suppose, where I'd caught movement in my peripheral vision. A woman drifting by in a green dress. A transparent highland cow poking his head around the corner of the castle. It was all very, well, *Scottish*, I guess. At least the mystical and moody Scotland I'd dreamt about as a kid when my parents had told me we still had a few relatives scattered about here.

And now here I was. In Loren Brae, planting roots for myself and making a name for my business, Iron & Ember, one day at a time. The village was pretty as a picture, and I'd even stopped into the pub after work a time or two with the lads from the forge. Though a few had made hints of flirting with me, I'd quickly discouraged any thoughts in that direction.

Work and sex did not mix.

I'd need a conversation with Thane at some point, if only to smooth his clearly ruffled feathers. It seemed he had more of an issue with our dalliance than I had. At least that was my story and I was sticking to it. Never mind that I could still taste the damn man's kiss on my lips.

Never mind that at all.

I had an appointment to keep, and a client, well hopefully two, to impress. Gathering my sketches, as well as some metalwork samples, I tucked them in my leather work satchel. Waving to the others, I made to leave, but Ian caught me on the way out. A nice man, though introverted, he cleared his throat and gestured with one hand awkwardly toward the parking lot.

"Sorry about Thane. He's ..." Ian trailed off, trying to decide on a word.

"Tricky?" I asked and a small smile ghosted his lips.

"Aye, that's one word for it."

"I'm not easily upset by others. You need a tough skin in this game." I shrugged and hitched the straps of the bag higher up on my shoulder. "I'm off for a meeting."

"Where to?"

"Common Gin."

"Shite," Ian mumbled, and I tilted my head.

"Problem?"

Ian glanced around and lowered his voice.

"Thane just went that way. He's, um, not happy."

It took me a second to gather Ian's meaning. When it did, my face flushed. *It was always the same.* No matter what, I constantly had to prove myself in this business. And now Thane, a local, was up at the distillery, likely trying to talk them out of working with me. Fury raced through me, and I tapped two fingers against my forehead, a silent salute to Ian.

"Appreciate the heads-up. I'll handle it."

Ian slipped back into the office as I stormed from the forge, annoyed that once more, some man thought he could one-up me.

The drive to MacAlpine Castle took about twenty

minutes, mainly because my car shook so hard every time I shifted gears that I feared one bolt would go flying and the entire contraption would explode like a toddler kicking a tower of blocks. Even so, I still managed to enjoy the wide expanse of Loch Mirren, how the water shimmered and shifted under the mid-morning sun that shafted through the clouds, and that strange shifting in my soul every time I looked at the perfectly circular island smack dab in the center of the loch.

If I was a betting girl, which I wasn't, I'd lay money on something being off about that island. *Was it even natural? There was no way an island could form in a perfect circle, was there?* Distracted by the view, I wound my way along gorgeous green hedges that lined an impressive drive that delivered me to a gravel parking lot next to the castle. Pulling up next to what must be Thane's truck, based on the Blackwood Forge logo, I sniffed at his fancy tires as I rattled to a stop.

He probably had heated seats too.

Annoyed, I stepped out and took a moment, like always, to admire the castle. Though I was sure the Scots likely drove past castles without barely a second glance, as an American, I couldn't help but internally squeal every time I saw a historic building of such grandeur. One of these days I'd take the tour, and likely fall in love with every curve and bow of the building.

But that was for another day.

Squaring my shoulders and hitching my bag up, I stomped across the garden toward the flurry of activity at the building site for the new Common Gin distillery. A stable conversion, they were blending both old and new to make a beautiful spot that would be welcoming and attractive for all. I was thrilled to be a part of what they were building here.

Thane paused mid-sentence on my approach.

Was I imagining things or did his eyes heat when he saw me? Ignoring the brush of desire, I squared off, ready for battle.

"Excuse me, Thane, but I have an appointment with Orla." Turning to the diminutive construction manager, I smiled, keeping my tone even.

"Oh, you two know each other? That's grand," Orla said, her face alight with interest.

"Aye, she rents space at our forge." Thane shocked me by touching a hand at the small of my back, as though to guide me away for a moment. "If you'll excuse us, Orla?"

He was going to hijack my meeting?

Absolutely not.

"Actually, it's you that will have to be excusing *us*." I stepped out of his touch and glared up at him, fury heating my temper. "I'm here to speak with my client, Thane, and I ask that you not be taking any more of her precious time."

Thane's brows dropped, a mutinous expression flashing across his face, before he gathered his control and smoothed his features out. Turning, he flashed a smile at Orla, holding his hands in the air in front of him.

Work-roughened hands that had wrung pleasure from my body.

Tearing my eyes away from them, I looked at Orla, who was now seemingly captivated by our interaction.

"As I was saying, Orla, we've worked together in the past and you're well aware of the quality Blackwood Forge can provide for you. For a project of this scope, might I suggest that my team would be better suited to the needs of Common Gin than …" Thane trailed off, seemingly unable to land on a way to voice his thoughts.

"Than what, Thane? A woman?" I crossed my arms over my chest and angled myself slightly closer to Orla, forming a team of two women who were used to men being jerks in our respective professions.

"Than a solo entrepreneur," Thane finished. "I suspect you'll be hard-pressed to deliver everything that Common Gin needs on your own."

He wasn't wrong, which made his words sting even more, and I turned to Orla, opening my mouth to plead my case.

"Just a moment." Orla squeezed my arm, giving me a sympathetic look, and I winced. She was going to side with him, wasn't she? "Tell me more about your partnership."

There was no partnership. I'd signed a simple tenant's lease, providing access to their equipment. My blood chilled as I realized he could probably revoke my lease and then I'd be unable to fulfill my side of the project for Common Gin anyway. I truly hoped he wasn't that kind of man, as I'd actually enjoyed his company in Edinburgh, but it was hard to say. We'd never touched on work or anything too deep, and one could never tell what a man would do to protect his livelihood. If I was a threat, he could eliminate it.

But I hoped he was a better person than that.

Even if just to assuage my personal shame for not picking the worst of the worst for a one-night stand.

"Kaia has leased space at our workshop, however she is independent of Blackwood Forge," Thane said, his voice clipped. "She joined our space while I was away in Edinburgh, working on Holyrood Palace."

Oof. That was a direct hit. Here I was coming from the States with a small portfolio and Thane was working on castles.

"I see." Orla tilted her head, her gaze bouncing between the two of us. "Didn't you mention you had spent some time in Edinburgh prior to coming to Loren Brae, Kaia?"

Despite myself, I locked gazes with Thane. Desire warred with anger, my stomach twisting in knots, and I raised my chin at him. He could stare all he wanted, but he wasn't going to rattle my cage.

"I did. Lovely city, but I do prefer the charm of Loren Brae."

"Mmm, is that right?" Orla tapped a finger at her lips, considering, and tilted her head to one side. "Here's the way of things, Kaia. I loved your portfolio that you showed me when we first met, and I'm looking forward to seeing your designs. However ..."

I flinched, my shoulders slumping.

"I also understand what Thane is saying about the

scope of the project. He's not wrong," Orla said, her finger still tapping at her lips.

"You're my only client." It came out as a whisper, and I cleared my throat, speaking louder. "I would live, eat, and breathe this project. My time and attention would be solely given to you, not divided across other clients. I can promise you, that I will deliver on your needs with an exacting and impeccable attention to detail."

Orla smiled, lines fanning out from the corner of her eyes as she did, her face softening.

"I don't doubt it. However, we are on a tight timeline. So here's what I think will be best. We need designs for the gates, the tasting room and pub, and the gift shop. I'd like to hire you both to do the work—"

At that, we both let out a soft exhale, our frustration evident. I refused to look at Thane, my blood boiling.

"Just wait," Orla said, her tone gentle. "We'll do a walk-through today, and you can both take a few days to come up with your designs for the different spaces. Kaia, when we originally spoke, the project's scope was just for the main gates, so you'll want to see the other spaces now. And once we see the designs, I'd like for you both to work on the project. Even if the design is not one of your own."

Damn. That was not what I'd wanted out of this job. Receiving credit for both the design and creation of the gates had become my ticket to future work in Loren Brae. I knew that Blackwood Forge produced incredible work, so I couldn't lie and say I didn't feel that my position was threatened here. Could I compete with Thane *and* secure subsequent prospects?

"Do you think that will be a problem?" Orla asked, her head swiveling between Thane and me. "Will you both be able to work together?"

I tried to put myself in her place. The scope of the project had changed since we'd last spoken, she had a finished project to deliver to her client, and it was possible I would delay her progress. She was being fair to me, while also including a local team she'd worked with previously and had an existing relationship with. I couldn't say I was particularly happy about this decision, but I also couldn't fault her for it.

I likely would have made the same choice in her position.

"Not a problem at all, Orla. I look forward to working on *my* designs for Common Gin. I'm certain I'll, I mean, *we'll*, be able to deliver a finished product that you'll be ecstatic about."

Thane bristled beside me, and I bit back a grin, knowing I'd annoyed him.

"Aye, Orla. It's always a pleasure working with you." *Okay, Blackwood, we all know you have a good working relationship with Clarke Construction.* Like I needed the reminder. The man had his hands in every project in the village and surrounding areas, and I knew it was going to be difficult for me to make a toehold in the business here. But still. There was work to be had, and I'd be happy to have it. Even if I had to share the project or fight for it.

"That's grand, then. All right, come along." Orla

nodded to a pile of hard hats in a box. "Hard hats are there. I've got twenty minutes for a quick walk around to give you the scope of our needs and then I have a meeting. And I believe Kaia does as well."

"Another meeting?" Thane glanced at me, lines hardening in his craggy face.

"Aye. With a potential new client. None of which is any of your business." I sniffed as Orla pressed her lips together, swallowing a laugh, and I took the hard hat she handed me. Taking a deep breath, I gave myself a mental kick. I needed to do better and not bicker with Thane in front of a client.

"I wish you good luck then," Thane said, strapping his hat on, and I nodded, not trusting myself to speak.

I didn't want to fight with him. I didn't want to have to prove myself to a client, or work side by side with a man who'd forever eradicated past lovers as mere jokes, nor fight my desire for him every time he unintentionally stepped close to me. Heat radiated from him, his presence hovering over me, as he walked behind me during Orla's tour of the tasting room. My insides had grown liquid, my body betraying me at his proximity, and I couldn't even begin to contemplate how we were going to work together over the next few months and pretend like nothing had happened.

Except maybe it *was* nothing to him. It hadn't been all that hard to pick him up, and he'd gone along with me readily enough to have a few drinks and a quick tumble in bed. Was I the only one who was quietly freaking out about being in his proximity again? His expression was guarded, and with only a quick ripple of awareness in his eyes when I'd first walked in, I couldn't be certain he was even particularly affected by my presence.

In fact, he'd seemed more upset by the fact that I'd taken a job from him than anything.

I needed to be an adult here, own my reaction to him, and just move on with my new life. Thane was a mere speedbump on my path to building a new foundation for myself and I wasn't going to let him slow me down.

By the time we'd finished our walk around, I was buzzing with ideas for the spaces that Orla had showed me. She left us at the front, with a promise to check in soon, and went off to her meeting. Checking my phone, I took off my hard hat, shook my hair out, and turned to Thane.

For a second, something flickered in his expression, before it smoothed out once more.

That something, though, had my mouth going dry.

Damn it, I had to stop imagining things on his part. Assumptions were not the way forward here.

"Best of luck with your designs," I said, pasting a fake smile on my face, letting him know that he was far from forgiven for this stunt he'd pulled today. "I have to get to my next meeting."

"Who are you meeting with next?" Thane's eyebrows drew up.

"That's hardly any of your business, is it?" Turning, I blew him a smooch with my hand and then walked toward the front door of the castle.

"Is it with the castle?" Thane called behind me, frustration soaking his words.

"Again, none of your business. Toodles." I waved my fingers at him and strode off, rolling my eyes at myself.

Toodles? Who even says that in real life?

I was off my game, and it was a stark reminder that my focus needed to stay on building my business one design after another. I'd never again lose sight of my goal due to a handsome and charming man. *Been there, had the heartbreak and humiliation to show for it.*

I needed to *not* let a man interfere with my dreams.

Even if he raided them every night while I slept.

CHAPTER FOUR

KAIA

Following instructions, I walked past the castle's main door, and around the side to a smaller door tucked at the back. Arched wood, with heavy iron hinges, and bolts that made me admire the handiwork of days past, the door was pretty much *the* perfect castle door. Did people even realize how distinctive styles of craftsmanship resulted in objects that stood the test of time? Admiring the handiwork, I trailed a finger over the iron bolt before swinging the door open and stepping into a rough-cut stone hallway lit with sconces in the shape of torches. Appreciating the blend of modern electrics with the nod toward the past, I paused.

I needed a moment to settle myself before I met with

Willow, an American fashion designer who had recently moved to Loren Brae and was working on designs for the castle gift shop. She'd approached me about an idea she had for chain-mail apparel, and I was meeting with her at her temporary studio today to discuss those designs.

Two very different projects, both creatively fulfilling.

At least this one wouldn't likely result in Thane trying to steal work from me.

My anger simmered, ripe and fresh, and I had to force out a few calming breaths lest I take that energy into the meeting with me. Willow was bubbly and fun, sunshine on a spring day, and I didn't want to allow recent frustrations to taint my mood during the appointment.

This would be fun. Creative collaboration should *always* be fun.

Taking a step forward, I slammed to a stop as something huge and transparent and fierce, leaped from the wall and skidded to a stop in front of me. Throwing up my hands, my tote going flying—directly through the apparition, mind you—I screamed the scream of a woman getting slaughtered in a horror movie.

The ghost highland cow shrunk back, his eyes rounding in concern, and he slunk into a corner of the hallway, his head hanging low as he watched me.

"What the hell?" I gasped, hand to my heart, tears pricking my eyes. I wasn't a fan of the ol' jump scare, not in movies or in real life. I'd never been one for haunted houses, even if I was certain that I had a propensity for seeing ghosts.

There was a stark difference between seeing a spirit drifting across the land, far enough away that you could still question if it was just a figment of your imagination, and one almost running you over in a dimly lit castle hallway.

Footsteps pounded behind me and even as I turned, I was being lifted, as though I weighed nothing. I was swiftly cradled against a muscular chest that I'd thought of in great detail many a night since I'd first been held against it.

He smelled like soap and cedar, and I burrowed into him for a second, knowing that this wouldn't last. We'd be back to rivals shortly, but in this moment, I needed him to steady me.

"What's happened, lass? Are you hurt?" Thane's voice rasped at my ear, worry in his tone, and I looked up, caught in the storm that raged in his eyes.

"Um." I licked my lips, my mouth having gone dry. "No, just a fright."

There was no way I was telling Thane that I'd seen a ghost. Men like him didn't seem the type to believe in such nonsense anyway.

"I didn't know you were so reactive."

At his words, my blood heated. Tilting my head, I shot him a look.

"Didn't you?"

Damn it. Damn it. Damn it. Hadn't I been lecturing myself ten minutes ago about making wrong decisions with men? And all it took was being cradled in this man's impossibly strong arms again for me to completely forget my resolution.

Heat flashed in his eyes and then his lips were on mine.

"Bloody hell." His words rumbled against my lips. "I've missed this."

Pressing my back to the stone wall, Thane kissed me like a man lost in the desert, discovering a few drops of rain caught on a leaf. His kiss consumed me, the intensity of his focus, his complete plundering of my walls leaving me liquid and warm. Reaching up, I dove my hands into his hair, pulling him closer. My breasts pressed against his chest, my nipples pebbling against his muscles, and I moaned into his mouth as he angled his head and deepened the kiss.

He licked inside, his tongue wet and hot, and a sharp stream of lust shot straight through me as flashes of the night we'd had together came back to me. Slick heat, rough hands against soft skin, his tongue laving across me and bringing me to pleasure, over and over.

I craved this man's touch, and no matter how much I'd tried not to think of him again, it had only taken one moment to reignite the desire I'd thought I'd successfully tamped down.

My body, that traitorous bitch, had other ideas. Hitching a leg up, I wrapped it around his waist, moaning into his lips as I felt his hardness brush against where I wanted him most.

"Ahem."

A throat cleared behind us and my head shot back so fast, I smacked it lightly against the stone wall behind me.

What the hell was I doing? I had a client meeting and here I was climbing this man like a maid sneaking out with the stableboy back in olden times. Closing my eyes, embarrassment heating my face, I eased my leg down and put my hands against Thane's chest, pushing him lightly back. Smoothing my clothing, I peeked around his shoulder, praying it was just some random passing by and not my potential new client.

Willow beamed at me from the end of the hallway.

No such luck today.

Furious with myself, and with Thane for throwing me off my stride, I pushed him farther back and crouched to pick up the contents of my tote, which had scattered across the floor when I'd tossed it in the air.

"Willow, I'm sorry about that. I had a bit of a scare and Thane came to check on me."

"Is that what he was doing?" Amusement danced in Willow's voice, and I stayed focused on gathering my things, trying to regain some modicum of composure.

"I'll be off then, lasses. Good morning to the both of you." Thane's voice was strained, his words proper and forced, and I didn't look up as his shadow disappeared from the floor and light streamed in the door.

"My God, I thought I'd have to put the firehose on you two." Willow's laugh was warm and bright, and finally I stood. She fanned her face, all smiles and amusement, and some of my embarrassment eased. "I might have to find my own grumpy Scotsman and reenact that whole scene."

"Willow, first may I say—I'm *so* sorry. That was not only unexpected, but deeply unprofessional of me. I hope you won't let this affect our potential working relationship. I can promise you nothing of that manner will happen again in the future."

Willow put her hands on her hips and threw her head back and laughed even harder than before. The sound boomed through the small hallway, and I realized just how much the space amplified sound. No wonder Thane had come running, he'd probably thought I was being murdered.

"I will certainly *not* make you promise that. From where I was standing it looked like it needed to happen again, and on repeat." A curvy woman with a larger-than-life presence, Willow wore wide-legged leather pants, slouchy boots, and a softly draped sweater in screaming hot pink.

"It can't." I hitched my bag up my shoulder and scanned the floor once more to make sure I'd retrieved everything.

"Hmm. Well, why don't you come in and we can chat about it?" Willow waved me forward.

"There's nothing to chat about." Horrified about discussing personal business with a potential client, I moved to follow Willow. She stopped, shooting me a glance over her shoulder.

"It's not all that long since I was also new in town,

Kaia. I'm offering friendship, because I know what it's like to feel untethered in a new place."

"Oh." Willow pushed open a door and ushered me into a large room with natural light, standing mirrors facing two fitting platforms, and two huge tables covered with fabrics, notebooks, and two sewing machines. Baskets of multi-colored swatches were tucked beneath the table, and Taylor Swift played softly over hidden speakers in the background. "I'm sorry, I hadn't thought about it like that. I'm really, just ... I'm a little flustered, I'll admit."

"Was that you who screamed?" Willow bent to a small fridge and opened it up, pulling out a Coke. Lifting it in the air in question, I nodded, and she handed me a cold can, then took one herself. Gesturing to two armchairs tucked in front of the paned glass windows, we both sat.

"It was. Again, I'm sorry."

"Please stop apologizing. I don't think less of you for being scared of something, nor do I think less of you for wanting to thank your hottie of a rescuer." Willow winked at me as my face flushed. "Tell me what spooked you."

"Um ..." *Right, how was I supposed to say it was a ghost cow?* I struggled to find the words.

Understanding dawned in her eyes and she pinched her nose. "Damn it, Clyde." Willow raised her voice and a plaintive moo filled the air.

I almost dropped my soda.

"You ... you ... can see him?"

"Clyde is our resident ghost highland coo. He's a big fan of scaring people. Like a toddler hiding behind a sheet and jumping out."

"A coo?" I asked faintly, taking a sip of the soda to cool my throat.

"Cow or coo, as they say here. He's harmless, though he did make Lia pee her pants. Something that she asks that we don't repeat, and we tell pretty much everyone."

"Who's Lia?" Distracted by Willow's chatter, I couldn't help but stare at the door to the hallway, in case Clyde decided to make another appearance.

"You'll meet her soon. Another American. She runs the restaurant at the castle. In fact, there are a few of us American ladies here. Sophie, you've met her?"

"Yeah, briefly." I tore my eyes away from the door and focused on Willow. "She's nice."

"She inherited the castle and has been recruiting people over the pond, so to speak, for various ... needs." The way she said that last bit had me tilting my head in question.

"What kind of—"

"So, anyway, Clyde's harmless, aside from the threat of wetting your pants. And not everyone can see him either, so that's interesting." Willow gave me a considering look.

"Is it?"

"It is. Do you see anything else?"

I blanched, uncertain how the conversation had taken such a turn. This morning was turning out to be a roller coaster—*for a lot of reasons*—and I was more than ready to hide in my cottage and lay on the fuzzy shag carpeting for the rest of the day, trying to process the series of events that had happened in quick succession.

"Um." I shrugged, noncommittal. "It's hard to say, right? Like, I sometimes think that I might, out of the corner of my eye, but it's always from afar. So it could just be, you know, a wisp of fog or something. Scotland is moody and dreamy in that way."

"Well, there are definitely ghosts here." Willow said it so plainly and cheerfully, as though she was commenting on the weather, that I just raised both my eyebrows at her. What was I supposed to say to that? Her laugh trilled, and she shook her head, wiggling her fingers at a cat that had just appeared at the door. "This is Calvin. He's my sweet angel, aren't you, baby?"

Calvin prowled closer, swiping under Willow's hand, before coming over to bump his head against my calf. Pleased with the attention, I bent and scratched the backs of his ears. When he glanced up, and tawny eyes held mine for longer than usual, I paused. Something tugged inside me, a knowing, like the same feeling I experienced when I looked at the island in Loch Mirren.

"Brap," Calvin half-meowed, half-purred, and jumped on my lap, settling in. Soon his little paws were digging in my thigh as I stroked his back, and I slowly relaxed into the soft leather of the chair.

"He's great, isn't he?" Willow asked, maternal pride in her voice.

"Really such a sweetie," I agreed. I nodded at the tote at my feet. "In the interest of not disturbing such a sweet boy, if you want to reach in my bag ... there are some samples of different types of chain mail. It should give you a better idea of what's possible and the weight of the material."

"Eeek." Willow clapped her hands and dug in my bag while I stroked Calvin's soft fur.

You're one of us.

I blinked down at the cat, a shiver dancing down my back. It was almost like he was speaking to me. The words formed in my mind, with such a stark clarity, that my breath caught in my throat.

That was odd.

"Oh, Kaia. These are so cool." Willow held up the rectangles of chain mail I'd made, each with varying sized links. "But they do look super time intensive."

"It's repetitive work, to be sure. I do find it soothing though." I tore my eyes away from Calvin, shaking off my thoughts of animals talking, and focused back on the conversation. "The finer chain mail takes longer, as the links are more intricate and require more time to hook together. You'd just have to price your pieces higher if you use that one."

"Hmm." Willow stood and walked to the mirror, pulling her pink sweater over her head and tossing it aside. Beneath she wore a simple fitted black tank. Holding the chain mail to her breast, she twisted and turned. "You know, I think the chunkier links look cooler. Almost has a steam punk feel to it."

"What are you thinking?"

Willow crossed the room and grabbed a sketchbook,

flipping through the pages before coming to my side. "See?"

The sketches showed women wearing simple T-shirts or tanks, with a few chain mail tops thrown loosely over the top of their shirts. One was in the style of a cropped tank, hanging loose over the white T-shirt. Another was in the style of a vest. A third was simply a body chain of sorts, chunky and edgier.

"That body chain is cool. You could throw it over a floral dress and edge it up."

"Yes!" Willow exclaimed. "That's what I was thinking. Mixing hard with soft."

"It's a unique idea. Depending on how many you want, it wouldn't be super time intensive. The real work that comes with chain mail is when you're making massive protective garments with it. But with these, since they're smaller and just a throw on over your clothes, the time would be far less. Particularly if you choose a larger link."

"Can you mock these three up for me? For a fee, of course. Not for free."

"Of course, no problem. I'll just need sizing and design requirements." Considering the vest style, I tilted my head as I thought. "And maybe for the vest, I'd like to do it in pieces so we could put the final product together ourselves? That way I won't accidentally follow the pattern wrong. I'm good at what I do, Willow, but I'm not a clothing designer."

"That's totally fine. Let me get you some measurements. I'll break them down into sections, and then we'll go from there?" Willow asked, excitement on her face.

"Perfect."

"And your price?"

I'd priced it out, considering my time and supplies, and then discounted it as she was a new customer. Quoting it, my stomach dropped when Willow frowned.

"That seems low."

"Oh." Relief filled me. "You're a new client. I wanted to offer an introductory discount."

"Nope." Willow shook her head. "I work for myself too, Kaia. You can't undercut just to get clients. It will only catch up to you. I'm happy to pay a fair price for good craftsmanship."

"Thank you." I wanted to protest more, but I still had to make a living. *Especially now that my income could be thwarted by working together with Thane.* Why hadn't I asked what differences would be made to the invoicing?

Willow beamed at me and returned to her chair.

"Now that business is concluded, why don't you tell me what's going on with tall, dark, and grumpy out there?"

"Nothing." The word came fast and hard and Willow pressed her lips together, amusement dancing in her eyes.

"If you say so."

"I say so."

"Because it really looked like you were stuck to him like a barnacle on a ship." Willow idly examined a nail, painted a brilliant tangerine.

"I wasn't ... it's not ..." I focused on petting Calvin like he'd be the lifeline that I needed to get out of this conversation.

"It's complicated?" Willow supplied.

"Exactly that." I kneaded my fingers in Calvin's soft fur, and he looked up at me again. "And I work with him now, so that's not a line to be crossed."

"Or is it?" When I looked up, my mouth dropping open at Willow's statement, she made a delightful purring sound. "Ramsay and I work together. And let me tell you ... that forced proximity can be ... delicious."

"Or make you lose your job," I grumbled, and Willow's eyebrows winged up.

"Oh no. Bad experience?"

"Pretty much. I was super gullible. I don't plan to put myself in the same position in the future."

Calvin shifted and jumped down from my lap, plodding over to Willow and bumping his head against her shin. She looked down at him and then up at me.

"Not to change the subject, but Calvin informs me we have bigger things to focus on at the moment."

"Does he?" Amused, but relieved about the subject change, I relaxed.

"He does. So ... not entirely sure where to begin, but I think you're here for other reasons than you may think." Willow looked up, her expression serious, and I glanced from her face to the cat.

"He told you that?"

"We know one of ours when we meet her." Startled, I glanced at the woman who had just spoken. Sophie

MacKnight, owner of MacAlpine Castle, stood in the doorway.

"One of yours?" I looked between Willow and Sophie.

"Fancy some lunch? We've got a lot to talk about …"

An hour later, I was sitting across from Willow and Sophie, my mouth hanging open.

Hilda, the caretaker of MacAlpine Castle, a woman with a scarily efficient air and a fiercely protective nature, refilled our tea while her husband, Archie, glowered at me from where he sat by the window tying flies for his fishing trips. I wasn't entirely sure if Archie was glowering at me because he thought I was slow to understand what Sophie was explaining to me, or if that was just his normal countenance. Either way, I needed to get up to speed. And fast, it seemed.

"The Order of Caledonia is made up of an enchanted group of people whose bloodlines run through Loren Brae. As descendants of prior members of the Order, we, too, can tap into our magick." Sophie held my eyes while I squirmed in my seat. What she said both made me feel uncomfortable and intrigued me. Magick. *Real* magick?

"It's wild," Willow said, tossing her hair over her shoulder. "But it's also an honor. Loren Brae needs our help to protect the Stone of Truth, and we're certain you're meant to join the Order."

"Me?" My voice might have squeaked a bit.

"Yes, you," Archie said with a snort. He leveled me a look under shaggy brows. "Is there any reason you doubt your ability to be a strong woman who can protect Loren Brae?"

The way he said it, as a challenge, had my blood heating, and my impulsiveness rose to the surface.

"I know I'm strong enough." This time I was the one who tossed my hair and straightened my shoulders.

"Thatta girl." Archie winked, and it felt like I'd won a prize.

I just wasn't sure if it was a prize I wanted yet.

CHAPTER FIVE

KAIA

It turns out I'm magick.
Yeah, I know. Even thinking that sounds wild to me, and yet, after hearing Sophie out, meeting Hilda and Archie, and going through an enchanted ritual to add me to the Order of Caledonia, I still couldn't quite believe it.

I'd thought I was having a wild day just dealing with working under the same roof as Thane, and then the universe threw me a massive curveball.

I *think* I was happy about it?

Maybe?

Honestly, my head was still reeling.

After Sophie had dragged me upstairs for lunch with Hilda and Archie—the castle caretakers who were in their early sixties and had me desperately missing my own parents—they had all dropped a bomb on me.

It seemed my suspicions about the island in the middle of Loch Mirren were correct—*no*, it wasn't a normal island and *yes*, it housed essentially the holy grail of magickal stones. Then I was treated to the history of the Order of Caledonia, a magickal Order of humans, like Sophie and Willow, who gain magick by accepting the responsibility to protect the Stone and keeping the Kelpies at bay.

No big deal, right?

That was the other thing. The Kelpies. I suppose that provided an answer to the otherworldly shrieks I'd heard in my dreams, but even I couldn't quite believe that mythological water beasts would rise from the water and terrorize anyone who drew too close to the Stone of Truth.

I was now sitting on the floor of my cottage, my toes digging into the awful green shag carpeting, and staring blankly at the wall as I tried to figure out what had just happened.

Instead of laughing in their faces and booking the first plane ticket out of Loren Brae like I should have, I had just nodded along and agreed to do their ritual.

Was I going to be one of those people that they filmed documentaries about? Like how a woman down on her luck joined a cult and then painted her skin with blueberry juice every day and weaved seagrass into her hair under the full moon? Or worse, joined some sort of ritual killing that ends up in the headlines worldwide?

Nervous, I picked at the threads of the carpet, ripping little tufts out and tossing them in the air, watching them drift down in front of me. I'd had an emotional morning. And then I'd gone and joined a magickal Order just because someone had asked me to. Was I that desperate to belong? What if I'd well and truly screwed myself?

"The Order of Caledonia has a steep history in protecting both Loren Brae and the Stone of Truth from harm. Each member of the Order will need to pass three challenges to prove their worthiness, and those challenges will vary from member to member. It's on you to see how your magick will manifest. It also isn't unlikely that you've already seen some glimmers of it in your past life, since membership is passed down through your blood."

Archie, with thick white eyebrows and a stern look to his face, had lectured me thoroughly and succinctly about my responsibilities to the Order of Caledonia, while Hilda had piled sandwiches on my plate and shooed dogs away from my feet. It had all been very cozy and, well, normal. Up until I'd walked the property with them and spoken the words of the ancient ritual, holding my chisel—my chosen weapon, *apparently*—and felt something shift inside of me when the ritual was complete.

Yeah, *that* had been wild.

Now I was sitting here, buzzing with this unknown energy, wondering how I was supposed to pass these challenges, what it meant for my time in Loren Brae, and yeah, well, how the hell was I going to work with Thane on the Common Gin project? Did he know about the Kelpies? Did he know that magick existed? Was this just something that everyone in Scotland knew about and was comfortable with?

I threw another tuft of carpet in the air, not caring that I was destroying something I was going to rip out anyway, and thought back to Archie's words.

My bloodline.

Pulling the phone from my pocket, I checked the time and called my dad.

"Honey!" My dad's face appeared in the screen, as he fumbled with the phone while pulling his glasses down from where they were perched on his forehead. "Mary, it's Kaia!"

I grinned, waiting for my mother to join him, and their two faces leaned in from either side of the screen, neither wanting to push the other out, but both wanting a look at me.

"Hi, Mom."

"Are you sitting on the floor? Did you fall?" Mom's forehead wrinkled with concern.

"Uh-oh, what's wrong, honey?" My dad leaned forward, worry in his eyes. They knew me too well. For some reason, I had a habit of sitting on the floor whenever I had something heavy weighing on me. It was as though the weight of the world was pushing me down, and I'd go to the ground to think it through.

I opened my mouth, and then paused, uncertain how to continue. I didn't keep secrets from my parents, but I didn't always tell them everything about my life. There were certain things it was natural to filter from one's parents, so I decided to leave the Thane conversation out. For now.

"Um, hmm. I wouldn't say anything's wrong," I said, rocking backward to lean my back against the worn couch. "But, maybe just weird. Can I ask you a question?"

"Of course," both my parents said at once.

"Well, I suppose this is more for Mom." Half-Scottish, half-American, Mom had grown up in the States but was still in touch with much of her Scottish family.

"Oh, is this a girls-only talk? I can leave," Dad said.

"No, no, not like that." I smiled. He really was the best father in the world. "I wanted to ask Mom if she knew of anything unusual in her bloodline."

"Oh, no, are you sick? I'll have to check the health records, but I don't think we have a concerning medical history." The furrows on my mother's brow deepened.

"No, not medical." I closed my eyes and counted to five. I was going to need to just say it. "Anything, um, magickal?"

"What?" My dad laughed.

"Oh," Mom said, and my dad turned to look at her with surprise on his face.

"You know what she's talking about?" Dad asked her.

"Yes, I do."

My eyebrows lifted to my hairline, but mixed with surprise was relief. The tension that banded my shoulders eased and I waited, knowing my mother would explain herself in her own time.

"I'm sorry, you did say magickal, correct?" My dad's head swiveled between me and my mother.

"There's ... a history in my family. Not much talked about, really, but not entirely hidden either." Mom's gaze darted off screen. "Is it too early for wine?"

"You need a drink for this?" Dad was getting worried now.

"No, no," Mom said, firmly, and put her hand on my father's arm. "It's fine, honey. I promise. It's just that there was talk of my grandmother being involved with a magickal Order. One that helped protect the town is all."

"Protect the town from what?" My dad's head looked like he was watching a Ping-Pong match.

"The Kelpies," I said at the same time as my mom.

"What are those?" Dad's voice went up a notch. "Are those the invasive beetles that look like ladybugs?"

I couldn't help it, but I snorted, amused.

"I wish it were that easy," I said.

"Tell me what happened," Mom said.

"Wait, Mary. Explain Kelpies to me. I don't like feeling like I'm out of the loop. It's not like you to keep secrets from me." Hurt filled my poor father's face, and my heart softened as my mom bumped her shoulder against his.

"I didn't keep a secret, darling. I just don't ever think about it. It's one of those family tales from generations ago that has always seemed too far-fetched to be true. Maybe it had popped in my head once or twice since

Kaia's gone over, but truly I didn't think much of it. Until now, that is."

"Tell me about your granny," I said.

"Honestly, it was just a touch out there, you know?" Mom leaned back, jiggling the charm bracelet at her wrist in a nervous habit she had. "But it was said she would charm the gates. The doors. The entrances. Late at night she'd walk the village and speak spells unto houses, and stand before the castle gates, and some said, well, they said they could see a glow coming from her hands as she did her charms."

"How have you never told me this before?" My dad's mouth dropped open.

"I don't honestly know." My mom shrugged.

My heartbeat thundered in my ears at my mom's words, and I drew in a deep breath, as soul-deep understanding flowed through me. I didn't know whether my ancestors worked with metal or not, but I did know that most of the doors and gates of that time period were made using wrought iron. A metal I worked with and was quite proficient with. Would this be how my magick manifested?

It wouldn't be that far off. There was much said about the alchemy of working with metals, and long have there been myths around the ancient process of bending them to your will.

"Do you know what she did for a living?" I asked.

"I ... I can't quite say. God, that would have been what ... like early 1900s? I'm not sure she had a profession so much as she was a homemaker. But I can ask. I'll reach out to the family and see if they have any more information for us."

"Where is Gran right now?"

"She's at a two-month yoga retreat in Costa Rica." A bemused smile crossed my mom's lips. "Living her best life I'm told."

My grandmother, fully Scottish and living life to the largest, was agile and constantly on the move. She'd married rich, saved like a miser, as many Scots do, and since my grandpa passed, she'd been spending his wealth doing anything and everything she pleased, just so she wasn't stuck at home feeling lonely. It was working tremendously well for her, though I knew she still missed my grandfather. Theirs had been a love match for the ages, as were my parents. Four years ago, I thought I'd found that for myself. *How I hate that my confidence in my future has been rocked by my first serious relationship.*

I only hoped I'd one day find the same for myself.

My thoughts drifted to Thane, and how good his lips had felt on mine, but I forced myself not to think about that right now.

This was not the time to consider entertaining a relationship with anyone. *Maybe my love match is still out there and I'm yet to meet him.*

"What does this have to do with you, honey?" my dad asked, pulling us back to the point of the conversation.

"Right, so. Basically ... the new owner of MacAlpine Castle asked me to join a magickal Order to help protect Loren Brae from the threat of the Kelpies, as well as basically the holy grail of magickal stones, and I, well, I did. I joined it. Like, just up and joined. Did the ritual and everything."

"Ritual," my dad gasped, bringing a hand to his mouth. "Did you kill someone?"

"What!" My mouth dropped open. "Do you honestly think I'd kill someone for a ritual?"

"I don't think you'd murder someone, with or without a ritual. But it just sounds …" My dad waved his hand in the air helplessly and the phone jostled. "The word ritual doesn't sound *great*, honey."

"No, admittedly it does not." I sighed and plucked out another piece of the carpet, flinging it up into the air. "It was just like an honorary ritual. A joining of the Order. We walked the cardinal points of the property, I said that I'd willingly help Loren Brae and protect the Stone of Truth, and then I felt … different."

"Different, how?" My mom leaned closer.

"Good." The word popped out of my mouth, but once I said it, I realized it was true. "I feel good. Like I've plugged into a side of myself that maybe was always there?"

"That makes sense." My mother tapped a finger at her breastbone. "I've always felt like I've had a bit of something, too."

"You have?" My dad swiveled to look at my mother in surprise again.

"Oh, George. You know that. Remember how I told you I felt I could see things at times? Or get a read on the way of things to come?"

"Yes, I suppose you're right there. I just thought it was woo-woo stuff. Not a big thing." My dad waved his hand in the air again, punctuating the *woo-woo* of it all. "Not rituals and ancient Orders and our daughter pledging allegiance to something."

"There are levels, I suppose. Some more intense if you're actually in Scotland." My mother brushed away my dad's next question and focused on me. "The real question is, are you happy? Are you okay? Do we need to come out there?"

"I think we most certainly *do* need to go over there," Dad insisted.

"No, no, no." I shook my head. While I appreciated their willingness to ride to my rescue, I needed to figure this out on my own. I'd agreed to join something, an Order that made power hum in my veins, and I needed to explore what that meant to me for a bit. On my own. This was my time to figure things out, and if having magick was part of this, well, so be it. I'd made my bed, so to speak, and it was time to lie in it. "Truly, I'm fine. I just wanted to see if there was any connection through Mom. It makes me feel better to know that this was something in our family and that it isn't as far-fetched as it first seemed."

"I mean, it feels pretty far-fetched to me. What are your responsibilities as part of this Order? Did they give you a job description?" My father leaned in, pushing his glasses up his nose with one finger.

I laughed.

"No, no job description for this one. I need to pass

three challenges, potentially of my character more than physical, I'm told. Though I do feel confident I could do both." I held my arm up and flexed for my parents and my mother nodded approvingly.

"That's my strong girl."

"Kaia, I'm worried about all this," Dad said.

"I know you are. And I'm a touch worried too. But it actually feels right. I've made some new friends who are also new to the area and have had to adjust to having power as well, so I think … I think it's going to be okay. At least I hope it will. I just wanted to talk it out with you both. I'm feeling much better now."

"You're sure? I have no problem coming over to help." That was my father in a nutshell. He might not understand the problem, but he'd show up and help fix it if I needed him to. I loved them both, fiercely, and a pang of longing hit me.

"I do miss you both, but I think I need to do this on my own. And not like in a 'ritual cult push my family out' kind of way. Just in a 'me growing into my own' kind of way." I blinked as tears threatened.

"You just say the word, honey, and we'll be there." Mom gave me a brisk nod. "I'm proud of you, you know. I get the feeling this was a really good decision for you."

"Oh, do you? Is this one of your magickal feelings I'm not privy to?" My dad huffed, glaring at my mom. She swatted his arm.

"Oh hush, don't be in such a fuss. It's not my fault you didn't take me seriously when I told you about this stuff."

"How was I supposed to know that magick was actually real?" my dad seethed and I grinned, knowing they'd be at it for hours now.

"Gotta run! Love you both."

"Bye, honey, love you!" Both my parents waved enthusiastically at the screen, and I clicked off, sinking back against the couch.

Tufts of shag carpeting lay in piles around me, and little holes showed on the carpet in a semi-circle around where I was sitting. At least this was one mess I'd be able to clean up easily. Needing to work, to stay busy to let my thoughts ponder, I stood and stretched. It was time to see what type of floors we were dealing with under this carpeting.

CHAPTER SIX

Thane

"Uncle Thane! Uncle Thane!"

I looked up from my desk to see my niece, Audrey, and my sister, Lauren, standing in the doorway. Was it already noon? Glancing at the time on my computer, I sighed. I'd been so focused on my design work, as well as catching up with the accounts, that I'd barely looked up since I'd arrived at seven this morning.

"Are you finally showing up for your shift?" I asked my niece, pretending to check my watch, as though Audrey was late.

"Uncle Thane." Audrey said my name with the level of dramatics only a seven-year-old could muster, and then she rolled her eyes at me. She was blond, cute as a button, and next to my sister, the most important person in the world to me. My sister had been handed a raw deal, losing her husband when he'd taken off with his best friend's wife, and she'd been raising Audrey on her own ever since. I'd stepped in as much as I could, and Audrey had become a welcome addition around the shop. She knew the safety rules and would often spend a few hours coloring or playing in my office while my sister got some much-needed time alone. As it was Saturday today, I had promised Audrey tea, and then she was allowed to paint my nails. The lads had learned long ago not to say a word about the nail painting, and now they just complimented whatever color Audrey chose that week. Usually I'd keep it on for a day and clean it off for the start of the week, but sometimes I'd leave it on if Audrey had done a particularly decent job.

"She's full on today," Lauren murmured, plopping a tote bag covered in pink sparkles on the desk. "You be good for your uncle, okay?"

"I'm always good." Audrey poked out her lower lip.

"Is that the way of it? I'm not so certain you were that good when I told you to eat your brekkie this morning and I came in to find you face first in a bag of crisps."

Audrey's eyes widened. "That was not me."

"No? Who was it then?" Lauren tilted her head and gave her wee daughter a considering look.

"The elves."

"Was it the elves then? The same elves that will take your toys away if you don't eat breakfast?"

"No." Audrey gasped and held her hands to her

chest, dramatic as hell. "They'd never do such a thing to me. The elves love me."

"If so, then why are they letting you get in trouble for their bad deeds?"

That question stumped Audrey and she twisted her hands. Laughing, Lauren ruffled her hair and then leaned over the desk to kiss my cheek.

"I should be back by half five or so."

"Take all the time you need. I can keep her tonight too if you want a night off."

"Nah, I'm good. No plans tonight. Just going to watch a movie and go to bed early."

I glanced up to see shadows beneath my sister's eyes. She was working long hours to make ends meet, stubbornly refusing my help. I wished she'd just let me pay for her rent, or something, but she adamantly refused assistance. I tried to make up for it in other ways, but I had to respect her choices. I didn't want to risk pushing Lauren away, so if she needed to do this on her own, then I'd support her the only way I knew how—by offering my time and babysitting services as needed.

"Everything good?" I asked. I tried not to get too pushy when it came to worrying about if she was taking care of herself.

"Aye. Work's just been tricky lately. Seems everyone's on holiday at the moment. Will be nice to have a wee afternoon off and then early to bed should sort me right out." Bending, Lauren kissed Audrey's cheek and then gave me a wave before leaving my office. Facing off with the tiny terror that now stood in front of me, hands on hips, pink sparkly skirt swirling under her purple jumper, I glowered at Audrey.

"No pink today, Audrey."

"I'm going to make you booo-tee-ful." Audrey ignored my glower and drew the word out, twirling around my office.

"Aren't I already beautiful?" I asked, hitting *save* on my computer and closing up my programs. When I was with Audrey, I liked to be fully present. She deserved to have a good male role model in her life, one that actually spent focused time with her, and made her feel seen. Unlike her deadbeat dad.

"No." Audrey giggled when my mouth dropped open and then squealed when I launched myself from around the desk and chased her across the office. Grabbing her, I turned her upside down as she shouted, laughing as I shook her.

"Just making sure it's really you and not some mean elf that's pretending to be Audrey."

"It's me, it's me," Audrey shrieked, and I righted her, giving her a kiss on the top of her head before setting her down on the ground.

"Just checking. Now, madam, what can I get you for your tea today?" I moved to the little fridge in my office where I'd already prepared a selection of her favorite mini sandwiches, as well as a few sweeties for after she'd finished her lunch.

"Earl Grey, please." Audrey stuck her nose up in the air and I grinned. The kid was too cute for words. Twenty minutes later we were seated at the desk in my office, a tray of sandwiches spread out before us, and two cups of tea at our sides. Audrey cradled my hand and examined my nails with the look of an artist contemplating their canvas.

"What's it going to be?" I asked, taking a sip of my tea with the other hand.

"I'm sorry, Uncle Thane." Audrey looked up at me, a sober expression on her sweet wee face. "But I think it will have to be pink."

"Again?" I sighed, though I fully knew she'd pick her favorite color. She'd been on a pink kick for the weeks leading up to my time away in the city, and anticipating this, I'd picked up a few new bottles for her while I was there.

"I just think it's the best." Audrey bit her lower lip, shrugging as though there was nothing to be done about it, and reached for the small bottle of fuchsia pink she'd pulled from her tote.

"Or, you might want to see what I have?" I asked and Audrey paused, frowning up at me.

"What do you have?" Audrey whispered.

"I just think you might enjoy some variety." I pointed to the paper bag I'd brought to the table and Audrey gasped, slapping both of her hands against her cheeks.

"Did you get me more colors?" Audrey demanded, reaching for the bag.

"I did. I felt bad that I had to be away for so long."

"That's okay." Audrey dove into the bag. "I'm used to people being away."

Her dad barely called her, let alone sent gifts, and I hated how much she normalized this part of her life.

"Purple! And pink! And sparkles!" Audrey pulled out three bottles, her eyes huge. "They all have sparkles. I *love* them."

"I thought you would. Particularly the sparkles." I nodded toward her skirt.

"I'll do something different today then," Audrey decided, shaking the purple bottle. "Let's try this purple and see how it looks."

"I think that's a great idea," I said. I didn't care what color she chose, so long as she enjoyed herself and we got to spend time together.

"Ohhhh, look. It's so pretty," Audrey whispered in awe, and I lifted my hand to dutifully admire the sparkling purple nail, which was painted surprisingly well. We'd been working on her technique, and very little strayed from the nail to the cuticle.

"Ian?" I glanced up at the knock at the door and froze as Kaia gaped at me, looking impossibly lush and gorgeous in gray canvas trousers, a simple black top, and a dangle of sparkly earrings at her neck. Her hair was pulled up high off her shoulders in a bouncy ponytail, and her mouth was slicked with some sort of lip gloss that made it look juicy and succulent.

My mood shifted. I was already angry at myself for not securing the Common Gin job on my own, let alone for kissing her again like the damn fool that I was. Now she was seeing me in a private moment with my niece, when I really just wanted to keep all barriers up between us.

"Oh, I'm sorry. I didn't realize ..." Kaia trailed off, looking between me and Audrey.

"Is there something you need?" I bit out, furious with myself for how excited I was to see her again.

"Just had a question for Ian. I didn't mean to interrupt you and your *daughter*. My bad." The way Kaia said the word daughter had my eyes flashing to hers. There was anger there. Before I could respond, she left the office, and I stood abruptly.

"Be right back, Audrey. Your coloring book is there if you get bored."

"Okay," Audrey sing-songed, carefully capping the bottle of nail polish. "Just don't get your nail messy."

"I'll be careful," I promised. I held my hand up and blew on it and she nodded her approval. Leaving my office, I cruised through the empty workshop to where Kaia stood at her worktable.

"Kaia," I said, and she turned, looking me up and down with disgust.

"What's up, *Dad*?"

The way she phrased it wasn't remotely sexual, and yet I immediately got a vision of her on her knees calling me "daddy," even though that wasn't a particular turn-on for me. I had *no reason* for my brain to conjure that image since she'd never used a pet name with me, and yet my thoughts somehow ended up there. It seemed simply being in her vicinity was enough to distract me and I needed to learn some self-control. Like, yesterday.

"She's not my daughter."

"Ah, just steal someone else's kid then?" Kaia glanced to my nails. "Nice color."

"Thanks, I got it in Edinburgh." At that, Kaia's eyes flew to mine. I couldn't help myself, I gave her a slow, searing grin. Surely I couldn't be the only one remembering how incredible our night together was? How was she so unaffected by this? Was I over-romanticizing the night we'd had?

Maybe I was. Maybe it was just me who couldn't stop thinking about it. And yet, she'd been extremely responsive yesterday, wrapping her leg around my waist and threading her hands through my hair. She'd kissed me right back, stopping my heart for a moment as her tongue had met mine, hungry for more. I didn't want to assume that she was all about me or anything, but she certainly wasn't ambivalent to my presence.

"I'll be out of your way shortly."

"Audrey is my niece," I explained, leaning one hip against her table. "*Not* my daughter."

"Okay," Kaia said, pulling notebooks from her table and adding them to her bag.

"Would it have bothered you if I was a father?" I asked, curious.

"Of course not," Kaia said, turning.

"But it feels like I've made you angry," I said, straightening.

"It's not ... I'm not ..." Kaia waved a hand in the air and clamped her mouth shut, clearly frustrated with articulating her thoughts.

"Uncle Thane?" I turned to see Audrey poking her head from the door.

"Yes, sweetie?"

"Do you think your friend would like to get her nails painted?" Audrey's tone was hopeful, and I turned to look at Kaia, interested to see how she'd respond.

"You don't have to if you don't want to," I said, not wanting her to think I was cornering her into spending more time with us. Though secretly I wanted to high-five Audrey for asking.

"No, it's fine. I like kids," Kaia said.

"Then why did it bother you to think I had one?" I couldn't help but ask as Kaia hitched her bag onto her shoulder and made for my office.

"Because I've been with people before who have hidden things from me."

"Yeah, but, lass, it was just one night we had together. Surely you can't think you'll get a life story in just a night?" I dared to touch her arm, drawing her up short, wanting to have this conversation before we got to nail painting time.

"No, it's more that where there's a child, there's usually a mother." Kaia raised an eyebrow at me. "And sometimes men on work vacations will hide a ring."

"Och, lass. No." I shook my head, realization dawning. *Who the hell hurt this woman?* If there was something I hated, obviously given what Lauren had been through, it was cheaters. I'd never been one, that's for sure. "That's far too much fuss. You'll get it straight from me, hen, I can promise you that."

Damn it but if Kaia didn't lick her lips at that. My body warmed and I took a deep breath, reminding myself where I was and who I was with.

"That's good to know." Kaia ducked inside my office, and I took a moment to collect myself, while I heard Audrey's squeal of excitement over being able to paint another woman's nails. By the time I went into my office, I'd done a good job of getting my libido under control, though I still wanted to know who the arsehole was who had hurt Kaia. That was clearly a conversation for another day.

"Pink is definitely the way forward," Kaia said and Audrey bounced in her seat, excited.

"You're next, Uncle Thane. I get to do Kaia's nails pink and then yours purple."

"And then I'll do yours," Kaia said, and Audrey almost fell off her chair in excitement.

"I hope you do a better job than Uncle Thane."

"Is he bad at it?" Kaia asked, amused, sliding a glance at me.

"Not horrible, but I'm better," Audrey promised, reaching out with the brush. "Hold still so I can do this. Why do you talk funny?"

"Audrey." I laughed. "Kaia is from the United States of America. Which means she has a different accent than us."

"Oh." Audrey shrugged one shoulder, unconcerned. "Are you dating my uncle?"

"No," Kaia said at the same time I said, "Yes."

Kaia's eyes rounded and she glared up at me.

"Ohhhh," Audrey said, giggling and looking between us.

"We've gone on a date before, but aren't dating now," I clarified. I tried to never lie to my niece, or anyone, really.

"Did you not like him?" Audrey asked Kaia. "Sometimes he can be scary."

"When am I scary?" I demanded.

"Like that," Audrey said, dutifully focused on spreading paint on Kaia's nails. "His voice gets all tough."

"That's not being scary, Audrey. That's just how I talk."

"Some of the kids at school talk like that to me." Audrey's voice got small, and I straightened, narrowing in on her words.

"Who—"

"Audrey, can you give an example?" Kaia shot me a look to shut me up, even as anger roiled inside me.

"Just like how I don't have a dad around. Or when I want to play pretend they say I'm being a baby."

I was going to punt those kids off the playground if they hurt my Audrey. Fury made me clench my fingers.

"Does this hurt your feelings?" Kaia's voice was soft, soothing Audrey.

"Sometimes. It's mainly Dylan. He says I smell."

"Ah, okay. Here's what you should do ..." Kaia leaned over and whispered in Audrey's ear and soon my niece was giggling.

"Okay!" Her eyes lit and I didn't care what Kaia had told her to do, so long as Audrey was smiling again.

Shoving the anger back down inside, I made a mental note to talk to Lauren about what was going on at school.

"There, all done." Audrey carefully capped the nail polish bottle and then waved to me. "Next!"

Switching places with Kaia, I tried not to inhale her soft citrus scent as she brushed past me.

"Now you wait right there and let them dry." Audrey pointed to a chair and Kaia sat, while I held out my hand for my niece to finish the job she'd started. "Uncle Thane, don't you think Kaia is pretty?"

"I do think she's pretty." I caught a faint hint of blush on Kaia's cheeks.

"Mum says all the pretty girls want to date you."

"Is that right?" Kaia leaned forward, suddenly interested. "Tell me more."

"I don't know." Audrey shrugged, bouncing in her seat as she tried to paint my nails and stay still at the same time. "Just that all the pretty girls love him, but he only loves work."

"Ah, I can understand that. Work can be consuming."

"But I think Kaia's pretty. And she's nice. You should take her on another date, Uncle Thane."

"And you should mind your business, or I'll take my nail colors back." I didn't risk glancing at Kaia, though I was extremely curious to see her reaction to Audrey's suggestion about going on another date.

No, there can be no further dates. We. Work. Together.

"You'd never," Audrey gasped.

"No, I wouldn't." Audrey knew she had me wrapped around her thumb.

"Are you scared?" my terror of a niece continued. "Do you think she won't go on a date with you?"

"*Why*? Why do we need to keep talking about this?" I griped.

"Because I think you're scared. And you're always telling me to do the things that scare me anyway," Audrey said.

"What if it's not me who's afraid?" I asked, neatly throwing Kaia under the bus. Her mouth dropped open and I grinned as she lowered her brows and glowered at me.

"Are you?" Audrey turned to Kaia.

"No, I'm not," Kaia bit out, her eyes on me. *Liar, liar*, I thought. *What the hell am I doing? I can't date this intoxicating lass.*

"Good. Then you can go on a date now, right?" *What the hell?*

I didn't have it in me to break Audrey's excitement. She'd been watching Cinderella and other fairy tales on repeat lately and had become somewhat focused on finding love and happy endings. I'm sure it stemmed from not having her dad in the picture, but I didn't want to dissuade her from the idea that a happily-ever-after could one day be on the horizon. For her *and* her mother. But now, sitting here looking at Kaia as she gaped at me, unsure with how to move forward, I grinned.

Why the hell not?

Playing with fire, Blackwood.

"Yes, Audrey. We can. Kaia, would you like to have dinner with me tonight?"

Kaia's mouth worked and her eyes darted between a hopeful Audrey and me. Caught, like a deer in headlights, my grin widened as her shoulders hunched.

"Sure, Thane. That would be nice."

"Yay!" Audrey squealed, smearing purple nail polish across my thumb. "You two love each other."

"I'm not sure it works as quickly as that," I cautioned my enthusiastic niece.

"Maybe, maybe not. I'm only seven, how should I know?" Audrey grimaced at the mess she'd made on my thumb. "Sorry. I'll fix it."

"Nae bother." With that, I met Kaia's eyes, issuing a silent challenge. She lifted her chin, understanding my meaning.

It looked like I had a date tonight.

Bloody hell. That should not be happening.

But how could I backpedal on my word to my niece? It was something I never did, nor would I ever do.

But what about Kaia? She'd clearly been badly burned before, so she'd feel obliged to ignore her gut feelings here as well.

Did she want to, though?

That was the question I had no bloody idea what the answer was.

CHAPTER SEVEN

Kaia

The last thing I needed was to go to dinner with Thane. Not only was I still trying to come to terms with this whole Order of Caledonia indoctrination, but I also had mixed feelings about working with him on the Common Gin project. His presence was larger than life, in all things, from painting his nails with his niece to leading his employees at the shop.

But holy hell.

I hadn't expected the punch of seeing him—with a tiny girl in pink sparkles wrapped in his arms—and how that made my heart melt on the spot. Thane was just so physically strong, with a personality to match, so when he'd picked Audrey up to give her a massive hug, I'd had to look away before I told him that I wanted that too.

Not just a hug.

But *that*.

A family. A unit. A belonging.

Which was absolutely the wrong way I needed to be thinking about things. I'd been down this road before. I had to work with this man on potentially one of the biggest projects of my life. Despite Willow's insistence that work and pleasure were a fun mix, I really did try to learn lessons from my previous experiences.

Yet here I was, walking into The Tipsy Thistle pub, wearing a slinky silk top draping my curves that I'd almost taken off ten times before I'd forced myself out the door. It wasn't like the man hadn't already seen everything that I had, right?

The Tipsy Thistle reminded me of the Scottish pub you'd see in the movies—complete with the hot Scottish bartender wearing a waistcoat, and his sleeves rolled up to reveal intricate tattoos. His name was Graham, and I'd met him briefly when I'd come in with a few lads from work. Now, seeing me alone, his smile widened, and he nodded to an empty seat at the bar while he filled a pint.

Glancing around, I saw the pub was about half full, not as busy as I'd expect for a Saturday night, but Thane hadn't arrived yet. The pub was hodgepodge in the way of rooms added on through the years, with low doorways to duck through, and stone walls showcasing vintage Guinness posters and various art pieces from the area. A stone fireplace dominated one area, though it wasn't lit now, but I could imagine it would be cozy in the winter months.

"How's it going then?" Graham asked, leaning forward and giving me a slow smile that I'm sure melted the bras right off many a woman. "Kaia, right?"

"That's right." I smiled right back, because, well, it was almost impossible not to. Did Scotland just grow their men handsome, tall, and strong?

"I always remember the names of beautiful women that frequent my pub." Graham propped an elbow on the bar and leaned forward. A woman next to me sighed and turned, shaking her head.

"Please tell me you're smart enough not to fall for this." The slender woman with stunning eyes and a swingy crop of curls gestured to Graham.

"I mean, the view's nice." I grinned as Graham's smile widened.

"See, Agnes? I'm just giving people what they want."

"Och, I'll admit you've a pretty face, lad, but you need to work on your lines. They're getting tired." Agnes sniffed and Graham brought a hand to his chest, wounded.

"Tired? Was that line tired? I thought it was a nice compliment." Graham looked to me for confirmation.

"Mmm. So-so." I wiggled my hand back and forth in the air before finally giving it a thumbs down.

Graham gasped, bringing the back of his hand to his forehead as though he was going to faint, and Agnes and I both laughed.

"It's just a line that I've heard before." I tried to soften the blow.

"See? You're unoriginal." Agnes tapped a finger on the bar.

"What have you heard before?" Thane's voice at my shoulder sent a shiver rippling across my skin and I turned. He was in dark denim, a simple white button-down shirt, and a gray tweed waistcoat. He'd pulled a newsboy cap over his head, and his eyes glittered beneath as he looked between me and Graham.

"Graham was just informing Kaia here that he remembers all the names of the beautiful women that visit his pub."

"Is that right?" Thane's voice went dangerously low, and Agnes's eyebrows shot up in amusement. A look passed between the two men.

"I'm not sure how to respond here, mate," Graham admitted. "If I take it back then I'd be implying Kaia isn't beautiful, as she is, but then if I admit to saying it, it seems I'll be stepping on some toes."

"No toes to step on," I promised to Graham just as Thane wrapped his arm around my shoulders and growled—yes, *growled*—at Graham.

"Hoooo, lassie." Agnes fanned her face, her eyes lighting in appreciation. "You've got yourself a fierce one here."

"No, I don't. Nobody has anything and nothing is happening." I waved my hands in the air, trying to dispel the implications bouncing around between us.

"Shall we take a table?" Thane asked, stiffly, his eyes still on Graham.

"Kaia, can I have a quick chat with you before you

do?" Agnes leaned forward and I grabbed on to the lifeline.

"I'll get our drinks?" Thane looked down at me. "Guinness?"

"Please, thanks." I slid off the stool, happy to be out from under his arm. His touch was driving me crazy, my body singing with excitement from being close to him again, and I was already kicking myself for going on this date with him. It was too easy for me to remember how good we'd been together.

Agnes directed me to a quiet spot in a back room of the pub, with a few cozy tables tucked in a nook lined with shelves of vintage whisky bottles.

"I just wanted to properly introduce myself. I'm Agnes, owner of Bonnie Books, and also sort of your unofficial historian when it comes to the Order of Caledonia."

My eyes widened. "Oh! *Oh*. Hello then, nice to meet you. So you know about all this magick and Kelpies and Order and whatnot?"

"Very much so. Sophie told me you'd taken quickly to learning about the history of the Clach na Firrin." The Gaelic words for Stone of Truth sounded lyrical on her tongue. "She said you were pretty stoked about doing the ritual and jumping in to help."

"Yeah." I shrugged, sheepish. "I tend to jump head-first into things at times. It's kind of had me a bit worried now that I've gone and joined so quickly."

"That's fair. I mean, it's not the easiest thing to explain to people, particularly if you're new to the area. I *will* say that we appreciate you joining as the sooner we have a full Order, the sooner we can banish the Kelpies that threaten Loren Brae."

My eyes flew to the window, where I could just see moonlight trailing across the dark surface of Loch Mirren.

"I'm still having a hard time believing they're real. But at the same time, I swear I've heard things in my dreams."

"Aye. They're real. Very much so, I'm afraid. We're all doing our best to keep them at bay, but we need to finish this up and do a closing ritual to banish them once and for all. The Stone needs to know it's protected."

"And somehow I'm meant to just have magick, pass a few challenges, and help with this all?" I laughed, shaking my head, and looked down at my hands. "Magick."

"It's a lot, I'll agree. Living here, I'm used to it. Not all is as it seems in Loren Brae. It's not just the Kelpies that are magickal, my new friend. It's everywhere."

"Are you magick?"

"No, not that I'm aware." Resignation passed across Agnes's pretty face.

"How do I start?" This was the question that had been bugging me all along.

"I'm not rightly sure, to be honest. Our past members have all discovered it on their own, and it's often intertwined with their own passions or hobbies. For example, Shona, our garden witch, was able to help heal a grieving heart with her tinctures."

"Ah." At that, I nodded. Finally, some sort of direction. "So for me it might be connected to being a metalsmith?"

"Potentially. I'd see if you can spend some time while you work and see if you feel any different? Maybe infuse some magick into your metal?" Anges shrugged. "Hard to say. It's going to be a personal thing to you."

"I'd love to get together, to talk about this more, sometime. I'm feeling a bit lost and overwhelmed." *Likely because you uprooted your whole life, jumped in headfirst to a new place, joined a magickal Order, and basically slept with your boss again.* Mentally, I rolled my eyes at myself. I should get *impulsive* tattooed on my wrist.

"Naturally. I'd love to. And I'm sure a few of the other women would like to meet you as well. I'll speak to Orla and see what Lia's schedule—"

"Orla?" I grabbed Agnes's arm in surprise.

"Och, aye. She's part of the Order too."

"I didn't get the rundown on who else was part of it." My heart hammered in my chest. If Orla was a member, like me, would my designs get the advantage? Was it an unfair advantage? Was this something I should disclose to Thane? Uncertainty warred with excitement in my gut.

"Then we'll definitely have to chat. Tomorrow's Sunday. Meet at the castle? We'll talk shop." Agnes grinned at me when I laughed, shaking my head in disbelief.

Shop.

Like magick was just another skill to be acquired.

I supposed it was, even though it didn't make much sense to me.

Yet.

But I was a fast learner and certainly had no issue with picking up new skills, so if I just gave myself time to learn, I was certain I could master this new and intriguing aspect of myself.

"Yes, let's." I glanced over my shoulder at where Thane sat at a table in the corner, glowering toward the bar.

"Tall, dark, and grumpy is waiting for you," Agnes said, an amused smile on her face.

"It's not like that." I was beginning to sound like an echo chamber, even if just to myself. Maybe I thought if I repeated it enough, I'd believe it?

"You keep telling yourself that." Agnes patted my shoulder and brushed past me. "Trust me, I know the feeling." Her last words were low, and I almost missed them, but it had me tilting my head at her in question. *What did that mean?*

Crossing the room, I joined Thane at the table, and if anything, his glower deepened at my arrival.

"We can't do this," Thane and I said at the exact same time.

"*I'm* not doing anything," we again echoed each other's words.

My mouth fell open and he held a finger in the air, commanding me to wait.

"I don't like lying to Audrey, and I don't like disappointing her, which is why I agreed to this date."

"Gee, thanks." I bit my lower lip and took a sip of my Guinness, trying to stifle the annoyance that rose inside me. "I'm sure there's a way to phrase that so you sound less of an asshole."

Graham materialized at the table just as I spoke, and a slow grin spread across his face.

"This one bothering you, darling? I'm happy to toss him out if need be."

"Och, piss off, Graham." Thane leaned back and crossed his arms over his chest, his brow furrowing.

"Let's just see what the lass wants, shall we?"

"It's fine." I shook my head, not ready to deal with this pissing match between the two men. "Nobody needs to get thrown out. Yet."

Graham laughed. "Or you'll do it yourself?"

"I just might." I grinned, appreciating him, and maybe I enjoyed Thane's scowl deepening *just* a bit too much.

"Can I take your order?"

"Mac and cheese," I said, cheerfully.

"Guinness stew," Thane ordered, and we handed our menus over.

"I'm sorry," Thane said, before I could speak, and I paused, surprised to hear an apology from him. "You're right. I was being a right arsehole when I said that. You ... bother ... me."

I raised an eyebrow at him. *This was intriguing.*

"I'm still struggling to see where this is less asshole-ish."

Thane huffed and rubbed his hand over the short

beard at his jawline. I tried not to stare. When I'd first met him, I'd been convinced he was the most handsome man I'd ever seen in real life, and that feeling had not changed. Granted, I was far more annoyed with him now than I'd been before, but that didn't change that just looking at him made my mouth water. His sheer size hulked the bistro table between us, and I swear I could feel the warmth radiating off him when he looked at me with those soul-searching blue eyes.

Yup, dinner had been a bad idea. I couldn't be this close to him, like we'd been in Edinburgh, tucked over a small table, attraction ramping up between us. It felt much the same, being here, like this, together again.

And all I wanted to do was ask him if he lived far from the pub.

No, bad Kaia. Intrusive thoughts. This man owns your business lease. You're competing with him on designs for your client.

"You're right. That is my problem, not yours." Thane took a sip of his Irn Bru, his eyes stormy, and God help me, but I wanted to be a boat riding the waves of his turmoil. The man's gravitational force was impossible to ignore, and my body tingled with awareness in his presence. "I don't mix business with pleasure."

"On that, we're agreed." I couldn't help but raise my glass to his, and he tapped his against mine, a light dawning in his eyes.

"Bad experience?" Thane asked, leaning back in his seat.

"You could say that. I was naive. My first, and well,

only real boss out of school. Stars in my eyes. Thought everything was falling into place. Turns out he was married with a baby on the way." I shrugged one shoulder, taking a swallow of Guinness to soothe the shame that burned at my throat. "I've mostly worked for myself ever since."

"Mine was a client." Thane shook his head, and I glanced up, surprised to see understanding on his face, and his eyes free of judgment. "She used me to make her businessman boyfriend jealous. He traveled a lot for work, so he was never around, and I assumed she was single. Until he walked in on us, and I saw the delight on her face. She got what she wanted and a hell of a deal on a beautiful new wrought iron dining table."

"That's shitty," I said, meaning it, and pressed my lips together. People could really be awful. And it surprised me that Thane was being so honest about it too. He was a good man. *What was done to him was cruel.*

"Aye, it was. But I guess lessons learned don't come cheap, do they?"

"Which is why—"

"We don't mix business and pleasure," Thane finished for me just as our food arrived, brought by a lad with a dishtowel tucked at his waist.

"So, it's decided then." I breathed out a sigh of relief, some of the anxiety banding my chest easing, and inhaled the scent of gooey mac and cheese. Comfort food at its finest.

"Aye, lass. Not that I don't think of you. And our night together."

My eyes flashed to his, desire coiling low, and my breath caught at the ragged look of yearning on his face.

"You do?" My heart hammered, and a thread of happiness wound through me. *It hadn't been just me.* He'd been just as into it as I had.

"Aye, lass. Every damn night." With that, Thane stabbed a fork in his pie, his expression disgruntled.

"Oh." What was a woman supposed to say to that? Particularly when we'd just agreed not to act on any attraction we had for each other.

"You're not an easy woman to forget, Kaia."

"I'm not?" Damn it, but I shouldn't be pleased by his words, but I was positively glowing under his terse compliments.

"You left. Without a note. A number. Anything. Bloody hell, but that bothered me."

"I'm sorry," I said, softly, reaching out to touch his arm, but then dropping my hand before I did. There was to be no touching. "If it makes you feel better ..." I hesitated. "I thought it was best to just start my new life fresh. With no—"

"Complications?" Thane huffed out a laugh and shook his head. "Well, looks like you landed yourself smack dab in the middle of one hell of a complication."

"But we can do this, right?" I straightened my shoulders, lifting my chin at him. "We can work on this project together and not step on each other's toes?"

"When she chooses my designs, I'll be delighted to let

you work on them." Thane positively beamed when I curled my lip in disgust at him.

"There's nothing I love more than taking down an overly confident man," I said, smiling brightly.

"May the best man win, then." Thane laughed again when I let out a low growl, and then focused on my mac and cheese. I refused to let him ruin my comfort food.

His knee bumped mine under the table and a shiver danced down my spine. We'd sat just like this in Edinburgh, both of us crowding over a tiny table, our legs and elbows bumping as we'd laughed and talked and had ended the night with pure bliss.

Damn it, but I wanted that again.

I shouldn't.

And I couldn't.

But still.

The thoughts lingered and refused to go away. What was it about wanting something you couldn't have that made it much hotter? I was an adult. I was in control of my actions and my emotions. There was no reason I couldn't carry on a normal conversation with Thane and learn more about his business and life in Loren Brae. And talk we did. He was such an interesting man, but he also asked me questions about my work and family. The time went quickly, especially while devouring delicious food with excellent company.

By the time he'd paid the bill and we were walking out, I was thrumming with desire, like a guitar string plucked, and I hastily waved goodbye to get the hell away from one Thane Blackwood as fast as I could.

"Hey, where are you going?" Thane called from where he stood in the cool night air in front of the pub.

"Walking home."

"Och, lass. I can't let you do that on your own." Footsteps sounded and I picked up speed, needing some space from him, lest I do something crazy like ask him to recite the alphabet with his tongue. Down there.

"It's not far." I trained my eyes ahead, the cool night air a slap to my heated face.

"I'll be seeing you home safe then, Kaia." His tone brooked no argument, and I only then remembered the threat of the Kelpies. Even though we were walking away from the loch, I glanced over my shoulder to see moonlight shimmering across the surface. Were they large? Or were they small and fast—like zombies? Should I even be turning my back on the loch? A million thoughts darted through my mind, but they all stalled when Thane brushed his hand at the base of my back, nudging me forward when I'd stopped.

"Best to get on home."

I wanted to ask him if he knew about the Kelpies. But I hadn't been able to bring myself to tell him about the ghost coo the other day, so what made me think I could casually drop the Kelpies on him now? Instead, I focused on thinking pure thoughts as we walked to my "wee" cottage tucked at the end of a sparsely populated lane on the edge of Loren Brae.

Puppies.

A bold red poppy flower in a green field.

My delicious mac and cheese.

Paint colors for the little bathroom I wanted to freshen up.

Relief filled me when we arrived at my cottage, and I hurried forward. I'd left a lamp on, and cheerful light spilled from the front window, highlighting the shifting branches of two trees that arched in front of the house. It still didn't feel real, this tiny house of mine, but it pleased me to no end to have a place to call my own.

A Stan-free place to call my own. Initially, he'd called me repeatedly after I'd left the States, but finally, the calls had tapered off. I hoped he finally got the picture that we were nothing more than friends. And barely friends at that. Certainly not someone I wanted to be intimate with.

Damn it. The moment my brain landed on the word intimate, desire caused my body to flush with heat. I fumbled at the door, trying to work the old key in the lock, refusing to look over my shoulder at Thane.

"Kaia." His voice was a rasp in the darkness, and I swallowed against my suddenly dry throat.

"Lock sticks a bit," I murmured. How could I be so warm in this cool night? Thane shifted behind me, his body cocooning me, as he reached around me to take the key from my hand to slide it effortlessly in the lock. I squirmed, caught between him and the door, desperately trying to pretend I was anything but interested.

The door swung open.

"Bloody hell." Thane's breath drifted across my neck, and I shivered.

I should have stepped forward.

But I didn't.

I waited.

And when his hand came up, brushing the hair back from my ear, his mouth warm at my neck, my breath caught.

"We shouldn't."

"I know." I did. I truly did.

However.

There was some invisible thread tying us together, pulling me to inch closer to him, to lean back just enough until his lips met my ear, and my shoulders touched his chest.

"Kaia." His lips brushed the lobe of my ear, and I rubbed my thighs together, needing his touch.

"Maybe ... maybe we just need to get it out of our system?" I suggested, hopeful. *Bad girl, Kaia. You know better.* I shoved those thoughts aside and instead focused on the way my body tensed as he leaned close.

His forehead pressed against the side of my head, his breath ragged.

Something about the sound of him physically trying to get himself under control emboldened me.

I'd never had a man want me like this before.

Maybe I barely knew Thane, but what I did know about him, well, *mostly*, I liked. If we ignored the whole trying to take my client away from me thing. But everybody had their faults, and he was trying to protect his own career. I could hardly blame him. Or could I?

The moment stretched out and my heart hammered in my chest.

My God, I want this man. Right now. Right here.

"Och, just to get it out of our system then."

Every nerve ending in my body cheered, and I squealed as Thane scooped me up like I weighed nothing more than a bouquet of flowers, and kicked the door closed behind him.

"Thank God," I breathed, and Thane took me to the floor.

CHAPTER EIGHT

Thane

I'd be lying if I said that I hadn't thought we might be heading here all along. It was impossible to be around Kaia and not think of touching her. My rules were important to me, and clearly *her* rules were important to *her*.

And, yet.

Breaking them suddenly seemed a lot more fun than following them.

A *lot* more fun.

Two steps into the room, I took Kaia to the floor with me, cushioning the fall so she rolled on top, her hair cocooning my face as she laughed at me in surprise.

"Thane! I'll squash you."

"Nope," I said, wrapping my hand around a hunk of

her silky tresses and pulling her head down until I could taste her lips again. Kaia gasped against my mouth so I slipped my tongue inside, seeking her heat. She met me, fire for fire, and we feasted. Sliding my hands down her back, I cupped her generous bum, loving the feel of that soft roundness in my grip, and pulled her more tightly against me. Shifting, I trailed my hands down the backs of her thighs, forcing her legs to straddle me, and arched my back. Hard met soft.

"Thane," Kaia gasped against my mouth.

"I like it when you're on top," I said, rocking against her. Those moody blue eyes widened at my hardness, and I rocked again, all heat and friction and desire.

"That ... oh, yeah. Just like that." Surprise flitted across Kaia's face, and I sucked at her bottom lip, delight filling me as she whimpered into my mouth.

"Think I could make you come undone? Just like this, lass?" I whispered against her lips, licking inside her mouth, loving how responsive she was to my touch. Now she rocked against me of her own accord, riding me, her thick thighs pinning me to the floor. Her soft breasts squished against my chest, and I ached to bury my face against them, to lick my way down her stomach and taste her sweetness again.

But there was time enough for that. *I hope.*

Right now, I was enjoying watching Kaia surprise herself at how much fun *she* was having. She had this beautiful mixture of sexy siren and ingénue about her, and I remembered the same from our night in Edinburgh. At times she'd be shy with her words, uncertain of what she was going to say next, and others she'd be animated, her hands waving in the air, her face alight as she spoke about something that interested her.

I wanted to watch her take full control.

And honestly, it might be my undoing if she did.

Wondering if I could get her to do so, I gripped her bum again, my hands sinking into her soft flesh.

"You set the pace, lass. I'm just here for your taking."

Kaia reared up, gaping at me, caught between pleasure and surprise. Pink tinged her cheeks, and the silky top she wore clung to her breasts, driving me crazy as she shifted over me, centering herself directly on my hard length.

Friction built, and even though I hadn't done this since my high school days, I couldn't help but get caught up as Kaia rolled her hips forward, her breasts bouncing as she rode me with cheerful abandon, until she was crying out over me, and I was damn near exploding in my trousers. Unable to last a minute longer, I rolled, taking her under me, and caught her lips with my own.

"I don't think I've ever dry-humped before." Kaia laughed against my mouth.

I laughed too, surprised that I could do so when I was so close to losing my mind with the need to be buried inside of her. It had been the same the last time we'd been together. Slick heat mixed with laughter mixed with deep-seated desire.

A heady combination, and one that had stuck with me after she'd left.

"It's a lost art, to be sure." I pulled Kaia's top over her

head, almost whimpering at the sight of midnight-blue silk against creamy white skin.

"Is it though? Is it really?" Kaia laughed again, sarcasm deep in her tone, and I buried my face between her breasts, inhaling her soft citrus scent that reminded me of a refreshing glass of lemonade on a warm summer's day.

"I would forge you in wrought iron," I said, licking against her skin, and blowing a breath to watch her shiver against my mouth. Reaching behind, I worked at the clasp of the bra as I explained that *she* was a true piece of art. "All twists and curves. Interlocking at the center with glorious copper elements woven in."

"Oh, Thane." Kaia's voice grew soft, her eyes luminous.

"A statue, not dainty, no." I almost whimpered when the bra finally sprang open, and her creamy breasts spilled free. "But a goddess. A warrior. Both strong and soft, forged in fire, every man falling at her feet." I took a nipple into my mouth, swirling my tongue around the soft nub, and she arched into me, mewling as I scraped my teeth over the sensitive skin. I wasn't going to last. As much as I wanted to worship at the altar of Kaia, I'd been dreaming of touching her again for weeks now and I needed to be inside her.

Kaia was already ahead of me, working to get me naked, and we both paused, doing the quick awkward dance of pulling the rest of our clothes off and flinging them across the floor. Sheathing myself with a condom from my wallet, I grabbed a cushion from the faded couch behind Kaia. Hitching her up, I slipped the cushion under her hips and paused, taking in the glorious sight before me.

Muscular legs sprawled open, leading to generously curved hips, a softly rounded stomach, and gorgeous breasts, her body was a playground for a man like me. I wanted to take her hard and fast now, but it wouldn't be the first time tonight, oh no. If we were going to get this out of our system, I'd make the most of it, and I planned to be exceedingly thorough.

Kaia's hair spread out around her, inky silk against the carpet, her eyes heavy with lust in the warm light from the lamp. Reaching down, I trailed my thumb over her to find her wet and ready for me.

"Bloody hell, but you're gorgeous, Kaia." I slid a finger up, massaging in a circular motion, and Kaia's hips jerked against my hand. Oh yeah, I was going to take my time with her tonight. But for now? I needed to feel her around me again.

To see if we were the perfect fit like I remembered.

Positioning myself at her entrance, I bent over her.

Kaia's eyes fluttered closed as I teased her with my tip.

"Uh-uh, darling. Eyes open. I want to watch as I fill you."

Kaia's eyes sprung open in surprise at my words, and her mouth rounded in a perfect O as I slid deep inside her, her tight wet heat almost sending me over the edge.

"Thane," Kaia moaned, lust clouding her face.

"Aye, lass?" I slid out and then drove in again, seating

myself deeply inside her, the cushion angling her perfectly to receive me.

"Oh my God, that's so damn good," Kaia gasped.

"It is, Kaia. We fit, don't we?" I didn't even really hear the words I was saying at this point, I was so caught up in her slick heat, and the beautiful rhythm of sliding back and forth, and when she started to clench around me, I caught her lips in a searing kiss.

"We're not supposed to fit." Kaia arched her hips into me, meeting me thrust for thrust. "But why is this so damn good?"

"Just like the first time." I'd obsessed over the mysterious woman who'd left me in the middle of the night and now here I was, once more buried deep inside her, my mind focused solely on bringing the both of us as much pleasure as possible.

We broke at the same time, shattering together, and I devoured her shrieks on my tongue, completely lost to this woman. Our bodies slid together, slick with desire, and her fingers dug into my back as she shivered around me.

Needing a moment, I arranged myself over her, pressing my forehead to hers, and we both caught our breath.

"Tell me you have more condoms," I finally said, already needing her again.

"Thane!" Kaia laughed up at me. "Don't you think that was enough?"

"Do you?" I arched an eyebrow at her.

"Um, I mean ..." Kaia pursed her lips in consideration. "It was certainly one for the books."

"You said you wanted to get this out of your system. And if I'm to do what you've so nicely requested, I suspect there's more work to do. As every good blacksmith knows, Kaia, you've got to keep the fire at a consistent high temperature." I stood and reached out my hands for her, hauling her naked body against mine. "And what do we need to do that?"

"Constant attention," Kaia murmured against my mouth, and I lifted her, wrapping her legs around me as I walked her backward.

"Exactly. Please tell me there's a bed around here somewhere." I glanced over her shoulder to see a door to another room and the faint outline of a bed. "I think I have rugburn on my knees."

"And on my back." Kaia started laughing again, the sound soft and low against where she trailed kisses against my jawline. "Dry-humping and rugburn on the knees. Should we play spin the bottle next?"

"Sure. We'll play 'body parts for me to kiss next.'"

"Eeep!" Kaia exclaimed as I dropped her on the bed and dove between her legs.

Night slowly gave way to morning, the murky light reminding us we should sleep, and finally spent, after hours of vigorous creative play, I slipped beneath the duvet with an already sleeping Kaia and pulled her gently back against me.

A shriek split the dawn.

Kaia jolted against me, trying to spring up, and I pulled her back more tightly against my chest.

"Shhh, it's all right. I've got you."

Another shriek sounded, loud enough to rattle the windows, and Kaia whimpered.

"What *is* that? Should we go—"

"We absolutely should not go. No, lass. We'll be staying right here."

"What if it gets in?" Kaia snuggled more tightly against my body, and I tightened my hold even more.

"Can't. From what I'm told at least."

"Is that the Kelpies?"

"I guess." I still had mixed feelings on what to think about the Kelpies, but so many people in the village believed them to be real, and here we were listening to them scream in the wee hours of the morning. It was hard to deny such things when you could hear them so clearly.

Kaia twisted so her eyes searched my face.

"You don't believe in them?"

"I haven't seen them." I couldn't help but lean over and nibble at her kiss-swollen lips.

"But you can hear them? I mean, the whole of Scotland can probably hear them. Man, I thought that was just dreams I was having. But this ... it's real. They're real. Holy hell, what have I done?"

"What do you mean, *what have you done*?" I squinted down at her in confusion, but Kaia just shook her head. I wonder if she just meant she regretted her decision to move to Loren Brae. I certainly hoped not.

Not that we were doing this again or anything.

As soon as my thoughts drifted there, I shoved them aside.

Even if this was meant to be a one-night, well technically, two-night, thing, I was going to savor our time together now.

"Shh, lass. Go back to sleep. I'm here, all right? I've got you."

Burying my face in her neck, I inhaled her sweet scent, and prayed the Kelpies would be quiet so I could enjoy this moment of solitude with this warm, witty, bold, and terribly irresistible woman. What had surprised me even more? Watching her interact with my niece. It had opened something in me, a door I'd long held closed, and suspiciously felt like yearning. How was I going to walk away from someone that I could chat with about everything from work to sports, sink into her glorious body, and then cuddle gently in the early hours of the morning?

Somehow, even though my body craved her, and my lips longed to taste her, I was going to have to learn how to forget.

CHAPTER NINE

Kaia

When I woke, my tiny bed was empty, and I was rested in a way that I hadn't been in a very long time. Stretching, I noticed twinges in my muscles, and when I closed my eyes, flashes of the night before brought a smile to my lips. Thane had been true to his word, ensuring that if we were to get this out of our systems, that no stone would go unturned, so to speak. Now I had to somehow pretend it hadn't been the best night of my life.

Burying my face in the pillow, I breathed in his masculine scent and silently berated myself for my choices. Because, *really*, how was I supposed to pretend he hadn't dominated every inch of my body and brought me so much pleasure that I might have competed with the Kelpies for shrieks in the night?

Remembering the early morning disturbance, I sat up and reached for an oversized hoodie I used as a robe. Pulling it over my head, my mind whirled at the memory of those otherworldly sounds. Was I meant to be helping with ... that? Were the other women out there in the early morning hours, fighting off Kelpies, while I'd slept blissfully in Thane's arms? I wouldn't even know what to do. I mean, I'd picked a weapon, I guess, but what did that even mean? Would I be stabbing a Kelpie in the eye with it? And if they were really made of water, would it even do anything?

A thousand questions whirled as I stumbled out of the bedroom, my sights on my bathroom, when I skidded to a stop.

Thane stood over my kitchen counter, a cup of coffee in his hand, wearing no shirt and a smile on his lips as he perused my sketchbook.

"Hey!" I exclaimed, rushing over to slam the book closed. "Those are my designs for Common Gin."

"They're good." Thane took a sip of his coffee and regarded me over the rim of his cup.

"They're not ready." I slammed the notebook back on the counter and glared at him. "And that's cheating. Now you owe me a look at your designs too."

Thane's smile widened, and he stepped forward, caging me against the counter. Putting his coffee down, he placed an arm on either side of me, forcing me to pull my attention away from his exceedingly well-muscled chest and up to his face.

"Okay," Thane said, simply. The lines around his eyes were softer today, as though some of the tension he habitually carried had eased, and I narrowed my eyes at him, suspicious.

"That seems too easy."

"I'm in a good mood." Thane shrugged and before I could stop him, he bent and gave me a kiss. It was just a brush of lips, soft, but when I sighed into his mouth, he angled his head, deepening the kiss, and it took everything in my power to bring my hands up to push him back.

"We ... we can't." I struggled in a breath, and then took another, forcing myself to abide by the agreement we'd made. In the light of day, it was a touch easier to remember that we had very real responsibilities, plus, I had to figure out this whole Kelpies and magick thing. There wasn't much room for me to be breaking my own rules this early into a new life, one that I'd carefully saved for and dreamt of, because if I burned bridges with the only man who owned a forge in town, then I'd be stuck. It would take me a while, but I'd be able to save up enough money to build my own, but until then? I was at the mercy of the man who owned the equipment I needed to successfully do my job.

And I'd just slept with him.

Again.

"If that's the case, then why are you caressing me, love?" Thane asked lightly, and my eyes rounded in horror. I'd gone from pushing his chest away to gently running my palms over the smooth contours of his muscles.

"Damn it." I snatched my hand back and glared at him. Ducking under his arm, I moved away. "I ... just give me a second. And stop snooping."

Making quick use of the bathroom, I stared in the mirror as I brushed my teeth. I looked ... well, hell, I looked like I'd been thoroughly pleasured the night before. My skin had a nice flush to it, and a touch of beard burn could be seen at my neck if I angled my head just so. My hair was a mess, in knots and springing out around my head, but the tension lines in my forehead had eased.

Rinsing my toothbrush, I took a moment and stared at myself.

Would it be so bad if this could be a thing? Thane and me?

No. Bad.

I dried my hands and left the bathroom. My new life hinged on the grace of this man, and I couldn't muddy the waters.

Though the waters may be a *touch* opaque after last night.

Thane grinned at me from where he sat on the couch, still with no shirt on, scrolling his phone.

"Why are you smiling at me like that?"

"You look beautiful. And annoyed, which I find even more appealing for some reason."

"Stop complimenting me," I grumbled and went

over to where the coffee had been made. At least that was a perk of having someone here and waking up before me. Pouring myself a cup, I turned and leaned against the counter, even though I wanted to nestle on the couch next to Thane.

"Fine. That mop of yours needs a good tidy." Thane gestured at my hair, and I winced.

"But ... I just woke up." I patted the mess of my hair —which he'd had a large part in contributing to—and glared at him.

"It might be time for a shave too, lass." Thane's eyes dropped to my bare legs, and I gasped.

"I didn't know I was taking someone home with me last night," I argued.

"And ye snore like a banshee." Thane laughed when I slapped my coffee cup on the counter.

"I do not snore." I pointed at him. *Did I? Maybe I did*. Stan had never complained, but it wasn't like we'd shared a room.

"Just cute wee ones," Thane promised, and I stomped a foot, eliciting another chuckle from him.

"Thane," I said, my tone serious, and he sobered.

"Aye, lass?"

"We can't ..." I picked up my coffee and moved forward, settling on the arm of the couch across from him. "This can't ... we have to not do this again."

"Aye, lass. I reckon you've the right of it. Too bad, as it was a belter, wasn't it?"

"A belter?" Distracted, I cocked an eyebrow at him,

wondering if he was referencing how loud I got during our, ahem, activities the night before.

"Och, a belter, lass. We use it to describe someone or an experience as outstanding, fun, fantastic. You know, you're watching the match and it's a pure belter, you ken?"

I blinked at Thane, enjoying the rhythm of his Scots and wanting nothing more than to crawl into his lap. Forcing myself to stay focused, I cleared my throat.

"Right, um, yes, it was a belter. But it can't happen again. We got it out of our system."

"Did we, love?" Thane's eyes glinted in the sunlight that streamed through the window and my heart twisted. How was I going to keep a professional distance from this man?

"Aye, we did," I said, mimicking him.

"If you say so."

"Thane, this is serious." Taking another sip of my coffee, I furrowed my brow, needing him to understand why we had to stop.

Even now, years later, I could still remember the looks of my co-workers when they realized I was dating the boss. I'd thought they were jealous at the time, unhappy that maybe he was giving me the better jobs. It was only *after* that I'd realized it wasn't jealousy but judgment in their eyes. An experience I didn't wish to repeat.

"Och, Kaia. I know it." The smile finally dropped from Thane's face, and he leaned forward, something shifting in his eyes. Was it sadness? "I was just enjoying the afterglow a bit, I suppose. I know you've the right of it. It's in both of our best interests to remain as colleagues."

"Right." Why did that suddenly annoy me? This was exactly what I wanted, no, needed. But hearing the words come out of his mouth was a touch annoying. Frustrating, even. The dopamine center in my brain just wanted more of him, but Thane was not a drug I could get addicted to. So I needed to pull my big girl pants on and move on. "I'm starting my life over in Loren Brae. And that includes the need to establish my business. And you … well—"

"I own the space that's allowing you to work and start your business. And if I think with my cock instead of my head, I could potentially screw this up for you, and you'll be out of a place to work."

"Erm, yeah, that's pretty much it in a nutshell. I can't … I just can't afford to do it all on my own. Not yet. At some point I might be able to afford my own shop, but not to the extent you have built up. The forge is a vital piece in my journey here."

"And you don't want to just come work for me then?" Even as he said it, Thane winced.

"Oh, right. That would go over so well." I shook my "mop" of hair. "We're already on rocky ground with me leasing from you. How would the guys feel if you gave me a salary and then I was sleeping with you? Think that would go over well for me?"

"Och, no. Not likely so." Thane pursed his lips.

"So. No more of this." I pointed a finger between the two of us.

"That's fair, lass. From this moment forward, strictly platonic." Thane held out his hand to shake and I took it, his rough palm warm against mine. I swear it felt like an electrical current vibrated between us, and I saw the desire flash in his eyes. I'm sure he imagined pulling me into his lap. As much as I could see myself straddling him and starting the day in a more exciting way than sucking down a cup of coffee and getting work done on my sketches, I dropped his hand.

"Right. So ..." I gestured toward the door. "I'll be seeing you around then."

"May I grab my shirt before you toss me out?" Humor gleamed in Thane's eyes and I rolled my eyes.

"Yeah, yeah. Just get on with it, would ya? I need to work." Plus, I wanted to get in touch with Agnes and see what time she wanted to meet later.

"On a Sunday? That's dedication." Thane stood and picked up his shirt, which was draped over the back of the couch, and put it on. Though I was sad to see those muscles disappear, I also knew it was for the best.

Or so I needed to remind myself, over and over, until he left and I was no longer tempted by his nearness.

I just nodded, not wanting to encourage conversation, needing this moment to be over so I could examine my emotions in private. It wasn't just that Thane Blackwood had a hot body and knew how to pleasure a woman. He had layers I hadn't noticed on our first night together. He didn't say much about his sister the night before, but the love and reverence in his eyes for his niece? The closest I'd ever seen that before was in the way my mom and dad looked at each other ... and at me. That little girl may not have a father in her life, but man, did she have an exceptional uncle who would never let her down. I'd love to find a man like that for myself.

He's a colleague. You need to keep this platonic moving forward. You've already crossed way too many lines. Time to be an adult and put your professional boundaries up, Kaia.

Thane checked his pockets, making sure he had his keys and wallet, and then went to the front door. I stood and walked to him.

"Thanks for the ..." I paused, my brain scrambling at what word to land on without sounding entirely too salacious or inviting.

"Fun?" Thane supplied and I raised both eyebrows, nodding in agreement.

"See you at work, pal," I said.

"Aye. Catch ya later, *mate*." Thane lightly punched my shoulder, and I pursed my lips, wanting to laugh at the ridiculousness, but I honestly felt somewhat bereft as I watched him walk away in the soft morning light, whistling lightly. I waited until he was out of sight, and never once did he look back.

Why did I feel despondent?

I'd just had my body rocked six ways to Sunday, had orgasmed more than I could possibly count, and would likely walk with a slight limp for days. I should be exuberant, bouncing around the room, and instead I lingered at the open door, watching the leaves shift on the branches in the soft morning breeze.

A raven landed at my feet.

At least I thought it was a raven. Maybe it was a crow. But this bird was bigger than a crow, which likely meant it was a raven if I could call upon my limited knowledge of birds. Feathers like midnight, eyes polished onyx, it tilted its head at me and dropped something at my feet.

"Well. Hello there, my friend. Aren't you pretty?" I admired the deep sheen of inky blue tucked among its silky black feathers. The raven backed up a bit, and then bent its head, nudging the item closer to me with its beak. "Is this for me then?"

Yes.

Surprised, I gave the bird a considering look. Had it just spoken in my mind? Or was I assigning it attributes it didn't have? It wasn't uncommon for me to anthropomorphize animals, because I enjoyed the idea that they had thoughts and feelings just like humans did. But this felt different. The voice in my head was rough and abrasive, not my own, and it gave me pause.

"That's ... interesting." Bending, I examined the gift at my feet as the raven hopped back a few steps. "Is that nail polish?"

A half-empty bottle of pink sparkly nail polish lay on the stone path in front of my door. Picking it up, I held it in the air and looked from the bird back to the bottle. The only pink sparkly nail polish that I'd had contact with of late was Audrey's.

"Is this Audrey's?"

No.

"But you're wanting me to think of Audrey, aren't you?"

Was I having a full-on conversation with a raven? Yes, I was. But at this point, did it even matter? Kelpies were screaming in the night, ghost highland coos jumped out of walls, and apparently cats called Calvin could speak into your mind *and knew strange things about you*. Maybe ravens did talk in Loren Brae.

Help her.

My eyes flew from the bottle to the bird, concern kicking up.

"Is she hurt?"

No. Help her. You can.

I pondered the bird's words, holding the bottle tightly in my hand. An idea formed.

"You mean with my magick, don't you? The bullies at school?"

Aye.

Of course it was a Scottish bird. Smiling, I lifted the bottle in the air at the bird. "Thank you, my friend. You've given me an idea. Do you have a name?"

Murdoch.

"Nice to meet you, Murdoch. Thanks for stopping by. If you need anything, you'll, um, let me know?"

Blueberries.

"Um, right. Okay. I'll see if they have some at the store then."

Murdoch bowed his head at me, fanning his wings out behind him as he dipped, and then he was gone, arcing gracefully into the sky. I stood for a moment, watching him soar away, clutching the bottle in my hand.

He wanted me to help Audrey. And if my magick worked how I hoped it would, I might just be able to do that. I wouldn't even need to go to the forge for the idea I had, at least I didn't think so. Turning, I went inside, closing the door behind me. For a moment, I just leaned back against the door and took a few deep breaths to steady myself, as memories of the night before flashed through my brain.

Thane had been … all-consuming. Larger than life, both in person and personality, he'd dominated my body, my thoughts, and my feelings. I'd never met someone so … potent as he was.

And somehow I had to figure out how to work with him.

Could I use magick on myself? Maybe I needed to make an amulet that would help me forget the intensity of my attraction for him. Sighing, I went to my crate of jewelry-making tools and soon had a mini workshop set up at the counter. Pulling out my phone, I put on a mellow Spotify playlist and picked up my tools.

I wanted to make a symbol of protection for Audrey to wear.

At first I thought about a bracelet, but I wasn't sure her wrist size or if she was allowed to wear bracelets in school. So instead, I decided upon a necklace she could tuck under her shirt. What I needed to do was form an amulet that, in theory, I could infuse with my magick to give her courage, as well as protect her from harm.

No small order, that. Considering I didn't even know the first thing about magick. I paused. Should I search for magickal spells on the internet? How did one just start doing magick?

But, typical of my nature, I felt pulled to just carry on, so I did.

Sunlight streamed through the small window above the sink, illuminating the counter cluttered with tools, silver wire, and an assortment of gemstones. My fingers moved deftly as I twisted and shaped the fine silver wire, coaxing it into the delicate outline of a thistle. Using pliers to curl the filigree into tiny leaves and a gently curving stem, I secured each detail with care. The process required patience, but I didn't mind. It gave me something to focus on other than Thane. Instead, I considered my intent with this piece and what mixture of attributes I should infuse the amulet with.

At the thistle's heart, I set a small sapphire cabochon, the stone polished smooth and glowing with its own quiet brilliance. Wrapping the wire snugly around the gemstone, I formed a protective cradle. There, I worked slowly, an evil eye motif emerging naturally, the sapphire's deep blue center framed by intricate spirals of silver that radiated outward like lashes. Holding the almost-finished piece in my palm, I felt the weight of my responsibility. A pendant like this wasn't merely a charm, it was a guardian. As I worked, I thought about Audrey —small, vulnerable, and braver than she knew. And yet, especially while sitting with her uncle, she was so strong. Confident. Her resolute trust that he'd never belittle or ridicule her showed that he'd spoken that unconditional love into her life. *And yet, she didn't have a dad ... and kids teased her about it.* How horrible for her. She was the cutest, sweetest kid I'd met, and I hoped that I truly would be able to help.

Once finished, I held the pendant between my palms and closed my eyes. I wasn't entirely confident in the mechanics behind finding or feeling my magick, so I just did what felt right to me. Warmth shimmered inside me, a glow that seemed to roll over me like a soft wave on a pink sand beach at sunset.

"May you shield her from harm," I whispered, my voice strong, "and grant her courage to face the shadows." The pendant pulsed faintly against my skin, as if breathing in the power I offered. I opened my eyes, and the thistle glinted with a subtle, otherworldly glow, the sapphire's gaze unblinking and watchful. No forge had been necessary—my will, my skill, and my magick had been enough.

Or, at least I hoped it had been. There was no surefire way for me to determine that I'd actually infused the pendant with a protection spell, but either way, it felt right to me and that was enough for today. Pleased, I carefully threaded the piece on a silver chain and then wrapped it in tissue paper, tucking it in my purse to give to Thane for Audrey. We were friends, right? It shouldn't be seen as anything more than a friendly gift for his niece who was struggling. I didn't have to tell him it was magick, in the real sense, and therefore didn't need to reveal any of this side of myself to him. I wasn't sure I was ready to share that with anyone, to be honest, since I still really had no clue about how any of it worked.

Speaking of, I needed to contact Agnes. Picking up my phone, I sent her a text and she responded immediately.

> Hi Agnes – Kaia here. Did you still want to meet today?

> Good morning! I was hoping to hear from you. Want to pop by the castle later this afternoon? A few of the girls are getting together.

I PAUSED, pursing my lips. A girls' night? I mean, I knew there were others in the Order and that I'd have to meet them, but still. Groups of women sometimes intimidated me. Either way, I was in it now.

> Sounds great. Can I bring anything?

> Nae bother. Lia loves to provide the snacks.

. . .

> Cool, see ya later!

It looked like I'd be spending my day at the castle. Pleased, I headed for the bathroom. I needed a long, hot shower, another coffee, and some time with some new friends. And all would be right in the world.

Just so long as I could stick to my guns and keep myself from wrapping myself around Thane like the ivy that clung to the walls of my cottage.

CHAPTER TEN

Kaia

Apparently, I was going to have a girls' night. Or late afternoon, really, as I walked toward the castle after lunch. Agnes had invited me to meet the others, and I hated to admit that nerves had me taking the long way around the village instead of heading directly down Main Street and past the loch. It had been a long time since I'd tried to make new friends, particularly ones of the female variety, since I worked in such a male-dominated field. Would they like me? Or would they think I was an oddball? I reminded myself that Orla was a member of the Order and she ran a construction firm, so I had at least one similar soul in the group. And Willow had been nothing but kind and welcoming to me, even if I was going to be working with her, and she'd point-blank asked to be friends. *Everything would be just fine.*

Still, nerves were nerves, and they were hard to entirely dismiss as I walked along the hedge-lined drive toward the castle. The hedges were immaculately trimmed, tall, obscuring the castle from view until the very last turn. It had to be demanding work keeping everything pristine, and I hadn't even had a chance to wander through the castle's famous walled garden yet. I was told between the castle tour and the beautiful gardens, tourists often made a point to visit Loren Brae on their way out to the Isle of Skye. Though, with the rumors of Kelpies plaguing the town, the tourism industry had been hit hard and the dearly needed visitor income was drying up. Even though I'd only called Loren Brae my home for a few weeks now, I already cared about its future. Everyone I'd met thus far had been welcoming to me, and the town itself could be a picture on a postcard.

Pausing as the castle came into view, I held up my fingers and framed it in a rectangle. Pretty as a picture, the castle stirred some deep-rooted emotion inside of me. Pride? Longing? Maybe it was just the idea of connecting to something that had lasted through centuries. Generations of families had lived and fought for what was theirs here, and now I, too, was joining them. Because, somewhere between uprooting my life and moving to Scotland and accepting a role in the Order of Caledonia, Loren Brae had also become mine.

Mine to protect.

Mine to stand for.

Mine to love.

And for some reason, that made me think of my mom's words about my great-grandmother.

"But it was said she would charm the gates. The doors. The entrances. Late at night she'd walk the village and speak spells unto houses, and stand before the castle gates, and some said, well, they said they could see a glow coming from her hands as she did her charms."

Had that been ... passed down to me somehow?

A barrage of barking stopped me in my tracks as Sir Buster and Lady Lola, a chihuahua in a kilt and a corgi mix with a tartan collar, rounded the corner and headed straight for me. Crouching, I held out my arms awaiting their arrival, because I'd always been a dog person.

Movement blurred, and the ghost highland coo, which had nearly given me a heart attack, jumped out from the hedge and sent Sir Buster about ten inches straight into the air.

I choked on a laugh at the horrified look on Sir Buster's little face—his eyes wide with terror—as Lady Lola skidded backward and tumbled onto her generous rump. Clyde pawed one hoof and bellowed into the sky, and the dogs recovered themselves, their barks ferocious. Clyde, seeming to realize his mistake, turned tail and ran, the dogs at his heels. I held a hand to my heart, torn between shock and humor, as I straightened from my crouch. Supposedly, I'd get used to Clyde and his antics, but at the moment I was certain I'd never get over seeing a ghost in broad daylight. Or at night. Or whenever, really. The barking trailed away as the dogs chased the coo into the garden, and I just shook my head, amazed at the sight.

"Och, it's every day with those three." I turned to see Archie, a tall, thin man with a shock of white hair and bushy eyebrows, squinting after the trio of animals. "Clyde pretends he doesn't know what he's doing, and Buster flies into a rage every time it happens. Lola just goes along for the fun of it."

"And that's just become the norm, now? Ghosts and all that?" I waved a hand toward the gardens.

"I don't reckon I have much say in it either way, lass." Archie slapped his gardening gloves in his palm. "Magick is a part of Loren Brae. Those of us tasked with protecting her have learned to expect the unexpected."

"But how?" I was someone that liked a road map for things. I liked understanding how systems worked, and why things were the way they were. "How do you protect? How do you accept magick?"

"We protect in many ways." Archie started walking and I fell into step next to him, intrigued. "We use spells, rituals, magickal weapons, tools. All handed down from generation to generation. There will always be a push-pull with anything magickal. A give and take. We use the knowledge given to us and do our best to be good stewards of the gifts we've been given, and the responsibilities we've accepted."

"I tried earlier," I admitted, pausing as we drew closer to the castle. "To use my magick, that is. I'm not sure if it worked or if I did it right."

"Did you bring your chisel with you?" Archie slanted a glance at my bag.

"I did." Wondering why he needed it, I pulled it out and handed it to him. Archie held the tool in the air and turned it, squinting.

"Is that new?" Archie tapped a finger around a copper band that now wreathed the handle.

"It is!" I took the chisel back from him and examined the band that shimmered around the handle. "How on earth?"

"Looks like you passed a challenge. Which means whatever you did, you used your magick correctly and the Clach na Fìrrin approved." Archie raised his bushy eyebrows.

"I made a protection pendant for …" I paused, not sure if I was ready to talk about Thane with anyone. "A young girl in need."

"That'll do, lass. That'll do." Archie patted my shoulder once and then whistling, wandered off into the garden.

That was it? A pat on the back and no further instruction on what the hell I was doing here? Shaking my head, I wandered toward the side door where I'd been instructed to enter the castle and tapped lightly on the door.

"Oh, hi. Are you Kaia?" I whirled at a voice at my back to see a pretty blond woman carrying a hedgehog.

"I am." Smiling, I stepped closer to peer at the sleepy hedgehog in her arms.

"I'm Shona, and this is Eugene." Shona gestured

with the hedgehog who let out a little yawn and burrowed back into the crook of her arm. "He's been a little clingy lately so I thought I'd bring him along."

"He's very cute. So you're ..." I glanced around and lowered my voice. "One of us?"

"Aye." Shona laughed at me, blue eyes twinkling. "I'm a garden witch and have my greenhouse down the way along the loch."

"A garden witch?" Huh, what did that make me then?

"Aye. The magick helps heal the plants, grow them strong, and I can mix them into medicines and tinctures and whatnot. Pairs nicely with Lia's talents."

"And Lia is?"

"I'm a kitchen witch." I jumped and looked up at another woman who had appeared around the corner of the castle. A fellow American, based on the accent, with curls springing around her head and a leather book in her hands. "And you must be Kaia?"

"I am, nice to meet you." I shook both of their hands.

"Let's head on in. Sophie said to meet in the library." Lia pulled the door open and my eyes were immediately caught on the beautiful foyer with soaring ceilings and elaborate wainscotting. I loved buildings with character, and it was such a treat to see inside the castle. I followed the women down a hallway hung with portraits of what must be various ancestors that had lived in the castle, with sconces designed to look like torches lighting our way. A mix of modern and antique.

Lia pushed through a set of double doors and my

heart sighed as we stepped inside a beautiful library. Floor-to-ceiling shelves lined each wall, and a fireplace on one end was bookended by two large windows with dog beds beneath. A long table dominated the other side of the room, and there we found Sophie, Willow, Orla, and Agnes. A charcuterie board had been set in the middle of the table, and wine was open and breathing next to a set of glasses.

"Ladies! Just in time." Sophie held up the bottle of wine and we all nodded in agreement.

"Kaia, do you know everyone?" Willow drew forward, giving me a quick hug, and I nodded.

"I do."

"Hi, Kaia." Orla gave me a sheepish grin.

"So …" I winced. We were due to give her our designs this week, and I wasn't sure what the protocol was with mixing work and … well, ancient magickal organizations?

"Och, I know. I couldn't rightly tell you what I was until I knew you were one of us." Orla tugged at the braid over her shoulder and shrugged. "But I am glad that you're a part of us, and I promise that I'll be fair when the time comes to look at the designs."

"Oh, good." I exhaled. "I was a bit worried that I'd have an unfair advantage. Not that I don't want to win the bid, but I guess I want to do it on my own merit, not because we're part of"—I waved a finger in a circle—"this."

"I promise that I'll be honest with my feedback." Orla squeezed my arm, lightning quick, and then drew her hand back like she wasn't used to touching others.

"Soooo," Agnes trilled, raising her glass of wine to mine. "How was the rest of your date last night?"

"Date?" Sophie perked up from where she perused the cheese. "Who with?"

"Thane," Agnes supplied before I could say anything. "The owner of Blackwood Forge."

"Oh, I suspected as much," Orla said, and my cheeks heated.

"I promise we'll treat your project with the utmost professionalism." Damn it. I hadn't wanted Orla to learn about Thane and me, lest she decide that working with a romantically involved pair was off limits for her.

"I'm sure you will. Don't worry, Kaia, I found love at work also." Orla's pale skin flushed when the others all made soft cooing sounds of delight.

"I told Kaia we wouldn't judge her." Willow lounged against the table, picking up a grape between fingers with nails painted a screaming red. "You work with Finn, I work with Ramsay, Sophie works with Lachlan, and Shona even rented her house to Owen. It's just Lia that doesn't work with Munroe, but she might as well since he's building his damn business about two steps from the front door of her restaurant."

My head spun with all this new information as I gaped at the group of women all beaming back at me.

"Thane and I ... we're not ..."

"It was weird, but I was certain his lorry was still in the parking lot of the pub this morning." Agnes neatly threw me under the bus.

"Um." I choked, my face flaming.

"Ohhhhh, it does sound like your date went well." Sophie laughed and waved me over. "He's quite a muscular man if I recall?"

"Och, he's class," Orla agreed. "Short with words, all gruff and muscular. I can see the appeal, Kaia."

"Oh God." I wiped a hand over my face.

"Here. Sit. Drink. Then give us all the details." Willow pushed me into a chair and shoved a glass of wine in my face, and I took a long sip, the cool liquid soothing my burning throat.

"It's nothing," I said, and the women all laughed at once. And in that moment, I wished I could have called Marisa and told her all about it. We both hadn't done the best job at keeping up regularly, missing each other's calls with the time difference, but I missed her dreadfully. I'd never had a large circle of female friends, and I'd always attributed that to not having much in common with them. But this? Instant, warm friendship? It was a gift, and I was grateful. *But I do need to steer them away from Thane.*

"I've said that before," Sophie insisted. She slid the charcuterie board toward me. "But humor us. Why is it nothing? It doesn't sound like nothing."

"Based on the way I found them wrapped around each other in the hallway the other day, I'd say they're more than nothing. They're something. Something very hot and exciting." Willow fanned her face.

"An illicit tryst in the castle hallway? Even sexier." Sophie laughed at my chagrin.

"Oh my God. Okay, just listen. It's complicated, all

right?" I took another sip of my wine and rushed to explain. "I actually met him in Edinburgh. Except I didn't know it was him, him. Like I didn't know he lived in Loren Brae or that I would be signing a lease at his forge. He was supposed to just be a one-night stand." I blanched as soon as the words were out. Now these women would think I was a slut or something. Not that there was anything wrong with having a one-night stand. I was allowed to seek my own pleasure, wasn't I? It just wasn't certain how this information would be received.

"They always are, darling, they always are." Lia saluted me with her wine, and I grinned, relieved, catching the faint trace of Boston in her accent.

"I just ... it was kind of like a 'hey, I'm starting my life over and haven't dated in a long time so I can let myself have some fun' kind of thing. We met at the museum, had drinks, hung out, and well ..."—I waved a hand in the air—"it was hot. It was great. And then I snuck away in the middle of the night, moved to Loren Brae, and thought that was the end of it."

"Until he got back from the Holyrood project in Edinburgh," Orla surmised, her eyes alight with understanding.

"Bingo. I'd already been working in the forge for a few weeks, drumming up business, working on meeting new clients, and in strolled Thane."

"He didn't know who you were? As someone who signed the lease?" Shona asked. She'd laid a napkin on the table and was currently cutting up a tomato for Eugene who had gone from sleepy to very interested in what she was doing.

"We never gave last names or exchanged contact information. In fact, we never even talked about our jobs." I sighed. "It was just this moment in time. Where we could exist and have fun and not talk about anything serious."

"Sounds fabulous," Sophie said. "And then what happened? When he came here?"

"He wasn't happy about it. And even worse, he was furious that I had gotten the Common Gin project from under him, I guess."

"Och, that makes even more sense now." Orla winced. "He was pretty worked up when he came to see me about the bid."

"He tried to take the bid away from you?" Lia gaped at me. "That's ridiculous. Orla, you can't let that happen. Should I speak to Munroe?"

"No," Orla and I said at the same time.

"He didn't try to take the bid necessarily," Orla continued. "But he was trying to show me that the scope of the work would require a team, not just a single blacksmith, and unfortunately, he's not wrong."

"No, he's not," I hastily admitted. "It's a huge project, and the scope has broadened since we first spoke."

"My solution was to ask that they both present their designs, we'd decide on the best ideas, and they'd then execute the work as a team. I figured it would be a win-win for them both." Orla gave me a sympathetic look. "I hope you know it isn't me dismissing your abilities or anything of the sort."

"I understand. Truly, I do. It stung, a bit, that he went straight to you instead of speaking to me, but I think I'm beginning to understand him better. He's pretty rough around the edges."

"Which, I, for one, find to be incredibly hot." Willow winked at me.

"Ramsay's favorite word is 'no,' and his second favorite thing to do is kick people out of his shop." Sophie laughed. "He's as grumpy as can be."

"He doesn't tell me 'no' all that often though." Willow preened and we all hooted with laughter.

"To be clear, Orla, we've agreed to move forward as colleagues only."

"Colleagues who sleep together?" Agnes arched an eyebrow at me.

"We got it out of our system," I rushed on, pressing my lips together. "It's fine. We're certainly capable of doing our job well and remaining respectful colleagues."

"Uh-huh," Willow said. "You two aren't going to be able to keep your hands off each other, at least from what I saw. Girl, that chemistry is palpable."

"It's fine," I repeated. "Everything's fine. I can handle this."

"Can I just ask …" Shona fed the delighted Eugene a bit of tomato, and he grinned as he ate it, tomato bits dripping from his mouth to the napkin below. He looked a bit like a cute, prickly serial killer. "Why won't you date him?"

"We've both made the mistake of dating in our work environment before. It didn't end well for either of us. Keep in mind that he owns the forge that has all the supplies I need to do my job. If things soured between us, it would take considerable capital to build what he already has. I'm just not in the position to do something of that nature. Yet. In time, when I have more customers, I'll be able to build my own shop, but I'm not there yet. Which means I have to rely on keeping a good working relationship with Thane. And, well—"

"Sex muddies the waters," Sophie finished for me.

"Exactly." I blew out a breath and picked up a square of cheese. Eugene caught the movement and rushed over to me, grinning his tomato-spattered grin. "Does he eat cheese?"

"No, best to give him more tomato." Shona handed me a small piece and I fed it to Eugene, surprised by how gently he took the piece from me.

"Okay, he's super cute."

"He's a sweetie," Shona agreed, an adoring look on her face.

"Wait until you meet her gnomes," Willow said, and I started.

"Gnomes?" Did Shona collect garden statues?

"Her familiars." Agnes drew my attention to her. "This might be a good time to pause and explain a bit more about our magickal friends here. One of the more interesting parts of stepping into power is you often gain a familiar of sorts who helps you along the way. Not always, but many of the women here have them."

"A familiar? Like ... the black cat with the witch?"

"Except mine's a tabby." Willow nodded to the cracked door where Calvin, her cat, sauntered through as if on cue. "I can speak with him."

"You weren't lying?" I gaped at the cat who flashed me a look.

I told you she wasn't.

"So I really can hear his thoughts," I gasped.

Willow looked at Calvin. "Is that right, baby? Can you communicate with Kaia?"

Calvin swished his tail and jumped up on Willow's lap, kneading his paws into her thighs.

Hi, Kaia.

"Incredible," I murmured, amazed.

"I have a broonie," Lia said, and my mouth dropped open.

"What in the world is that?"

"It's a brownie, or broonie, depending on where you were raised. Kind of like a little house elf. He helps me in the kitchen."

My eyes widened.

"I have gnomes. Gnorman and Gnora. They're impossible and absolutely delightful."

"I have, well, *had* ... a ghost companion. The Green Lady. She was my guide for years."

"And I suppose Clyde would be mine," Sophie mused, "though I wouldn't say he does much guiding, more goofing." A plaintive "moo" sounded from above and I glanced up as the other women laughed, but Clyde was nowhere to be seen.

"Um, so that's all kind of wild." I fed Eugene another piece of tomato. "And I'd usually just kind of like scoff at all of this, I guess, except, I think I might have met mine. My familiar that is. Maybe."

"Is that right?" Agnes leaned forward, her eyes dancing. "Do tell."

"He's a raven. Murdoch. He brought me a bottle of nail polish this morning and I was fairly certain I could hear him speaking. It kind of threw me, to be honest, but it did set me in motion on trying out my magick." I looked up, but only saw interest and acceptance on everyone's faces.

"What did he bring you?" Shona asked. She tapped the table lightly and Eugene scurried back to her. Calvin watched, interested, but made no move to pounce on the little hedgie.

"A bottle of nail polish." At the confused looks on the other women's faces, I continued. "But I knew what he was getting at. See, Thane has a niece named Audrey. And I went into work the other day and we all had tea and she painted our nails."

"Thane let his niece paint his nails?" Willow interjected, and I nodded. "That's hot."

I had to agree with her.

"And during that time she mentioned getting bullied at school for not having a dad."

The women all shifted in their seats, and my eyebrows winged up. It was subtle, but immediate, like a banding together against evil. Their mutual expressions of outrage signaled that I'd read their movements correctly.

"So I got this idea to make a protective pendant for her. And I did. I just ... I don't know ... tried to infuse it with my power? With my thoughts? I sort of just poured my intent into it?" I shrugged, uncertain how to explain what I'd done. "It's meant to both protect and give her courage. And well, then this happened."

I put the small chisel on the table and pointed to the band of copper on the handle.

"You passed a challenge!" Sophie crowed and leaned over to high-five me.

"I guess?"

"Same happened to me. I got bands of gold on my hammer." Orla tapped a finger on her lips, smiling. "This is good."

"Right, well, I guess what I need to know is—just how are we meant to be fighting these Kelpies? Or helping the Order? I'm confused."

"The Kelpies won't be fully banished until the Order is restored. In the meantime, I do my best to use my voice and my power to hold them back," Sophie explained. "The others are using their powers and their familiars to help Loren Brae. As the Stone of Truth has remained unprotected, the consequences have been far-reaching. It's not just the tourism industry that's hurting, it's everything. Shona's helping with orchards that are struggling, Lia's bringing in guests for her restaurant, Willow's creating a tourist draw with her fashions. Between Lia and Shona, they're working on tinctures and tonics to help those suffering more sickness of late here. What's happening is the Stone is testing us. It becomes a touch insidious if it believes that we can't protect it, and it begins to crack our foundations. It's part of why the challenges you have to pass are as much about strength as they are character. You're proving your worth to the Stone, but you're also helping Loren Brae."

"That's ... that's some high-level magickal shit, isn't it?" I didn't care if I sounded crude, as my thoughts were racing. The Stone of Truth would end up being the downfall of Loren Brae if we didn't get the Order of Caledonia together. *And somehow, through divine intervention—maybe?—I was a part of it.* Had my great-aunt known when she'd bequeathed her little house to me? *Was that why she had left it to me?*

"It is." Orla pursed her lips. "Every day we're working to make Loren Brae safer and more prosperous. It will be an uphill battle until we complete the Order though and banish the Kelpies."

"Right and how does one go about banishing a Kelpie?" I asked.

"A ritual. And in the meantime, we use our voices. Our weapons. Our power. We push them back, over and over, and do our best to protect others from them."

"And the sooner I complete my challenges the sooner we find the next person?" I asked, squinting at Agnes.

"Maybe. There's nothing that says we can't find the next of the Order sooner than that." Lia held up the book she'd brought with her. "I'm constantly reading through this for hints. It's a magickal recipe book and journal of sorts, passed down through generations. Let's see if your family is in there. What's your last name, Kaia?"

"Bisset, but my mother's is MacCrimmon," I said, faintly, as Calvin jumped off Willow's lap and padded across the table to me. He bumped his forehead against my hand, and I stroked his silky ears. Wait, we might need Gran's mother's maiden name. "And Gran's mother's maiden name, if we're thinking this is passed down, was MacKendrick."

"Eithne MacKendrick. Forge witch. Or Ore witch. Looks like both are one and the same, but that depends on who was writing about it." Lia looked up and turned the book to me so I could see the list of names.

My heart twisted, and something caught in my throat. *Eithne MacKendrick*. I didn't know her, but my gran might be able to fill in some of the gaps. Either way, I had a name.

A name connected to me, who had once lived here. Fought here. Made magick here. The same feeling of connectedness and longing I'd experienced whenever I looked at MacAlpine Castle filled me and a sheen of tears coated my eyes.

Calvin bumped his head against my face, and I buried my head in his fur for a moment, collecting myself.

"It's powerful, isn't it?" Sophie asked, leaning over to pat my shoulder. "We all feel the same, discovering we're a part of something so much more. You've got roots here,

Kaia. And we want you to feel welcome. We're more than just friends, you see?"

"I do." I looked up, gratitude filling me. I wasn't about to spill my guts about how hard it had been growing up. I had a great family network, but I didn't have many girlfriends. I'd always been the oddball, digging in the dirt, building things, never much interested in school gossip or joining cliques. I'd grown comfortable with being a loner, allowing myself to hyperfocus on whatever new project I was creating, and the friendships I did build were carefully and painstakingly curated. I'd grown better at socializing, as it was a necessary part of working with and selling myself to clients, but I still succumbed to awkwardness at times when I was around new people. "I've never really had a group of girlfriends before, but this feels like something so much more."

"I get that." Orla reached over and squeezed my hand, the touch brief once again. "I was an orphan, Kaia. I've been searching for a long time to feel connected somewhere. These women here will stand for you. It's powerful, these friendships. Outside of the magick, even. It matters. *We* matter."

"Och, you're going to get us all going." Shona fluttered her hands in front of her eyes and I hiccuped out a laugh.

"Right then, this cheese isn't going to eat itself yet. So, Agnes, when are you going to bang Graham and put him out of his misery?" Sophie asked, and Agnes gasped, laughing as she shook her head.

"Never." Agnes rolled her eyes.

"Uh-huh." Sophie gave her a skeptical look and I watched the exchange with interest. I'd definitely caught some vibes off those two the night before.

"Moving on. Lia, anything else interesting in the book about Kaia's ancestors?" Clearly Agnes had deflected this topic many a time. *Interesting.* Graham was a handsome man, but Agnes must find him lacking. How long had they been dancing around this?

Two hours later, I walked home, lightly buzzed, and feeling the calmest I'd felt in years. Orla was right. Discovering I was a part of the Order of Caledonia and finding a tight-knit group of friends—magickal ones at that—felt like a piece of the puzzle clicking into place for me. It even made me feel less worried about anything ever happening with Thane, because I trusted my new friends would help me figure out an alternative solution if I ever needed one for my business. Thoughts of Thane had me pausing at a stone wall that lined a part of Loch Mirren, and I peered out across the dark water. Clouds hugged the sky, obscuring any light from the moon or stars, but the streetlights reflected on the surface of the water, smudges of light against inky darkness.

What if there was something more between us?

Movement shifted in the water, and I gasped as a column of dark water barreled toward me, a bone-curdling shriek freezing me in place. I had no time to react, to move, to do anything really, other than put my hands up as icy water crashed over my head. It flung me forward, my head cracking against the stone wall, and I slumped to the ground, burying my face in my hands as icy water rained down over me.

"Get out!" a voice screamed at my side, and I looked up, my sight blurry between the hit to the face and the water cascading over me, to see Sophie with a sword in hand, Lachlan at her side. "I command you to get back."

Instantly, the threat disappeared, as Sophie stabbed the Kelpie with her sword, and it shattered into a thousand drops of water that splattered to the pavement around us. I held my hands to my face, my body shaking, tears streaming. It had all been so fast, so unexpected, that I didn't know how to react.

"Kaia." Sophie dropped to her knees, the sword clattering at her side. "Let me see, hon. Here, just let me look." She pulled my hands away and examined my face, worried.

"I'm fine," I said, automatically, though I clearly felt anything but fine. I felt like a wuss, frankly, as I'd done nothing but cower on the ground while Sophie had fought the Kelpie.

"You're bleeding. And your face will bruise." Sophie shot a look to Lachlan, who I'd only met briefly once, and he crouched at my side.

"I don't think stitches though." Lachlan's voice held the Highlands in it, and he reached out to tilt my head into the light. "How many fingers am I holding up?"

"Three," I said dutifully.

"Follow my finger. Tell me when it moves." Lachlan went through what I assumed was a concussion protocol before finally dropping his hand. "I think you're fine when it comes to a concussion, but you're definitely bruising. You'll want to get some ice on that."

"Should we go get Lia?" Sophie worried her lower lip. "Or Shona? Between them they can heal you right up."

Now that I'd had a moment to collect myself, and touch my face gingerly, I realized that I'd be okay. I considered myself to be a fairly tough woman, and a few burns and bruises were all in a day's work for me. I knew well enough the protocol to ease some of the swelling.

"I just want to go home," I said.

"We'll walk you."

I started to protest, but realized I'd feel better if they did, so I said nothing as they scooped me up and each took an arm. We set off down the street, the loch now silent.

"I hate that I froze up there," I admitted, swallowing against the embarrassment that burned. "It happened so fast. I didn't know what to do."

"That's normal. Trust me, it took a while for me to figure out how to stand up to them. You had no way of knowing they'd attack." Sophie leaned in front of me and shot Lachlan a worried look. "They just attacked one of their own, Lachlan. This is happening more often now. You'd think the Stone would want us protected."

"Kelpies don't discern friend or foe. Everyone's a threat now," Lachlan murmured.

"We need to warn people." Sophie sighed as we passed the main street and turned down my lane. "Things are getting worse. No walking by the loch at night."

"Aye, lass. I'll get the word out."

The light shone from my front window, and I fumbled with my keys, ready to be inside and out of my soaking-wet clothes. I was in pain, out of sorts, and just completely flustered.

"Let me stay. I'll help you," Sophie insisted, wringing her hands at the door to my cottage.

"No, truly. I'm fine." I just wanted a moment to lick my wounds in private, if I was being honest with myself. "I'm going to take a hot shower, put an ice pack on my face, and bury myself under the covers."

"Should I call Thane?" Sophie asked.

"Thane?" Lachlan inquired, a curious look on his face, and guilt flashed over Sophie's face.

"Sorry," Sophie whispered.

"No, it's fine. I'm fine. Truly. No need to call anyone. I'll check in with you in a bit. I just want to shower and get in dry clothes. I'm tough, I promise. Just a bit rattled is all."

"Okay, but I expect a text message within the hour. If not, I'm coming back with my jammies and staying the night."

"Promise. One hour."

A Kelpie attacked me. Holy hell.

This was hard to process, I was in pain, and I really just needed them to leave. Much had happened in the last twenty-four hours, and I wasn't sure my emotions could handle anyone mothering me right now. I wanted a shower, my comfies, and my bed. In that order. Giving Sophie a quick hug, I went inside and locked the door, waving through the front window before making a beeline for my bathroom and turning the shower on as hot as it would go. Only then did I dare look in the mirror.

"Shit," I breathed, staring at the bruising on my face. There was no way makeup would cover this. Resigning myself to some uncomfortable questions, I stripped and stepped into the steaming hot spray of water, turning so it warmed my back. Leaning my shoulder against the wall, I let the tears come and made a promise to myself.

I wouldn't let myself be in that position again. My parents had raised me to be resilient, so I'd learn from this experience tonight and grow from it. I was armed with my weapon, I would get more magickal training, and I'd be on alert moving forward. Much like the hard lesson learned from sleeping with my boss, I wasn't going to make the same mistake twice with the Kelpies.

CHAPTER ELEVEN

Thane

Kaia had worked from home on Monday, and though I wanted to text her to check in, I couldn't quite come up with a reason that would justify my intrusion into her life in such a manner. There were no rules about when she should or shouldn't be in the shop, as she simply leased her space from me, and she was capable of managing her own hours.

Was she working on her designs from home so I wouldn't see them? From what I'd seen of her open sketchbook, she'd had great ideas, and frankly, I'd be happy to implement them at Common Gin so long as my team got to work on the project as well.

Still, I craned my neck to look out of my open office door every time I heard a car pull up and a door slam.

"You've got the phone call at half ten with Grange Farms," Ian reminded me, and I glanced at the clock on my computer and reached for my desk phone. Business must go on, and I really needed to push all thoughts of Kaia from my mind. My sister was dropping Audrey off at lunch, a rare half day of school for her due to teacher conferences or something like that, and I needed to wrap up my work so I could be present for my niece when she arrived.

An hour and a half later, I'd worked through most of the day's admins, signed off on accounts, looked over stock orders, and arranged site visits for three potential clients. Pleased, I looked up as Ian hovered at my desk, an odd expression on his face.

"What's up?" I'd known him long enough to know something was bothering him.

Ian glanced around, then crossed to close the door. Worry had me sitting up straighter. I dearly hoped he wasn't about to quit. Ian was an integral part of my business running smoothly, and I'd be hard-pressed to find someone as knowledgeable as him to help me.

"You're worrying me," I said, when Ian dropped into the chair on the other side of my desk.

"It's just ..." Ian glanced over his shoulder and lowered his voice. "It's not my business. Or anyone's really. But ..."

"Just spit it out, mate."

Ian pressed his lips together and then met my eyes. "Kaia's here."

"Oh." Excitement immediately bloomed, but I

shifted in my seat, keeping my expression blank. "And? Did something happen?"

"Not to me. Or the forge or anything. It's just ..." Ian pursed his lips and then tapped a finger to his eye. "She's bruised."

"What?" I straightened, leaning closer over the desk.

"Her face. She's got some cuts on her forehead, and half of it's quite bruised."

I was already rising.

"Wait, Thane. You can't just go barreling in there. You'll embarrass her. Pause for just a second."

Rage, hot and sharp, sliced through me as a multitude of potential scenarios raced through my mind. Had she had an accident? Had someone hit her? It wasn't all that easy to get bruises to the face. Not really. I needed to know what had happened. And I needed to know, *now*.

"Tell me everything you know," I bit out.

"She said she had an accident. Tripped and fell, hit her face against a fence. But she wouldn't look me in the eye when I asked. She promised me it's fine, that it looks worse than it is."

That was all I needed to know before I was flinging the door open so hard it slammed against the wall. A few of my men in the shop glanced over at me, watching as I stormed across the room to where Kaia sat at her workbench, headphones on, working on small rings of metal.

"Kaia."

When she didn't look up at me, I took a second to study her face. *Bloody hell*. Ian was right. This was bad. Bruises stood out against her cheekbone in sharp red and deep blue, the edges a murky yellow and green. A few scratches on her forehead had scabbed over, and it looked like she hadn't bothered to cover anything with makeup. Maybe it had been an accident, if she wasn't trying to hide it, but seeing her beautiful face bruised and battered did something to me that I didn't want to examine too closely. Barely coherent, I pulled the headphones off her head and lightly lifted her chin, angling her face toward mine.

Her mouth dropped open on a gasp, and she whirled with her tool in hand.

That was odd.

"Who did this to you?" The words came out, sharp, furious, as I held her face still so I could see the extent of the damage.

"Thane, it's not ..." Kaia's eyes shifted, and she looked up and away, refusing to meet my eyes. Reaching up, she gently removed my hand from her jaw, while I scrambled for control of my emotions. I didn't want to scare her, but I was going to murder whoever put hands on her.

"Don't lie. Not to me." My voice was gruff, my fury barely contained, and Kaia's lashes fluttered furiously at her cheeks.

"It was an accident."

"Hell of an accident," I bit out. "Try again, Kaia. Who did this? I want a name." *For the second time in our brief time of knowing each other, I wanted the name of who had hurt her.* I wasn't going to examine that too closely either. What the hell had she gotten herself into in the time since I'd seen her? Was this why she wasn't at work yesterday?

"I did it. Me. I tripped and fell." Again her eyes shifted, and she glanced around at the shop. I looked up to see my men watching me, with equal looks of interest and caution. I know they respected Kaia, and I gave them a reassuring nod to let them know I'd take care of this. Whatever it was, I'd seek justice on her behalf. If only she'd tell me what really happened.

"I find that really hard to believe, darling." I lowered my voice. "I'm well aware that you're fairly agile. Seems pretty odd you'd fall and not catch yourself with your hands."

"I was carrying something?" This time it came out as a question and I squeezed my eyes shut and counted to ten.

"Try again."

"Thane, seriously. It's not a big deal. Bruises happen sometimes. You know that well enough in our line of work." Kaia shrugged and turned, as though she was going to go back to work and dismiss me.

"Uncle Thane!" I looked up as Audrey burst into the workshop and made a beeline for me. My sister waved from the door and turned, heading back toward her car, and I moved to intercept Audrey before she saw Kaia and asked too many questions. But my niece was fast and in a second she was hugging my leg, looking up at Kaia's bruised face, tears already brimming.

"What happened?" Audrey whispered, the tears

spilling over, and instantly Kaia was out of her chair and crouching by Audrey.

"Shhh, it's okay, Audrey. I promise it was just an accident."

"No, it wasn't." Audrey turned and buried her face into my thigh, and I bent and picked her up, hugging her to me. I knew the last time she'd seen bruises like that had been on her mother's face—*something I hadn't bloody protected Lauren from* ... though Kaia would have no idea why Audrey was so upset.

"It was. I'm just really clumsy."

"Why don't we go to my office?" I suggested, and Kaia stood, her eyes sad as she followed me to my office while I cradled Audrey close. Once there, Ian took one look at the situation and made himself scarce, closing the door behind him.

"Come on then, poppet. Everything's just fine now." I pulled back so I could see Audrey's face. The tears had stopped but her lower lip was still wobbly. I didn't blame her. I was equally as upset, and one way or another, I'd get answers.

"Audrey." Kaia came to my side and my niece twisted to look at Kaia. "I promise you that nobody hurt me. I hit my head on the stone wall by the water. You know the one that lines the walk down by the loch?"

Audrey nodded.

"I wasn't paying attention. It happened fast and it caught me by surprise. But I'm okay. These are just bruises, and I'm tough. See?" Kaia pretended to flex her muscles and Audrey gave her a shaky smile.

"You're really not hurt?"

"My face is sore. The bruises hurt a little, but I'm just fine, Audrey. I promise you. In fact, speaking of being tough, I also have a present for you."

"You do?" Audrey straightened in my arms, bouncing against me, and I let her slide to the floor. I knew there was more to Kaia's story, but I wasn't going to interrogate her in front of my niece, particularly now that Audrey had calmed down. But if Kaia thought she was getting out of telling me the full story, she was one hundred percent wrong.

"Yes, just let me go get it. It's in my bag." Kaia disappeared from my office, and I looked down at my niece.

"You all right?" I asked, tugging on one of her plaits.

"It was just scary," Audrey admitted. She went over to the table and dropped her backpack onto the floor.

"I know. I'll look after Kaia."

"Just like you did for Mum?"

"Aye." I looked up to see Kaia in the doorway, her eyes darting between me and Audrey, an unreadable look on her face.

"Here we go," Kaia said, her tone cheerful, and held out a small tissue-wrapped package.

"Is it more nail polish?" Audrey's voice went up an octave as she grabbed the gift from Kaia. I moved closer so I could see what Kaia had found for Audrey, pleased she'd even considered getting something for my sweet niece.

"Ohhhh, is it a necklace?" Audrey held up a small pendant on a silver chain. "This is really pretty."

"It is. It's an extra special necklace. Do you want to know why?" Kaia helped Audrey slip the necklace over her head.

"Why?" Audrey bounced on her heels, holding the pendant up in front of her face.

"It has magick." Kaia lowered her voice, as though she was telling a secret. "It's going to protect you from those nasty bullies at school and give you the courage when you need it."

"Really?" Audrey's eyes rounded.

"Really. Promise." Kaia crossed her finger over her heart.

"I'm a magickal princess." Audrey twirled, the tartan skirt of her school uniform flaring out, and Kaia grinned.

"Exactly that. You're going to be so powerful now with this necklace. Nothing anybody says will hurt you anymore."

My throat suddenly felt tight, as I thought about the kids at school bullying Audrey, and how Kaia had instinctively found a way to help my niece in a manner that I hadn't. And as much as I wanted to pretend that Kaia and I were just colleagues, my reasons for keeping it strictly professional with her were beginning to blur.

Ian knocked at the door, poking his head inside.

"Permission to enter? I just need to work on a few invoices."

"All good." I reached in a drawer of my desk and handed Audrey a new coloring book I'd picked up for her. "Have a go at this, poppet, while I have a quick word with Kaia. She needs to get back to work."

"Thank you for my gift," Audrey said, launching herself at Kaia and wrapping her arms around her waist. Kaia squeezed her close.

"You're welcome, sweet girl." She then followed me out of my office and into the car park where we'd be out of the hearing of everyone in the shop.

"Thane—"

"I'm not going to ask you again, Kaia." I held my hand up. "If you're not ready to tell me what happened, that's fine, but please don't lie to me."

"I ..." Kaia looked away and toed her boot into the gravel of the lot. "It's complicated, okay?"

"Who is he?" I asked, my voice barely above a whisper. I couldn't keep the menace out of it, and the fury that I had previously tamped down rose again.

"It's not a *he*." Kaia hiccuped out a half-laugh. "It's ... I just ... *listen*. Can I explain it to you later? Not here? I really want to make headway on these chain-mail designs for Willow and finalize the drawings for Orla."

I didn't want to let her off the hook. I wanted to push until I got all the answers I needed, until I could subdue the rage that simmered just below the surface, so I could take action to fix this for her. But I also had my niece inside waiting for me, and neatly drawn boundaries on my relationship with Kaia. I was stuck between a rock and a hard place and I didn't like it.

I hated not being able to fix a problem.

And Kaia's bruised face? Well, it was one hell of a problem.

Whether she liked it or not, she was going to get some formal protection. From me. At least until she could reassure me that her safety wasn't in jeopardy.

"I'm coming over after work is done tonight," I said, my tone brooking no argument. "And if you need me to bring locks or anything else to make your cottage more secure, tell me now. I have a wide range of security options for you." *Like knives or a cricket bat.*

Kaia pressed her lips together, started to speak, and then paused again. Her soulful eyes locked on mine and apparently whatever she read there made her back down.

"Fine. Come over after work and we can talk."

"I will. It wasn't an option."

"I should find this domineering side of you annoying," Kaia grumbled, pushing past me to go inside. Despite my anger, a corner of my mouth lifted. So she liked when I went full protective mode? Flashes of the other night filled my mind—holding her down while I ravaged her, her taking everything I had to give. A different heat flooded my veins and when Kaia glanced back at me just before she went inside, she must have seen it in my expression. Her eyes widened, and damn it, she licked her lips.

I stepped forward, needing to touch her, and panic flitted across her gaze. Turning, she raced back to her workstation and I dug my fingers into my palms, taking a deep breath to gain control of my roiling emotions.

Pasting a smile on my face, I went to find my niece and was determined to color until I could think clearly again. Audrey deserved the best of me, and if that meant rage-drawing princesses and fairies for the next two hours, then it looked like art therapy was on my agenda.

CHAPTER TWELVE

Kaia

"I just want to start by saying that both of you have done a great job."

My stomach twisted as Orla paged through both of our design proposals. It had already been an emotional day, and I hadn't planned to end it with a meeting at Common Gin, except Orla had called us in for a design review as her schedule had shifted for the week and she needed to move forward. Finlay, the project manager and Orla's partner, had joined us for the meeting. To his credit, he'd politely introduced himself, only briefly glancing at the bruises on my face, a flicker behind his eyes barely giving any emotion away. Thane, he'd already known, and they'd quickly caught up on mild chatter about the latest football match.

I couldn't help but watch how Orla and Finlay were together. He was slick in the way of accomplished men who carried themselves with confidence and that sheen of prosperity. Even though his boots were scuffed, his clothes were impeccably fitted, and he managed to have style in the middle of a job site. Whereas Orla wore her hair plaited and dusty dark green overalls with scuffed work boots covered in doodles and designs. From the outside, I'd never have put these two together. Yet the quick glances, simmering in heat, and the light brush of his hand at her back spoke volumes. There was an intimacy here that wasn't overt, yet you could see it if you looked for it.

It was what Orla had told me about working with someone you cared about. And Willow had echoed. It could be done, they'd insisted, but I just wasn't ready to put my future in someone else's hands. Already Thane was proving to be volatile, with the way he'd stormed across the workshop when he'd learned of my injuries. What would happen if we had a lover's spat or a falling out? Would I be able to count on him to allow me to fulfill my lease? He could create all sorts of problems for me and shut me out of the forge, no matter what my lease may say.

Slanting a glance at his profile, I considered the direction of my thoughts. He'd been fiercely protective of his niece earlier and had attempted to be so with me. Was he really a man who wouldn't honor a lease or would force me out of his workplace if we clashed?

My gut told me "no."

The issue was, could I trust myself? My instincts? I'd ignored red flags before and been burned. I'd just have to be extra careful in this instance and proceed with caution. That was all. Pulling my thoughts away from Thane, I focused on where Orla tapped an illustration in my design book.

"These gates are fantastic, Kaia."

Pride bloomed, and I smiled, leaning closer.

"I thought you'd like the design."

"Aye, we weren't expecting the name to be woven into the gates so seamlessly, but it's clever. Well done." Finlay nodded his approval, and I beamed at him.

Thane turned to me and I searched his eyes but only found the same approval there.

"Indeed. They're beautiful, Kaia."

"Oh." My mouth went dry. I hadn't expected his outright support of my designs. "Thank you." My gut was screaming. *See? This is the type of man he is. The type of man you want.*

By the time we'd finished going through the options for the different areas of the distillery, my heart was singing. Orla and Finlay had mostly picked my designs, aside from a few ornate table legs for the main tasting room, a design for one of the supply room doors, and some cupboard doors for the botanicals room. If one were to put a winner badge on either myself or Thane, it seemed like I'd earned it.

Mentally, I did a little dance and a huge squeal, but instead I kept my face still and pumped Thane's hand.

"Good job, Thane. I liked your designs as well." I could be magnanimous in my win.

Thane's lips quirked and he held my hand for a moment longer than necessary, his palm heating under mine, and little explosions of need burst inside me.

"I look forward to working with you on these," Thane said. I pulled my hand back as my body flushed, the mere thought of working next to him sending me into overdrive.

"If you can get the final budget over to us, along with the estimated timeline, that would be great," Orla continued and I dropped my hand, curling my fingers into my palm so as to hold Thane's touch a little longer. Damn it, but I had such a visceral response to this man. I had to get my head in the game and make sure I stayed focused on the long-term goal—establishing a business and life here. My reputation mattered to me, and this was a huge opportunity to build a good rapport with my clients.

My clients.

Excitement bloomed. I'd done it. I'd landed a huge client just a few weeks into my Scottish life, and I'd make sure that I *over*delivered for them just to set the precedent that I was trustworthy, reliable, and *damn* good at my job.

So long as I had the right tools and the space to work in, that is. Sliding another glance at Thane as he walked out of the distillery with Finlay, I worried my lower lip. I had such conflicting feelings when it came to him, but with Orla picking my designs, it helped clarify my path forward.

"Are you all right? After the attack?" Orla pitched her voice low beneath the bustle and hum of the construction site. Her dog, Harris, kept pace with us, undisturbed by the cacophony of noises. The distillery was well under way, the project coming to life, and I was itching to add my design elements to the space.

"I am, thanks. It was scary, that's for sure. Largely because it happened so fast and was so unexpected," I said. "Finlay didn't seem thrown off by it."

"I warned him. Sophie called all of us after it had happened, so Finn knew what to expect. I figured you wouldn't want questions about it, and I wasn't entirely sure what you were sharing with Thane."

"Appreciate that," I murmured, as we drew close to where the men had stopped at the parking lot. Raising my voice, I continued, "We'll get the final workup to you tomorrow?" I looked to Thane, and he nodded in agreement.

"Great. Looking forward to working with you both." Finlay shook both of our hands, and then stepped back. I caught how his hand automatically went to Orla's shoulder before he quickly dropped it. She must have schooled him about touching on the worksite. Smart woman. I couldn't count the number of times a customer had looked past me to the men on my projects to ask for insight. Orla seemed like she ran a tight ship, and I imagined she likely had a "no touching" rule for a reason on site.

"Shall we have a meeting in the morning to finalize things?" I turned to Thane after Orla and Finlay had walked away, keeping my tone light.

"Och, I'll be following you home, darling." *Darling.* I shivered at the way his mouth formed that delicious sound when he called me that. I blinked up at Thane, trying to ignore the instinctive urge to lean closer into him. Being close was magnetic, and it was a struggle to tamp down my attraction.

"There's really no need for that."

Thane raised a hand and brushed a finger, featherlight, down the side of my chin, and I quickly glanced over to the distillery to see if anyone was watching us.

"You promised me you'd tell me what happened. We can do that here or at your cottage. Which do you prefer?" There was steel beneath his words, and I knew I wouldn't be able to shake him until I gave him an explanation that he could accept. My stomach twisted. I didn't want to lie to him, but how would he take this whole magickal Order story? He'd been somewhat dismissive of the Kelpies when we'd heard them shriek in the early hours of the morning the other night.

"Um, my cottage I guess." I pressed my lips together, nervous.

Thane's eyes flew to my lips and his hands tightened into fists. "Don't fret, Kaia. I'll be taking care of whomever did this to you."

Oh shit, he was taking my nervousness about telling him as truth that someone had done this to me. I needed to nip this in the bud before it flew out of hand.

"I'll see you at my place."

Hopping into my ancient car, I argued with the gear shift until I managed to get the car moving, and then tightly gripped the steering wheel for the rest of the ride home, Loren Brae a blur past my window as I tried to work out what to say to Thane. By the time we arrived at my cottage, Thane's truck right on my bumper, my tension had ratcheted up.

It was one thing speaking to my parents about magick and ancient Orders and all that, as I never questioned whether they would love and support me. They'd always been a constant champion of me *and* my life choices, and their unwavering support had given me the backbone to be the woman that I was today. But it was entirely different to float the concept of magick out in front of someone like Thane. And at the same time, I suspected if I tried to lie to him about it, he was just going to bulldog me until he got to the truth anyway. Otherwise he'd be interrogating every man in town until he found someone who took responsibility for my injuries.

Murdoch swooped as I shut off my car, and despite my nerves, I smiled at the bird as he bounced around by my front door. I'd begged some blueberries off Lia before my meeting with Orla at the castle, and now I dug in my bag.

"Hi, friend," I said, holding out the bag. "Look what I got for you."

He cares about you.

I glanced over my shoulder to where Thane sat in his

truck, watching me and the raven, clearly not wanting to interrupt us. It showed he respected me, I realized, to not immediately storm me even though he had questions he wanted answered. Instead, he waited while I quietly fed Murdoch blueberries.

Again, my stomach twisted. From what I could tell, Thane was a good man.

"I'm not sure how much that matters or not," I whispered to the bird as I opened the bag of blueberries. "We need to just be colleagues."

He'll protect you.

"Do I really need protecting? Aren't I the one with the powers?"

Murdoch hopped forward and took one of the blueberries gently from my fingers.

There are different kinds of protection, little one.

I raised an eyebrow at that. Was the raven really calling me the little one? Though I supposed I did look quite tiny when he was flying overhead. Murdoch finished his blueberries and flew to a branch, clearly ready to settle in for the conversation.

Thane got out of his car, and I tensed as he strode over, his serious expression deepening the craggy edges of his face.

"Want to see the backyard?" I asked, inanely, I supposed, but I didn't want to go inside with him. Not with this much emotion pinging around inside me. It was a toss-up whether I wanted to jump into his arms and hug him for wanting to look out for me or push him back so I could live my own life free of overbearing men.

A colleague, I reminded myself. I dug my hands in my pockets and strolled around the corner of the cottage, not waiting for his answer.

And came to a dead stop at the sight that greeted me.

Thane slammed into me, not expecting my sudden stop, and I stumbled forward, but his arms were already around my waist, pulling my back to his chest, cradling me close. He tightened his grip, and shifted our bodies, just a bit, so our shoulders angled toward the backyard.

The backyard where a softly glowing unicorn stood, angling her head at us.

Yup, that's correct. A freaking unicorn.

My breath stuttered, my heart expanding at the sight, and I winced as though I was looking directly at the sun. She was incredible, a sight beyond belief, yet the longer we stood there the more soothed I became.

Her coat was opal white, a soft rainbow of muted colors shifted through her mane, and her horn was like a glimmering pearl. She tossed her head, shaking her mane out, and stomped a hoof.

"Her eyes," I whispered, covering Thane's arms with my own, hugging him back.

"A thousand worlds held within." Thane's voice was at my ear, his breath warm against my neck. He wasn't wrong, either. It was as though she could see our very souls, and I desperately hoped she didn't find us lacking.

Once more she bobbed her head at us, signaling some unknown message, and then turned and bounded into the trees. Trembling, I stared after her, surprised to feel tears prick my eyes.

I'd never seen something so beautiful. I wanted to memorialize this moment, to figure out how to forge it in gold or iron, to bring it to life so I'd always have it with me.

Thane turned me, and bent, bringing his forehead to mine.

"Did that just really happen?" Thane whispered.

"Incredible," I breathed.

His lips brushed mine, feather soft, and I jolted, forcing myself to step back. We'd just come from a meeting where I'd signed one of my biggest clients ever, and I needed to hold my boundaries. Unicorn or no unicorn.

"Sorry," Thane said instantly. He stepped back, raising his hands. "Got caught up."

"I ... I have no idea what to say." I glanced over my shoulder at the line of trees bordering the property. "Is this a normal thing for Loren Brae?"

"Och, lass." Thane barked out a laugh. "Not that I'm aware of. I'd have thought I'd well and truly lost it had you not been standing here with me."

"Wow, just wow." I turned and began to pace the back garden. It was a bit of a wild spot, as I hadn't had time to cut back the bushes or tame the long grass, but an old stone walkway and patio area allowed for some space. I needed movement to work out this frenetic energy that kicked around inside me, a mix of anxiety, awe, and unfortunately, arousal. I quite simply was over-the-moon attracted to Thane. "Every day, things just get wilder here in Loren Brae."

"What do you mean by that?" Thane leaned against the back wall of the cottage, giving me the walkway to pace, and I glanced up at a flutter of wings in the air. Murdoch had perched himself on the roof.

"Can I ask you something?" I stopped my pacing and looked at Thane. I continued when he nodded. "The other night? The Kelpies? Do you really think they're fake?"

"No, I don't." Thane sighed, his lips pressing into a worried line. "I want to, and that's the truth of it. I want to think this is all just a make-believe thing made up to scare the wee kids home by bedtime, but it's hard to dismiss. No matter how much I try."

I held his eyes for a moment, needing to make sure he wasn't having me on, and when I saw the confusion and frustration there, echoing his words, I nodded once and resumed my pacing.

"It's the Kelpies that did this to me, Thane." There. *Just ripped the Band-Aid off.*

His hands were at my shoulders in a matter of seconds, and he was turning me to him.

"Surely you're joking?" The color of Thane's eyes seemed to deepen, matching the storm of expressions that warred on his face.

"I'm not." I swallowed and forced myself to keep speaking. "I'm ... well, see there's kind of this magickal task force that's been put together to help conquer the Kelpies. And, well, I've been recruited."

I wasn't quite ready to mention the Stone of Truth. I

figured I could take this in steps and see how he handled it.

His fingers tightened slightly at my shoulders, and he tilted his chin up as he replayed my words. Murdoch let out a call, like a low knocking sound, reminding me he was here for me, I supposed.

"You have magick? As in, you'll be dancing under moonlight and singing spells and making things float in the air?"

My lips quirked.

"I don't think that's how it will be manifesting for me, no. I think, from what I can tell, it will be tied to what I can make."

"Alchemy." Thane nodded in understanding, and I supposed it made sense he'd immediately tie that together. I wouldn't be the first blacksmith in history to potentially have magickal power. But now that he said it, it did make all those old myths ring a touch more true. I'd have to go back and read some to see if any resonated with me.

"Maybe?" I shrugged one shoulder, conscious of his hands still on me. "I haven't yet been able to transmute anything. But I did infuse the pendant I gave Audrey with some power."

Thane's eyes widened.

"You gave my niece a magickal protection pendant?"

Shit. I gritted my teeth. Hopefully he wouldn't be pissed at me.

"Just a touch. For courage. And to ward off negative energy. Nothing bad, I promise."

"That's bloody awesome." A smile bloomed on his face, shifting the contours of his face. "Thank you."

Relief filled me.

Thane reached up, bringing one finger to my chin, and angled my face into the sunlight, examining my bruises more closely.

"This looks really bad, Kaia. Was it scary? I hate that I wasn't there for you. I had no idea the power they had, and now I don't want to let you out of my sight. Does this mean they're after you? Will they single you out specifically if they know you're hunting them?"

I blinked at the barrage of his questions. They made sense—I had phrased the Order of Caledonia as a task force—and now I'd need to explain that the Kelpies and I were working toward the same goal.

One a touch more aggressively, is all.

"We aren't hunting them." I shrugged again and took a step back, breaking contact with Thane. I needed a little space to breathe. His nearness often overwhelmed me, and I needed my head on straight to explain this in a manner that hopefully wouldn't violate too many confidences. "Um, so, we kind of have the same goal. Us and the Kelpies."

"I'm sorry, what's that now?" Thane held a hand to his ear, pretending like he hadn't heard me.

Murdoch gave out a series of calls again, those deep knocks reverberating across the backyard, and Thane turned to look up at the glossy bird on my roof.

"Do you know this bird?"

"Um, I do, actually." Probably not the best time to

tell Thane that I could also speak to animals apparently. "I'm calling him Murdoch. He's been bringing me little gifts, and I feed him."

"He's cool," Thane said, turning back to me. "Big."

"Yes, ravens are much bigger than crows. Anyway, um, so … right. Listen, Thane, a lot of this is not public knowledge. I don't know how much I'm allowed to tell. Let me just say that there are people here who are tasked with protecting something very important in Loren Brae. And because that particular thing has been largely left unguarded the last few years, the Kelpies have come to do the guarding. Once the task force is back to its full power, the Kelpies should disappear. Or go back to sleep. Or return to wherever they go."

"Protecting something very important." Thane repeated the words as he puzzled it out. "It's not like a nuclear bomb or something like that?"

"Oh, hell no." I laughed and reached up to wind my hair around my finger. "Trust me. I'd be the last person to get recruited as a secret government spy or whatever."

"Then what could be that important?"

I pressed my lips together, unsure of what I could say. I wanted to ask Sophie about it first.

"Right, you can't tell me. I'm guessing it's a treasure of sorts then?"

"Closer," I said, pursing my lips in agreement. "Listen, if I can tell you more, I will, is that fair?"

"Aye, that's fair. I'll stop pressing. But tell me about the Kelpies and more about your magick."

"Not sure on the magick. Still learning there. I

talked to my mom about it, did a little digging, and it turns out one of my ancestors might have had magick too. Like she would go around protecting homes and stuff."

"A sigil." Thane nodded. "Sounds like a hearthward."

"A hearthward?"

"Aye. It protects the home from evil."

"Hmm." I nodded, thinking it over. The idea resonated. "I like the sound of that. Maybe I'll try to work on something like that next."

"I'll take one. For Lauren and Audrey."

"Noted. As for the Kelpies ..." I shrugged. My stomach twisted as I thought about the sickly swell of panic seeing a two-story wall of water rise above me. "They're really fucking scary."

"Are they big?" Seeing my distress, Thane reached out and rubbed his hands down my arms.

"Massive. Two stories. And they just ... slammed over me. Took me down. I busted my face against that stone wall that lines the loch."

"Och, love." Thane brushed my chin with his hand, his eyes full of concern. "That's terrifying."

"I know. And supposedly I'm meant to help keep them back. But I did nothing. I didn't know what to do. It just happened so fast. It was Sophie ..." I trailed off, wincing.

"Ah, Sophie's involved in this." Thane nodded. "I'd heard tell of it. At least an excitement upon her arrival. That tracks."

"Please don't say anything," I said, miserable. "I

don't know who knows what and I don't want to get her or anyone else in trouble."

"Not a word." Thane tilted my head so my eyes met his. "Promise."

"Thank you."

"I will say though, I don't like this at all. It shouldn't be on you, or her, to be fighting these Kelpies. They're clearly dangerous. I'm surprised Lachlan hasn't put a stop to this."

I laughed and stepped back, some of the tension easing.

"Have you seen Lachlan? He's besotted with her." I'd only met Lachlan twice now, but he was head over heels for Sophie. She could tell him she was flying a dragon to the moon, and he'd ask what to pack in her bag for her flight.

"It's not right. We should be able to help you. Look at the nick of you, Kaia. Your face is a mess. It could be even worse next time. I won't be having it and that's the truth of it. You'll need to go."

"Excuse me?" I raised my eyebrows at him.

"You need to go. Until this is sorted out. It's the only solution. You've already been hurt once." Thane's chin took on a stubborn angle.

"I am *not* leaving." I pointed a finger toward the front of the house. "But you can if you keep up that talk."

"It's not right, darling. It's just not. I should be doing something to help you. Loren Brae isn't safe for you. You need to leave."

"Well, I'm not, so get used to it."

"Aye, you are." Thane leaned closer, frustration on his face.

"No, I'm not." I leaned in too and stomped my foot for good measure.

"You're going to leave even if I have to pack you up myself."

"I'd like to see you stop me from staying." I whirled and marched toward the cottage. I was two feet from the back door when he caught me, turning and lifting me so my legs straddled his waist and my back was pressed to the cool bricks of the cottage.

His mouth was on mine before I could protest, and I met him heat for heat.

"Damn it, lass, you'll be the death of me." Thane arched into me, his hard length rubbing against me, and I moaned. Rolling my hips against his, I shuddered at the delicious press of him against me. Reaching one hand down, I fumbled at the button of my jeans. I wanted him.

I was lying to myself every time I told myself he was just a colleague.

Thane broke the kiss, and seeing what I was about, he stepped back and let me slide down his body, so I could kick my jeans off. Digging in his back pocket, he unzipped his pants and quickly sheathed himself with a condom, before hoisting me back up and pressing me against the wall.

"I should take care with you," Thane gasped against my mouth, teasing me where I wanted him most.

"I'm stronger than I look, Thane." I tightened my admittedly muscular thighs around him and pulled him closer. "And I don't look weak."

"No, you don't." His hands gripped my butt, digging into the ample flesh there. "You're strong." He thrust and my eyes rolled back in my head.

"I am." My head lolled back as he thrust again.

"And soft." His mouth was at my breasts kissing me through my shirt.

"And ample." Another slick thrust. "And all-consuming. All woman."

I moaned as he picked up the pace. Pleasure built inside me, a coil ready to be sprung, and I tightened around him. A cool breeze shifted across my exposed skin, and being outside, surrounded by nature only heightened my pleasure. This felt raw, animalistic almost, like he couldn't tear himself away from my body. The very thought of how much he wanted me took me right over the edge and I cried out as I came undone.

Two more thrusts and Thane followed suit, burying his face into my neck, his moans muffled as he sought his release. When he finished, he just held me there, pressed between his hard body and the rough stone of the wall.

"Did I hurt you?" Thane asked, drawing in a breath.

"God, no." I laughed, leaning back to look up at him. "That was incredible."

"But your back? Your soft skin? Against the stone?"

"I'm fine. Trust me, I'm *more* than fine." I patted his chest and wondered how long he could hold me here like this. I was not a light woman, but he seemed to have no problem throwing me around with ease. "Thane. What are we doing here?"

"Likely making mistakes."

His words landed, hurting me, even though I'd been the one to push back against a relationship just as much as he had. Taking a deep breath, I covered my wound with a soft smile.

"Agreed."

I saw a flash in his eyes and wondered if my ready agreement had hit him the same way his words had me.

"So. Colleagues?" I asked, trying to restore the boundary. Which was *just* a bit hard to do when the man was still inside me.

"Mmm." Thane made a noncommittal noise and withdrew, allowing me to slide to my feet. I bent and picked up my jeans, pulling them on quickly while he righted himself. "Kaia, I'm serious about you leaving. I don't think it's safe here for you. I don't know how to protect you from the Kelpies so the only logical solution is for you to leave."

"Then you'd have to leave too." Annoyance flashed through me. "The Kelpies aren't just after me. They're after anyone who threatens what they're protecting. Don't you see? I could very well be saying the same for you."

Thane scoffed, as if the very idea that he wouldn't be able to protect himself was a joke. I sighed. *Men*.

"Thank you for your concern, Thane. But I'm fine. And we've got a job to do for Common Gin. When do you want to start?"

"I've got the men finishing two big projects for the Kinross farm tomorrow and the next day. So we likely won't be starting any actual design work until next week at the earliest. Let's meet for measurements and stock estimations tomorrow afternoon then?" Thane said the words reluctantly, as though he'd honestly expected me to listen to him and pack my bags that very second.

"Perfect. I'll see you after lunch then. In the meantime, I need a night to unwind." I slanted him a look and patted his chest. "Alone."

"Understood. You'll call me if you need me?"

"I'll be fine, Thane."

"Nevertheless?"

"I'll call you if I need you." I sighed.

"Thank you." Thane looked like he was going to lean in to kiss me, but I just shook my head, gently nudging him backward with my hand. Turning, he walked away, and in moments I heard his truck door slam and tires crunching on the gravel. Taking a shuddering breath, I stood where I was for a moment, blinking up at murky clouds gathering in the sky, the promise of rain on the horizon.

Murdoch swooped low, making his odd knocking call.

"Tell me you didn't watch that." I gritted my teeth, my cheeks heating in embarrassment. I'd forgotten about the raven.

Obviously not. I have little interest in the couplings of humans.

An idea occurred to me. I was still too keyed up to sleep, and it was only late afternoon.

"Want to come hang out?"

That would be nice, thank you for the invitation.

With that, I walked around the cottage and opened my door to the raven, marveling at what a turn my life had taken. Stepping inside, I glanced once more down the drive toward the loch, but Thane's truck was long gone, and the surface of the loch was smooth. For now, I could rest.

I firmly closed the door behind me and slid the latch closed.

CHAPTER THIRTEEN

Kaia

My feelings were jumbled up in knots inside me, and I was more than a bit out of sorts. But now I had a raven sitting on the back of my armchair, staring at me, as the first patter of rain hit the window.

"Listen. I want to hang out with you, but I'd also like a shower and to get into comfy clothes. Do you want me to open the window so you can leave if you want to while I do those things?" I asked.

I'm just fine. I'll come get you if I need anything.

"Do you want more snacks?"

I wouldn't say no.

I laughed as Murdoch lifted his head, feigning indifference.

"Right, let's see. Some more blueberries. How about nuts?"

I love nuts!

I made a small bowl of goodies for him and put it on the kitchen counter, and he flew over to enjoy himself. Ducking into the bathroom, I took a quick shower, my body loose and languid from my tryst with Thane, and I sighed.

Damn it, but I was screwing up again.

Finishing my shower, I dried off, got cozy in my soft clothes, and padded back out to the living room where Murdoch was still digging in his bowl. Walking to the window, I eyed the storm clouds before going around the room lighting candles. I'd found some brass pillar candle holders in the shed out back, ones with a handle that you could walk around with, and I'd brought them inside to use. I'd been lighting one each night, just for the charm of it, and I had to admit the candlelight added a rosy glow to the room.

Kind of like the rosy glow my body was feeling.

Murdoch flapped his wings out and hopped across the counter, before flying over to where I'd dropped onto the couch and pulled a throw over my legs. He hopped along the back of the couch until we were eye to eye.

"You're very handsome, you know." He really was. His feathers were such a beautiful inky color, and they had such a lovely sheen in the candlelight.

I'm aware. But I do enjoy the flattery. Murdoch preened for me, and I laughed.

"So how come you're hanging out with me,

Murdoch? Like, why *me* specifically? Is it because I'm new in town? Do you want to hear about lands far away? I didn't know any ravens in the States, I'm sorry to say." I didn't think I'd paid much attention to any birds at all now that I looked back on it.

I'm here to help you. You're mine and I am yours.

"Wait, what? Help me with what?"

Murdoch ruffled his wings and puffed up, bouncing along the back of the couch.

Anything. Everything. It's my job. It's a great honor to be a familiar you know. And my family has been with yours for generations.

I straightened at that, pulling myself higher on the couch to lean forward and meet his eyes.

"Your family has been with mine for generations? And a familiar? Like a witch has?" Even as I said it, I flashed back to Lia telling me she was a kitchen witch. What did that make me then? Was I really a witch?

Correct. Your family are forge witches.

"So it's real? Being a forge witch?" Lia had mentioned my ancestor, Eithne, when reading her ancient book.

Aye. Your power is in the metals.

"But I don't think my mother ever did much with metals." I paused, thinking it over.

Not all witches claim their power.

"Is that right?" I was still trying to wrap my head around being a witch, and I burrowed more deeply into my blanket as the rain lashed the window, and a low rumble signaled the approach of a larger storm. "I can't imagine not claiming power if you have it. Though I'm still trying to figure mine out."

Power doesn't suit everyone.

I thought again about my sunshiny, easygoing mother. Nothing much ever ruffled her feathers, and she'd been such a consistent, soothing foundation in my life. I supposed that was its own power of sorts. To mother with an easygoing and smooth nature was not for the faint of heart.

Murdoch tilted his head and hopped closer.

"Can I pet you?" I asked, curious.

Just my head. Light scratches. If you pet my other feathers, I'll lose my oils.

"Is that right?" I reached up and gently scratched the back of Murdoch's head, and he closed his eyes for a moment while I did so. "You're quite soft. Does this feel nice?"

It does. It's a tough spot to reach, so sometimes it is nice to have it scratched.

"If you know my family, and my magick, will you be able to help me? Do you understand everything going on with the Stone of Truth and the Order of Caledonia?"

I do and I can.

I brightened. That had been my hope when I'd invited Murdoch in. I didn't want to force anything out of him, but knowing he was willing to be my friend and knew more about my family, I hoped he could offer some insight into my magick.

"How is it that I can just have magick? And how does it work for a forge witch?"

Magick is always about intention. The Clach na Firrin has chosen your bloodline and given you the ability to tap into your magick. It remains latent, mostly, until the ritual to join the Order happens.

"Why do you say mostly?" I thought about the ghosts I saw before the ritual, and how Calvin spoke to me at Willow's.

Power is magnetic, lass. It's a multiplier of sorts. The closer you get to the source, the more you'll feel it.

"So that's why I always felt a pull to the island in the loch." I stopped stroking his head and Murdoch opened his eyes, settling down onto the back of the couch so his legs tucked into his feathers.

Likely so.

"And my magick? Is Thane right? Will I be able to make things float and turn people into puffins?"

That's a wee bit dramatic, lass.

Murdoch tilted his head and did that low call again that sounded like a series of knocks.

"Oh, right. *I'm* the dramatic one. Sitting here in my cottage talking to my bird after seeing a unicorn in the backyard. Excuse me for stretching the realm of possibility for a moment there."

Murdoch fluffed his feathers, digging his beak underneath a wing, and I waited.

You can infuse your creations with your magick.

"Thank you. So you're saying that my magick is specific to my metals. Can I create a sword or weapon with some type of magick?"

Aye.

"Interesting. What kind of magick? Like laser beams?"

Another low knocking call and a head buried in feathers. It appeared I was an embarrassment to my familiar. Likely to my entire people based on the way Murdoch turned his back on me.

"Right, got it. No laser beams. Protective spells. Charms. Courage, strength. What about love spells?"

You can use a spell to enhance attraction or to make people see what is right in front of them. But you cannot change free will.

"That's fair. I don't think I'd be pleased if someone was forcing me into a love spell either." My thoughts went to Thane, my insides tightening just thinking about our fast and raw coupling outside. What had I been thinking? It was like I literally couldn't trust myself to be around this man.

"Tell me a bird joke."

Murdoch flipped around and flapped his wings, and I leaned back so he wouldn't hit me in the face. Now I'd really gone and insulted him.

What kind of bird works at a construction site? Murdoch tilted his head, studying me.

"Hmmm, not sure on that one."

A crane.

I burst out laughing and Murdoch hopped along the back of the couch, clearly delighted with my response.

"Good one, Murdoch. I didn't expect you to have a sense of humor."

I am a bird of much depth.

I grinned, delighted with him. "Why you, Murdoch? Or your family? Why do you help mine?"

Ravens are highly intelligent, drawn to shiny objects like metal and gold, and we can help gather information for spells.

"Like how? What kind of information?"

Murdoch tilted his head, seeming to consider the question.

For particular spells, we can gather ingredients. For others, we can provide detailed intel. We can tell you where people are, if there are threats nearby, or what spells once worked in the olden times. We pass our knowledge down, generation to generation, and we like to help our people. You're now our people.

"Aww." Warmth spilled through me. "That's nice. Here I thought it might be hard to make friends in Loren Brae, but not only did I have my first real girls' night, but I also have you as a friend. That's pretty cool."

My phone pinged from the pocket of my sweatpants and I dug under the blanket to see Marisa's name. Guilt tugged. We'd gone from talking almost daily to not connecting at all since I'd moved here.

What would she think of all this? Would it freak her out that I had a raven friend and magick and Kelpies screaming in the night? Pondering it, I hit video call and almost dropped the phone when her face showed on the screen and she immediately screamed. Murdoch fluttered behind me and took flight across the room.

"Your face!"

"Oh!" I slapped a hand over my mouth and then

winced. I definitely should not be slapping my face with my bruises. "I forgot. I should have prepared you for that."

"What the hell, Kaia?" Marisa, with dark brown skin, soulful brown eyes, and a wicked sense of fashion, looked like she was an off-duty model. She strutted down a sidewalk in an oversized blazer, slinky white tank, and slouchy bag at her shoulder. We'd always been an odd pairing, me in my overalls and hoodies playing with metals and tools, and her obsessing over this season's Louboutins. But since the first day we'd met, rolling our eyes at a man trying to mansplain something to another student in our class, we'd clicked.

"Where are you?" I asked, trying to bring down the worry in her eyes.

"Chicago. What happened? You have ten seconds before I hang up and start looking up flights." She'd do it, too.

"It's a long story, but it was an accident. No man involved, I promise. Though there is a man."

At that, Marisa veered off the sidewalk, and from what I could see over her shoulder, into what looked to be a softly lit bar with funky mirrors hanging on cream brick walls.

"I'll have an old fashioned, please." While Marisa waited for her drink, giving me serious side-eye, I decided to join her and crossed the room to open a bottle of red wine. By the time we were both situated, her in a round booth with tufted black leather cushioning, and me on the couch with Murdoch back at my shoulder, Marisa was almost foaming at the mouth for details.

"You have a bird behind you." She stated this matter-of-factly, as though it was a common enough thing for me, and I grinned.

"I do." I angled the screen. "This is Murdoch. Murdoch, meet Marisa. She's my best friend in the whole world."

Murdoch tilted his head to look at the screen, and I smiled as Marisa did the same back.

"Girl, he's darker than I am. I approve. His feathers are gorgeous."

She's pretty.

"He thinks you're pretty," I said, reaching up to scratch the back of his head.

"He's got good taste." Marisa laughed. "Are you sure you're okay? I don't like the look of your face."

"It hurts, but just bruises. I ..." I took a sip of my wine and Marisa took a larger gulp of her drink, signaling someone off screen that she'd want another. I didn't blame her. There was a lot to unpack here. "Which part do you want first? The magick or the man?"

Marisa sucked in a breath, pressed her lips together, and made a funny little popping noise she always did when she was thinking.

"What kind of magick? Voodoo? I can get down with some of that. Don't know much about the rest of it though." Marisa gripped her glass with both hands and gave me a level stare. She'd always been this way, just sailing over the speedbumps of life, a steady hand on the wheel.

"Turns out it might run in my family. But now that I'm here, it's like returning to my ancestral home or something. Power's amplified." I shrugged. "Looks like I come from a line of forge witches. Others in my family worked with metals. My great-grandmother made hearthwards for the doors in the village. To ward off evil."

Marisa was nodding along with me, listening, not interrupting.

"And there's a group of women here. All with different kinds of magick. Like a kitchen witch, a garden witch. And we're tasked with protecting a great treasure. We're here to help the town."

At that, Marisa pursed her lips and drained her drink. She waved a finger in the air, motioning for me to continue.

"I know it sounds ridiculous. But it's not like ... I don't know, it's not like what you'd see on television or something. I did my first spell, infused a pendant with some protection magick."

"Like some evil eye shit?" Marisa asked, smiling as a waiter brought her a fresh drink.

"Pretty much. It was for a ... friend's ... niece. And I think it will help. I could feel it." I smiled at her, feeling confident with this for the first time. "Like inside me. I could pull at this power and feel it go through me and into what I was creating. It was pretty ... I don't know ... special, I guess."

"You've always been special," Marisa said, almost absentmindedly. "But I'm glad you're finally seeing it. And if this place is making you feel magick or do magick and it's a good thing for you, then I support it. Except the bruises, I don't like those."

"Yeah, that's the not so great part. There are these beasts called the Kelpies here. They're magickal water horses."

Marisa raised one perfectly manicured eyebrow, and I gulped down a laugh.

"I know. I know. It's what we're protecting the town from. I wasn't prepared and they crashed into me. Knocked me down."

"Not a fan of that," Marisa said, a scowl on her face.

"Nope. Me either. But I'm learning. I have friends who are helping me learn, including Murdoch. I can hear him."

"Right." Marisa nodded and switched to her fresh drink. "You've got magick now, you were attacked by water horses, and you can hear the bird. I'm trying here, Kala, I really am."

"I should have called you sooner. I'm sorry. It's a lot, even being here and experiencing it all, but I'm sure even more so trying to digest it in one conversation. I know you'll have a million questions, and I'll do my best to answer them. I'm still kind of absorbing it all myself."

"Did the bird really say I was pretty?"

"He did."

"And he's watching out for you?"

"He is."

"Humph, okay. I'll accept this new turn of events. Tell me about the man."

I shifted, sinking backward into the cushions, and took a sip of my wine.

"I met him in Edinburgh." I filled her in on the finer details and she cheered up until I got to the bad news. "And he's basically my new work landlord. I lease workspace from him, and now we're co-workers on a huge project for this new distillery called Common Gin."

Marisa's lips rounded, and she tapped a finger with a bright red nail with a singular crystal in the middle against her lips.

"First. Congratulations on the job! I bet that's exciting for you."

"It is!" I beamed at her. "Huge job, great company, and they liked more of my designs than Thane's."

"Naturally. You're brilliant." Marisa waved that away. *Why have I deprived myself of this?* Yes, she's completely biased, but she's also completely candid, which was incredibly uplifting. I loved this woman so hard. "This man ... Thane? Kaia, he's your co-worker. We've been here before."

"I know. I knooooow." I winced. "And we both keep agreeing that this can't happen again."

"And yet it does." Marisa accurately guessed.

"It does. I don't know what's wrong with me. It's like he's a magnet the minute I'm around him. We can't seem to keep our hands off each other."

"He's single?"

"Yup. Verified." The town was too small. None of

my new friends seemed the type to hide news of a wife from me.

"He's the friend with the niece then?"

"Correct. She paints his nails every week."

Marisa's expression softened.

"What's he look like?"

"He's massive. Just all tall and broad shouldered and muscley and lifts me like I weigh nothing at all."

Marisa fanned her face. "Go on."

"Moody eyes. Stormy expressions. Gruff. He's also a good boss, and everyone seems to respect him. He's just ... all sorts of in charge and ..." I sighed. "He almost lost his mind when he saw my face. I thought he was going to burn the town down until I told him what had really happened."

"This I like." Marisa saluted with her drink.

"But now he wants me to leave."

"Hmmm, *dislike*." Marisa hummed. "Why does he want you to leave?"

"He's worried I'll get hurt again so he thinks kicking me out of town is the only way to protect me. It's stupid. We're all here trying to help Loren Brae."

"I mean, I don't want you to get hurt again either. Do you really think that's a possibility?" Marisa's eyebrows drew together in concern, and she leaned closer to the phone.

"I don't know. I hope not. I've got support now, help, and tools. I think it's going to be just fine. I mean, there are people living here, going about their lives every day. It's a threat, but also not a threat, you know?"

"On a scale of Snickers to Three Musketeers, how worried should I be?"

We'd always used candy bars as a rating system for where something was at, with Snickers being the best. I thought about it.

"Mounds bar."

"Okay, I can handle that." We both loved coconut. "But you need to check in more now. I can't do this 'weeks of no contact' bullshit and then almost have a heart attack in the middle of the day. Look at me. You've got me drinking before five in the afternoon!"

"Apologies." I smiled at her. "I've missed you. It's just been a lot."

"No kidding. Just ... be careful with this man. I am giving you a very light approval rating with him. Maybe not a red flag warning, but a pink flag, okay?"

"You're not swearing me off him?" I looked at her, incredulous.

"It doesn't honestly sound like I'd be able to do much since he just banged you against the wall of your cottage."

Murdoch made a sound that distinctly sounded like he was laughing.

"See?" Marisa pointed a finger at the screen. "The bird agrees. He's smart."

I like her.

"He says he likes you."

"Good, because I like him too. Can he FaceTime? Someone's got to keep me updated on your chaos."

"I'll see about getting him a live stream." I took a sip

of my wine and smiled. "Now tell me what's going on with you. Dating anyone?"

"Girl, why do you think I'm in Chicago? I met a running back at one of his away games. You think your man is all tall and muscle-bound?" Marisa shook her head in exaggeration. "You have noooo idea."

I laughed and leaned back, glad I'd decided to call her, and to not keep anything from her. Even if she didn't believe everything that was happening to me, she didn't judge.

She has power too.

I took in Murdoch's words with a small nod. I'd ask him more about it later, but it certainly didn't surprise me. Marisa had always been a force to be reckoned with. Now that I knew magick existed, it wouldn't surprise me in the least if she had it.

Because maybe, just maybe, I'd always been meant to surround myself with magick.

CHAPTER FOURTEEN

Kaia

The next day, I took the morning away from Blackwood Forge to work on finetuning the final estimate for Orla, making notes where I'd need Thane's input on pricing per his contracts with his suppliers, and tried to narrow the timeline down. I knew Orla liked to keep to her schedule, so if we could deliver ahead of time, that would make everyone happy. It would depend on how many workers Thane could spare for this project, but either way I was feeling pretty pleased with how things were shaping up.

Murdoch had stayed the night with me, choosing the warmth and coziness of my cottage to the slashing rain outside. I'd enjoyed having him with me, even though I still marveled over my ability to communicate with him, and I had to admit that I felt just a touch safer having him in the cottage with me. Not that I was sure he could do all that much if I was under attack or something, but at the very least, he could sound the alarm or maybe peck someone's eyes out. I shuddered as I toweled off from my shower. I didn't want to think too deeply about that.

Craning my neck, I tilted my face into the light and examined my reflection. The bruises had turned to a nice yellowy green, but at least it was colors I could work with. Though I wasn't typically one for makeup, it was impossible to be friends with Marisa and not have learned some tricks over the years. Though my supply was basic at best, I did have a good foundation, an excellent concealer, and a few other bits and bobs to shine myself up when the mood struck. By the time I'd finished, even swiping a dusty rose sheen across my cheeks, I gave myself an approving nod. The bruises were well hidden, and I wouldn't scare anyone out in public today.

Even though I knew I was putting off going into the forge today, largely because I still hadn't managed to work through the disconcerting emotions that tangled in my gut every time I thought of Thane, I'd decided to detour to Bonnie Books to see Agnes's bookshop and bring her a bowl of soup from the pub.

I'd already called the order in and Graham was packaging it for me by the time I arrived. The Tipsy Thistle wasn't terribly busy for a weekday lunch, but far from what it could be, I was certain of that. Sophie was deeply worried about the lack of tourism in town and, looking around the mostly empty pub that was the main spot to eat in Loren Brae, I could see her concerns were valid.

"There's a bonnie lass," Graham said, his eyes twinkling at me. "Like a spot of sunshine on a cold winter's day."

"I shouldn't be charmed." I sighed, propping my elbows on the bar. "But I'll admit it, I am."

"Is that right?" Graham angled his head, his smile deepening.

"Charmed, I said. Not foolish." I laughed when he brought his hands to his chest, pretending to be wounded. I'd learned fairly quickly that Graham was harmless, and he complimented men and women alike from the ages of twenty to ninety. At least he was an equal-opportunity charmer. And what was the harm in that? He made people smile.

"Off to the forge then?" Graham asked, sliding the soup containers into a brown paper bag for me.

"Nope, just across the street to the bookshop. I'm taking Agnes lunch."

"Och, are you? Give me just a moment then." Graham ducked through a swinging door that led to the kitchen and I took the time to look around the pub again, trying to imagine it filled to the brim with people. It would be a happy place, and I hoped I could be a part of restoring business to the town. The door swung and I turned to see Graham with two more containers in his hands.

"Agnes likes extra rolls with her soup. And we've got

her favorite dessert on today, a millionaire shortbread, so I've added that in as well for the both of you."

"Oh, thank you." I reached for my wallet.

"Nae bother, hen." Graham waved it away and hitched the bag into his hands. "I'll just be carrying it across the way for you. Don't want you spilling the soups now."

"Can you leave the pub?" I bit back a smile as I went ahead to hold the door for Graham. I had a feeling he didn't offer hand delivery of his takeout meals for most of his customers.

"It's not a bother. I told the kitchen, and they'll keep an eye out."

The main street of Loren Brae was the kind of street that made me take pause. The buildings were colorful, clustered together, with the picturesque backdrop of Loch Mirren framed by rolling green hills. I couldn't imagine being a tourist and not wanting to stop and visit for a while. And if I angled my head just right, I could just see MacAlpine Castle peeking out over the rooftops. Yeah, it was a postcard of a town, and I wanted to do my best to help it.

Bonnie Books was a pretty stone building with large arched windows in front, and a cheerful sign over the door. I held the door for Graham, and a soft tinkling of bells announced our arrival. Celtic music lilted, wood beams lined the ceiling, and soft light spilled in the front windows showcasing a cozy room with woven rugs, shelves with rows of books, and tables piled with art and knick-knacks. Agnes turned, a smile on her face, and something flashed behind her eyes when she saw Graham.

I was right behind him, so it was almost like she was looking at me, and even I could feel the punch of it. *Oh yeah, these two. They were made for each other.* I wanted to fan my face, or hell, turn around and go find Thane.

"Special delivery," Graham said, holding up the bag.

"Are you a delivery lad these days? Taken on a new side job?" Agnes said, tucking a wayward curl behind her ear and turning to shelve another book.

"We do what we must in trying times." Graham put the bag down on what looked to be a desk and sidled closer. "I've heard it's proper to tip the delivery boy."

"Is that so?" Agnes turned and put her hands on her hips. "Well, it's not my order, is it? It's Kaia that will need to be doing the tipping."

"Awww, go on and give us a kiss, Agnes." Graham's smile deepened when her cheeks flushed. "I put your millionaire shortbread in."

Agnes sucked in a breath.

"You play dirty."

"It's your favorite."

"Fine. One kiss, but that's all the tip you'll be getting from me." Agnes pretended to stomp her foot and gave me an aggrieved glance. "He's shameless, this one."

"Don't look at me. I'm American. We tip for everything." I grinned as Agnes sighed and then leaned in to kiss his cheek.

At the last moment, Graham turned his head, and her lips met his.

I couldn't tell who was more surprised, and my breath caught in my throat as her hands gripped the flannel of his shirt. The kiss lasted no more than a breath, but it could have been hours, and when Agnes pulled back her eyes were shuttered, her emotions hidden.

Silence filled the store.

"You must really like shortbread," I said, breaking the moment, because I could tell Agnes needed a lifeline. Agnes opened her eyes and looked past Graham, who still stared down at her, as though transfixed, and gave me a wobbly smile.

"It's really good shortbread. I hope you packed enough for Kaia?" Agnes raised a look at Graham, who cleared his throat and shook his head as though to gather his thoughts.

"Of course, there's more than enough for both. Um, I'll just be—"

"Right, you'd better—" They spoke over each other, awkward, and I pressed my lips together. She definitely needed an assist.

"I'm super hungry, so I, for one, can't wait to dive into lunch. Shall we have our soup? Graham, are you staying for lunch?"

Graham turned and focused on me, seeming to realize where he was finally, and shook his head.

"No, I've got to get back to the pub. Enjoy your lunch, ladies." Graham turned back, awkwardly patted Agnes's arm, and then almost ran from the store.

Agnes watched him through the window. When she turned, I raised both eyebrows.

"Don't," Agnes said.

"I won't. If you don't want to."

"I don't."

"Because it looked like—"

"It wasn't." Agnes busied herself with opening the bag.

"Well if you ever need to talk about it …" I held up my hands when Agnes gave me a look over her shoulder.

"There's nothing to talk about."

"Well, I'm just saying … if there was something to talk about, I could listen. I'm a great listener. And I'm shit at advice. I keep jumping my co-worker and we keep telling each other we'll never do it again. I certainly have nothing to offer you."

Agnes snorted and ripped a piece of roll off, shoved it in her mouth, and chewed thoughtfully as she stared at the pub through the window.

"I have no idea what I'm doing."

"Same, sister, same." I took my container of soup and dropped onto a love seat tucked beneath the window.

"I don't think I'm ready to talk about it. This. I don't even know what just happened. Why would he ask for a kiss? Why did he turn at the last second like that?"

"Because he wants to jump your bones?"

Agnes leveled me a look and I waved my spoon at her.

"Trust me, I could feel the heat from here. Hell, I almost left to go find Thane and have him work off whatever residual heat you two were generating. That is a man who wants to worship at the altar of Agnes."

"That and every other woman in town." Agnes sniffed and brought the rest of the food over.

"Oh, is that the way of it?" That was tough to hear. I didn't want to hate Graham.

"Well, used to be. If I'm being honest, he's not been so bad of late."

"Because he's in love with you."

"Och, it's not ... no." Agnes shook her head emphatically. "*No*. It's not like that."

"Then why do you keep looking out the window at the pub?"

"I don't ..." Agnes trailed off as she realized she was doing just that. Turning, she narrowed her eyes at me, and I grinned. "And here I thought I was going to like you."

"You do like me. But, since my life is no more sorted out than whatever that whole thing I just witnessed and you're trying to pretend didn't really happen, I'm happy to move on. I hung out with Murdoch last night, my raven." I neatly changed the subject and Agnes seized it, clearly happy to talk about something else. We chattered through our admittedly delicious potato leek soup, and then moaned over the dessert.

"Damn it. I may need to go over there and kiss the man myself for this. It is *so* good," I said around a mouthful of caramel and shortbread.

Bells tinkled before Agnes could respond and a woman in her sixties walked in, slowly, with a much older woman hanging on her arm. The older woman used a cane, had a thick braid of bright white hair hanging over her shoulder, and brilliant blue eyes tucked in a face filled with wrinkles. Her gaze landed on me.

"Eithne!" the woman crowed, her face alighting.

My heart skipped a beat.

Eithne. Do I resemble my great-grandmother? If that wasn't freaky ...

"No, Mum, you've never met this woman before." The younger woman threw an apologetic glance my way.

"Welcome, ladies." Agnes slid me a glance and lowered her voice. "Maureen suffers from dementia. It's come on quickly and really changed their lives. She was quite active before the change."

"Ah. That's too bad."

"Go on and finish your lunch. We'll just prattle about."

"Eithne." Maureen said the name more sharply, as though she was upset I didn't recognize her, her eyes boring into mine. "Don't you know me, hen?"

"I'm ..." I paused and changed my tactic. "Hello, Maureen, how are you?"

"You sound different." Maureen tilted her head, confusion cluttering her face, and she reached up to grip a brooch she wore at her jacket, but it snapped off and tumbled to the floor.

"Och, Mum. You've dropped your brooch. Here, I'll get it." Her daughter bent and picked it up, examining the piece. "Such a shame. Looks to be broken."

"No." Maureen's sharp cry of distress had me standing and moving across the room.

"May I look at it? I make jewelry. I might be able to help."

"Would you mind? It's an important piece to her." Her daughter held it out to me.

It was a silver brooch, with what looked to be moss agate as the main stone, with intricate Celtic designs carved into the silver. It looked like she'd snapped the pin where it attached to the back of the brooch, an easy enough soldering job, but I'd need to bring it home with me.

"Would you be okay if I just popped home and soldered this bit? Would take maybe fifteen minutes tops, or so?" I held the brooch in the air.

"I can vouch for Kaia," Agnes said. "She works for Blackwood Forge and also has her own jewelry line."

"If it's not too much trouble." A relieved look crossed the daughter's face. "It's the only thing that brings her comfort these days. She always puts it on."

"Maureen." I reached out and gently squeezed the woman's arm. "I'm going to fix this for you, but I'll just need to be away for a short period of time."

"Of course you will, Eithne." Maureen gave me a brisk nod as though she understood what I was going to do, and then slowly made her way to a bookshelf, a relaxed expression on her face as she peered up at the books.

"That's her occupied now. She could look at the shelves for ages." The daughter shot me a look of appreciation, and I gave Agnes a quick wave before I tucked the brooch in my pocket and left.

A sound almost like a *"gronk gronk"* caught me, and I looked up to see Murdoch flying above me. It was a different call than the low knocking sound he did when he was hanging out with me, but it didn't sound like he was in distress or warning me about anything.

"All good?" I called.

Aye, lass. Maureen knew your great-grandmother.

"I wondered if that was the case."

A woman across the street pushing a stroller gave me an odd look, and I smiled, waving at her, and realized I likely looked a bit odd calling out into the air. Pressing my lips together, I hurried down the lane toward my cottage and made a note about talking to Murdoch in public.

I didn't want to get a reputation for being the weird newcomer who screamed at ravens in the street.

Once at the cottage, I made quick work of plugging my soldering iron in, and gently turned the brooch over in my hands, looking for a makers mark and to see if it was genuinely silver. Only then did I notice a small latch at the side. Easing it open, a tenderness curled around my heart. Inside, behind a little glass pane, was a singular lock of hair. This was more than just a brooch, it was a mourning pin. Common during Victorian times, people would often elaborately braid the hair of their deceased loved ones into their jewelry. This was just a simple memorial, for Maureen alone to carry, and I gently clicked the brooch closed again.

It warmed in my hand, and I could feel the love in this piece.

I wasn't sure how else to explain it, but it was more than just the context clues of what I had been given. I could actually feel it. When I held the piece, a quiet joy filled me, steady and sure, and when I put it down on the table, removing my touch, the feeling went away.

An idea occurred.

I stood and went back to my door, opening it and poking my head out.

"Murdoch?"

Aye, lass. The raven swooped low and landed at my feet, tilting his head.

"Can you help me? I want to help recover Maureen's memories. She's fighting dementia, and I'm told it's quite bad. I was thinking maybe I could do a spell?"

Of course. I'll collect the rosemary.

With that, Murdoch disappeared into the sky and I squinted after him. The rosemary? And how long would this take? I didn't want to upset Maureen by being away with her brooch too long. But Murdoch returned within a minute, rosemary in his beak, and I opened the door wider for him to fly inside.

Perching at the counter by the brooch, he dropped the sprig next to my tools.

"What am I meant to do with rosemary?"

Rosemary is traditionally used to help with memory. Add it to the locket, along with an intention spell to help unlock her memories.

I picked up the sprig of rosemary and looked from it to the locket. How was I meant to add this to the jewelry? Mulling it over, I went to a cabinet and pulled a bowl out. If I crushed it, I could likely add a bit into the part I soldered, and it wouldn't hurt the strength of the bond. Or so I hoped.

"And that's it? I just add it in and ask it to help?"

You need a spell to unlock her memories. Try this: By the breath of wind and roots of old, unlock the past, let memories unfold.

I repeated his words to myself and busied myself with turning on the soldering iron, getting my silver solder ready, and crushing the rosemary. When the iron was ready, I scooped the tiniest amount of rosemary out of the bowl with my chisel, touched the iron to the silver solder, and then gently picked up the minuscule amount of rosemary. Moving with precision, I quickly joined the broken pin back to the brooch, focusing on keeping the solder neat and tidy. When finished, I put the pin in its holder and eyed my work.

"Shit! The spell."

I'd been so focused on doing the work that I'd forgotten to add my intent. Annoyed with myself, I examined the brooch. Maybe I could shore up any areas that looked to be worn? Or add a small insignia on the back? Mulling it over, I spotted where one edge had worn down with time, on the back side of the brooch. Humming, I picked up the iron and added a small dab of silver. Once on, I pressed it flat, and then, squinting, I etched the tiniest of keys into the metal.

"By the breath of wind and roots of old, unlock the past, let memories unfold." I recited the spell as I reached for that thread of power inside me. For a moment, heat coursed through me, my skin tingling with power, and the brooch warmed slightly beneath my touch.

And then, just like that, it was done. Or so I hoped. I dabbed some pickling solution on the solder and glanced at Murdoch as I cleaned the top of my iron before storing it.

"Think that will do?"

Aye, lass. She'll be very pleased to have her memories back.

"I hope so." I stood up, pacing. "I feel good. Energetic. Like I want to go, like, race around the house or something."

That's magick. It can provide an adrenaline rush.

"Really?" I instantly thought about using magick during sex and my cheeks heated. Turning away, I opened the fridge. "Want some blueberries?" I needed to wait a few more minutes before I could clean the brooch and return to the bookshop.

Of course.

After I fed Murdoch, cleaned the brooch, and made quick use of the bathroom, I headed back to the bookshop. The sun shone today, with wispy white clouds threading the horizon, and a chilled breeze toyed with the frills of my hair.

"Oh good," Agnes said, when I walked in. "I was just going to call you. Maureen was getting restless without her brooch."

"Eithne, do you have my brooch?" Maureen asked from where she sat on the love seat.

"I do. It's all fixed now. Just like new."

"Here, Mum." Her daughter took the brooch and held it up so her mother could see it, before she pinned it back on her jacket. "There. That's you all sorted out."

"My brooch." Maureen reached up and curled her hand around it, her eyes on me. I waited, wondering if anything would happen immediately, or if it would take time.

A small gasp of air left her lips.

Her eyes held mine, incredulous.

"You're not Eithne."

"No, I'm not."

"You're her great-granddaughter, aren't you? You've the look of her though. In your eyes." Maureen's daughter was peering at her in confusion.

"Mum?" Concern filled her tone.

"I'm quite all right, dear." Maureen stood and without her cane she walked over to me, her gaze sharp and assessing as she looked up at me. She beckoned me to bend closer and reaching up, she gave me a hug. "It seems you've given me a key. And now I'll return the favor. She's left something for you. Step by step, you walk on me, beneath one tread, the treasure shall be."

Maureen whispered the last part, and I committed it to memory, though my mind whirled in confusion. *Step by step, you walk on me, beneath one tread, the treasure shall be?* What in the world?

"Mum, what's going on? Don't you need your cane?" Maureen's daughter stood, clenching her hands, her face hopeful.

"I'm much better and that's the truth of it, dear. I

can remember again." Maureen's daughter's eyes filled and the two hugged while I turned away to give them a moment.

"Well done you," Agnes murmured at my side, bumping my shoulder with hers.

"She gave me a clue of sorts," I murmured back. "From my great-gran."

"Even more interesting. I do love a riddle."

"I have to go"—I checked the time on the antique clock on the wall—"if that time is accurate."

"It is."

"I'm expected at the forge for budget meetings. We'll chat soon." Agnes gave me a quick hug before I could leave, something I still wasn't entirely used to with having very few female friends, and I stopped by the two other women on the way out.

"I'm Kaia, by the way. I don't even know if we were formally introduced, but I have to go to work. Hopefully I'll see you again?" I was dying to know what else she remembered about Eithne.

"Of course you will. It's a great gift you've given us."

My mouth rounded at her daughter's words as well as at her fierce hug.

"Oh, I just fixed the brooch. Wasn't a problem at all." I shrugged.

"I don't care what you did to it. It's brought Mum back to us and that's all that matters."

With that, I left quickly, before the tears that threatened spilled over. I couldn't imagine losing my mom or gran to dementia—they were both such shining lights in my life—and if nothing else came out of my stay in Loren Brae, this one moment might make it all worth it. It had been an honor to help Maureen, and I was delighted with the work I'd done today.

I'm proud of you.

Glancing up, I smiled at where Murdoch flew above me, my faithful sentinel.

"As I am of you. We make a great team, don't we?"

Aye, lass.

CHAPTER FIFTEEN

Thane

She'd asked me for space.

Granted, it was likely because I once again invited her to leave Loren Brae, and maybe was a bit pushy about it.

And it had also been in my office at the end of a meeting to go over the budget for the Common Gin product.

It was my screwup. I'd mixed business and personal again, but by bringing up the Kelpies. I'd barely slept the last few nights, my ears constantly straining for any sound of the Kelpies. I had no idea what I'd do if they screamed again in the night. I wasn't even sure I wanted to know what to do. From the sound of it, these beasts were terrifying.

Kaia had faced them alone.

Swearing, I gripped the steering wheel as I drove Audrey to her mum's house.

"Bad words, Uncle Thane."

"You're right, I'm not being very polite right now, am I?" My nails were black with silver sparkles today. Not that I much minded the pink or the purple, but when I'd spotted a slightly more masculine color in the market, I'd snagged a bottle for Audrey. She lectured me about the color, but the polish had still met with her approval based on the sparkles.

"I won't tell Mum. If you get me a sweetie."

I slid a glance into the rearview mirror where she grinned at me. Audrey was well aware that I couldn't resist anything she asked of me.

"I might have picked up a treat for you already. Or we can stop on the way home."

Audrey considered the options and then nodded soberly.

"I trust your decision."

Amusement made my mouth quirk up. "Well, that's very kind of you."

I pulled my lorry into Lauren's house, the end of a terraced row of cottages, and their cat, Pickles, jumped to the windowsill to look out.

"Looks like Mum's not back yet. Let's go on in." I grabbed my bag from the seat next to me, hooked it over my shoulder, and rounded the car to help Audrey out. In moments we were seated at the small kitchen table, while Pickles wound his way between my legs. Audrey propped her chin up on her hands and tilted her head at me. I noticed the glint of a chain at her neck.

"How has school been?"

Audrey shrugged. "Fine, I guess."

"Remember when you said some of the kids were being mean?"

Audrey nodded and bent over to pick Pickles up. The cat, a tawny orange fluff ball, poked his head over the top of the table to see if there was any food available.

"How's that been going?" I didn't want to push her on this, as she so rarely talked about things bothering her, but I hoped to get more intel.

"They stopped." Audrey kissed Pickles' head.

"Oh." I thought about it, my eyes going back to the chain. "That's good, right?"

"Yeah. It just kind of happened. One day I told them they wouldn't like it if someone said those things to them, and they all just stopped."

"You stood up for yourself."

"I guess. It wasn't really a big deal. We all kind of hang out now."

How I wished life was as simple as a grade school row to sort out.

"I'm glad to hear it. It's easier to get on with everyone if they're just being nice, isn't it?"

"Yeah." Audrey bobbed her head. "But I guess I just don't care as much either. Kaia told me I had power now, and I think that I do."

"Did she really?"

"Yup, and I believe her. I'm strong now. And I have

pretty nails." Audrey examined her pink nails, scrunching up her wee face as she looked for any chips or dents in the polish. "Can I have my sweetie now?"

"Och, right." I pulled out a package of Tunnocks tea cakes, her favorite, and her face brightened.

"Yay!"

Reaching for a paper napkin from the holder, I opened the package and put the sweetie down, then ruffled her hair. "Make sure Pickles doesn't get any."

Looking out the window, I saw the washing from earlier and stood. My sister had moved into this place after her divorce and though it was small, it was what she could afford. It had two bedrooms, one bathroom, and a cozy kitchen and living area. But the backyard was fenced, they had enough outdoor space for some games for Audrey, and most importantly, it was all Lauren's. Grabbing the laundry basket by the back door, I ducked outside to pull the clothes from the line.

Kaia's pendant had worked.

She was doing good here, and she'd only been in Loren Brae a matter of weeks. Already she'd discovered ways to help the community, even if that meant using her magick.

I shook my head as I pulled down a pair of jeans and gently folded them.

I'd had to take some time to think over what Kaia had said about her magick. It still didn't sit right with me, yet at the same time, I didn't think it was wrong either. It was more that it was just something I didn't really understand. I couldn't control it, and I didn't really know how it worked. Because of that, I'd reached out to Lachlan to see if he wanted to grab a beer. I'd mentioned I had a few things to chat about, and he'd readily agreed to meet me. Since I knew Sophie was involved, maybe he'd be able to put my mind at ease about the Kelpies and Kaia.

I wasn't stupid either. I knew what she said was right. How was I comfortable with staying in Loren Brae, hell —my sister was staying here with Audrey—yet I wanted Kaia to leave? Maybe it was because I felt like Lauren and Audrey were mine to protect.

And Kaia, well, Kaia didn't want my interference. In anything.

Torn, because I knew I was being hypocritical, and yet at the same time I was just so damn worried for everyone, I finished folding the laundry just as I heard a car door slam out front. Coming back inside, I put the basket by the door and scurried over to the table to make a big production of hiding the box of Tunnocks back in my bag.

"Shhhhhh. Don't tell your mum."

"It's our secret." Audrey giggled. The chocolate all over her face immediately gave the secret away and I grabbed a napkin to wipe her cheeks. I was just crumbling it into a ball when Lauren walked in, her face stressed.

"I'm sorry I'm late."

"Don't be. It wasn't by much. Just brought the washing in for you."

"Och, thanks. I forgot on our way out this morning."

"You lucked out. No rain." I gave her a quick hug and went to the door while she crossed to give Audrey a cuddle.

"Someone smells like chocolate." Lauren shot me a disapproving look.

"No idea what you're talking about." I tucked my bag behind my back and shrugged.

"Mm-hmm." Lauren swiped a finger down Audrey's nose while she giggled. "Go wash up. I'll have dinner on shortly."

Audrey bounded away with a quick wave to me and I hesitated at the door before I left.

"Sounds like things are better at school." I pitched my voice low, so Audrey wouldn't hear.

"I know. I'm so relieved." Lauren shot me a grateful look over her shoulder as she opened the refrigerator and pulled out a Tupperware container. "I don't know this Kaia of yours, but I like her. Audrey seems convinced she's given her magickal powers, and as far as I'm concerned, so long as it keeps the bullies off her back, I'm good with it."

"She's not mine. She just works at the forge."

"Uh-huh." Lauren raised an eyebrow as she pulled the lid off the container. "Audrey said you took her on a date."

"Only because your daughter manipulated me into one."

"Oh really? You can't say 'no' to a seven-year-old?" Lauren laughed and shook her head. "Never mind, based on the chocolate on her breath, I'll take that as a no."

"I gotta run. Meeting Lachlan for a pint. Need anything before I go?" I asked, neatly switching the conversation. I wasn't about to unravel my complicated 'situationship' with Kaia with my sister.

"All good. You'll talk to me, right? If you need me?" That was Lauren. Even as busy and tired as she was, she always made time for those she loved.

"I will. I'm figuring things out at the moment."

"Well, if it's any help, Audrey loves her. And I trust Audrey."

"Trust me for what?" Audrey said, bouncing back into the room.

"To not lie to me about secret chocolate."

Audrey slid me a guilty look.

"I'm outta here!" Laughing, I threw her to the wolves and left the house, their laughter music to my ears as I left. I hadn't heard Lauren laugh much after her divorce, so it was nice to see the tension had lessened. Dropping my lorry at my house, I changed and walked to the pub to meet Lachlan.

I wished I could detour and walk past Kaia's cottage, but I didn't want to seem stalkerish, so I didn't. But I wanted to.

Damn it, but the woman had me all tied up in knots. If I wasn't busy thinking about how to keep her safe, I was remembering what it was like to be buried deep inside her body, her softness surrounding me, crying out as I brought her pleasure. Every time I'd promised myself I'd had enough, I just kept going back for more. For better or worse, Kaia was in my system, and I had no idea how to extract her.

The Tipsy Thistle wasn't too busy when I arrived, a few regulars I knew from town playing cards at a table across the room, a TV showing a replay of a rugby match on low in the background. My eyebrows winged up when I saw Lachlan, Finlay, Munroe, and Ramsay all sitting at the bar. I shoved down my disappointment. I'd hoped to have a chat with Lachlan about Kaia, but it seemed he'd misread my invitation for a lads' night. Two of these men were now my clients, so I'd have to make sure to be as charming as I could. I bit back a sigh. It looked like I was working tonight.

"There he is." Lachlan spied me and waved me over. "How's it going, lad?"

We were friendly enough, having a pint here and there, but Lachlan and I were more acquaintances than friends. What I knew of him was that he was fiercely loyal to the town, a bit uptight about following the rules, and madly in love with Sophie. Ramsay I knew as well, though he was a man of few words, which was fine by me. I think I'd whiled away more than one afternoon watching a match with him with barely more than ten words spoken between us. We both liked it that way. I gave him a nod, and he tapped a finger to his forehead in response.

I reached around Lachlan and shook Finn's and Munroe's hands.

"Gentlemen. Good to see you both."

"Guinness, mate?" Graham asked, and I nodded my

thanks. He hadn't mentioned a word about Kaia to me and we were back on normal terms, at least from what I could see.

Lachlan pulled out a stool in between him and the other men, and I took it, relaxing a bit as Munroe and Finn argued about the placement of some piping for the distillery. Graham slid me my pint, and I took a sip, letting out a contented sigh.

"How are things at the shop then, Thane?" Lachlan asked me.

"Yeah, good, mate. Keeping busy. The Holyrood project took me away for a while, so it's nice to be back home."

"And Kaia? Is she settling in okay? Did you hire her?" Lachlan asked.

"No. She leased the space from us. I would, but ..." I trailed off when I realized the other men were all listening to me.

"But what?" Munroe asked. I winced. I didn't want to talk about anything personal in front of them.

"She wants to build something of her own." There, that was an acceptable answer. I certainly couldn't say it would muddy the waters even further when it came to our apparent lack of self-control around each other.

"I can admire that." Ramsay tilted his pint glass in a silent toast.

Lachlan grinned.

"All of our women are fiercely independent, mate."

"Except mine." Graham grinned from behind the bar.

"Yours is so independent you haven't even met her yet," Ramsay quipped, and we all laughed.

"It's why I try to date as much as possible. Playing the odds."

"I keep telling you to cut that crap out." Lachlan sighed. "It's not going to get you what you want."

I had an idea who Graham really wanted, but it was none of my business.

"That's easy enough for a man to say who's got someone to go home to every night." Something indiscernible flashed behind Graham's eyes. A bell from the kitchen dinged. "Excuse me."

Lachlan sighed as Graham disappeared to pick up food for the tables.

"They'll find their way soon enough," Munroe murmured, and Lachlan shrugged.

"It's his funeral."

I didn't say anything, though I was curious. I had worked around groups of men for years now and knew when to keep my mouth shut.

"Anyway," Lachlan said, draining his pint. "Thane is here to talk to us about Kaia."

I coughed, sputtering on my sip of beer, and Lachlan cheerfully pounded my back while I reached for a napkin to wipe my mouth.

"What the hell, mate?" I glared at him and then made eyes at the others.

"We know," Munroe said, smiling.

"There's nothing to know," I lied, protecting Kaia's reputation.

"Willow said you body slammed Kaia against a wall and the castle could have burned down around you two and neither of you would have noticed." Ramsay stated this placidly as he took another sip of his beer, his eyes on the TV.

"Och, so now you're a talker?" I glared at Ramsay as the rest of the men whooped in laughter.

"Who are we on about now?" Graham asked, having returned from delivering food.

"Thane and Kaia," Lachlan said, and I rubbed a hand over my face.

"Och, I could've told you as much. The lad almost eviscerated me the other day when I flirted with her. I've made sure to do it extra whenever she's about just to infuriate him."

The lads laughed even harder, and I grimaced.

"Listen … it's not. It's just …" I sighed and pinched my nose. "It's important to Kaia to make her own way here, on her own merits. Because she's leasing from me, she's worried that anything more will cause complications that could threaten her livelihood."

"But you wouldn't do that? Would you? If things went sour between you?" This from Finlay, my client.

"Of course he wouldn't," Lachlan answered before I could. "You may not know this, but Thane has taken over for his niece's absent father. Christ, look at his nails."

The men all looked dutifully at my sparkly nails.

"Nice color," Ramsay said.

"Thanks," I growled.

"I'm just saying ... a man doesn't take up for his sister and niece like that if he doesn't respect women." The men all murmured in agreement with Lachlan's words.

"Appreciate that," I said.

"And if you do, well, we'll fix it." Lachlan gave me a look.

"I wouldn't."

"So is that what's bothering you? How to work with her?" Finlay leaned in. "Because Orla's super strict on-site, and I just respect the rules she's laid out. It can work."

"And Willow just steamrolls and bosses me about and I let her because I basically stop listening when she goes on a rant and drool over her sparkly short skirt." Ramsay held up his glass for a refill.

We all hooted at Ramsay's admission. He shrugged. "It's just the way of it."

"It's that. And ..." I pressed my lips together. Nope, I wasn't going to do it. I certainly couldn't bring up magick to these lads. Maybe just Lachlan when I got him alone.

"The magick?" Munroe asked and I blinked at him in surprise.

Munroe was the owner of Common Gin, insanely wealthy, and married to Lia, the chef at the castle. Certainly not someone I'd thought I'd be discussing magick with.

"You know?" I asked, leaning forward and lowering my voice.

"All of our women are magick," Finlay said.

"Even Graham's. She's so magick she's see-through," Ramsay quipped and Graham stopped pouring his pint.

"I'll pour this down the drain, mate."

"Och, you're far too cheap to waste good beer," Ramsay protested. "But I'll lay off."

I just sat there, gaping at all of them.

"Wait, to be clear, you're saying that all of your women have magick?" I barely spoke above a whisper.

"Correct. They're all a part of the Order of Caledonia. Well, and Owen's partner, Shona. Not sure if you've met him?" Lachlan asked, leaning back on his stool.

"American lad? Movie producer?"

"Aye, that's the one. Shona's a garden witch." Lachlan held his hand out and ticked names off on his fingers. "Lia's a kitchen witch. Orla's a house witch. Sophie's the knight. Willow can see the future. And Kaia ..."

"She's a forge witch," I supplied.

"What's that?" Graham asked.

"One who can imbue her magick into metal. Or so I'm told. I've only just learned about it, and certainly haven't seen it in action. We ... had words."

"Och, mate. Were you hard on her about the magick?" Munroe glared at me.

"No. At least I don't think so." I swung my head around, but nobody else was paying attention to us. "It's just ... I think she'd be safer if she left town. Did you see her bruises? Those are from the Kelpies. I'm worried."

"Ahhhh." It was a collective sound of understanding from all the men.

Lachlan sighed and clapped a hand around my shoulders.

"Mate, I'll say this with the best of intentions. You're fucked if you try to kick her out of town."

"I am?" I glanced at him in surprise.

"Aye, if she's anything like my Sophie she'll kick your sorry arse for even suggesting she do that."

"It's true," Finlay said, nodding his agreement. "Our women are much stronger than they look. You'll not be able to run her from town."

"But how do you protect them?" I asked. "The Kelpies ... they're just terrifying."

"Makes your butthole pucker," Ramsay agreed, and I winced at the imagery.

"Basically, yeah."

"Willow saved me from them," Ramsay said, and my mouth dropped open.

"She did?" All of the lads here were strong, but Ramsay was massive. To imagine a woman rescuing him was almost impossible.

"Aye."

It seemed that was all I was getting of the story, and I could certainly understand that.

"So what do I do?"

Lachlan punched my arm.

"You just hang on for the ride, lad. It's all you can do."

"Bloody hell," I said, and signaled for another pint.

CHAPTER SIXTEEN

Kaia

I'd passed another challenge.

The day after securing the brooch, I discovered another slender copper band in the handle of the chisel I'd taken to carrying around everywhere with me.

I figured it didn't hurt

Not that I was particularly confident about what I could do against a two-story Kelpie with a small hand tool, but hey, best to be somewhat protected, right?

Either way, I was proud to have passed another challenge. Murdoch told me he was proud of me as well, and I gave myself a mental pat on the back as I got out of my car at the castle. I was meeting Thane on-site today to discuss a few design elements and then heading back to the forge to start implementing our first round of designs. I was itching to start creating, because I loved nothing more than seeing a project come to life.

Tires crunched next to me and I squared my shoulders. Turning, I pasted a polite smile on my face. I hadn't spoken much to Thane outside of anything to do with work the last few days after he'd asked me to leave Loren Brae again during a business meeting. Luckily, it had been just him and me in his office when he'd done so, otherwise I'm not certain I'd have held my temper in check. Instead, I'd simply stood up and requested he give me space.

Thane had followed my request.

Which had left me feeling oddly bereft the last few days. This, in turn, also made me annoyed. I wasn't someone who played games. It wasn't really in my wheelhouse to try the whole "play hard to get" thing, and if I did, I'd likely lose pretty fast based on my past experiences with the inability to see red flags. So I told him to leave me alone. And he did. And yet it annoyed me. I didn't tell anyone that it annoyed me. But I would say that a small part of me, which I wasn't particularly happy with at the moment, was having a tiny temper tantrum at his acquiescence.

Yes, I'm aware this was not logical.

It just was.

This was why I'd left the dating pool entirely. I didn't like games, and I was horrible at dealing with conflicting emotions. And right now, it felt like every other thought I had simply served to be contradictory to the other.

Yup, super fun times all around in my brain at the moment.

"Good morning," I said.

Damn it. He looked really good today. He wore one of those soft chambray button-down shirts, rolled up to reveal strong forearms, and dark trousers with cargo pockets. Something shifted behind his eyes when he saw me, a storm brewing, but he just gave me a polite nod.

"Good morning."

Great, here we were. This is what I had asked for. This was what I wanted. A colleague I could be polite with and build beautiful things together.

"It's a nice morning. I'm looking forward to seeing the progress they've made at the distillery."

I was told some of the cabinetry had gone in at the tasting room, so we could check our measurements for some of the wrought iron gated doors we'd be doing.

"As am I."

And that was it. No extra chatter, no small talk.

Murdoch gave a low knocking sound from the trees, but I ignored him, not wanting to remind Thane of the magick I'd told him about. I still wasn't sure where he stood on that front, but at least I knew he hadn't spoken of it to anybody at work because everyone still treated me the same. If not a little overprotective of me since I'd come in with bruises. Even though I'd reassured everyone it truly had been just an accident, I could tell the men at the shop were watching me more closely.

It was mildly annoying, but I knew they were just doing so because they cared.

"Och, now there's a handsome lad if I've ever seen one."

I skidded to a stop as Thane yanked me to his side, and we both gaped down at a tiny diva dressed in a pinup dress with curves for days. A female, um, *gnome* to be exact. A tiny talking female gnome that was currently strolling out of the bushes with her eyes set on Thane.

"Care to take me for a drive, darling?" The gnome blew a kiss up at Thane, and I slowly turned my head to look at him, my eyes wide.

"Och." Thane cleared his throat. "It's a crying shame that I can't, miss. But I've a work appointment."

"Gnora!" I jolted as another gnome shot out of the bushes, this one in a biker vest and with tattoos running up his arms. "Stop flirting with that man."

"I was just seeing if he'd take me for a drive, Gnorman. You know that I love a good ride." Gnora fluttered her lashes at Gnorman, and his face flushed an angry red.

"He will not be taking you for a ride. I'm the one that gives you a ride. You, sir, will leave my girl alone." Gnorman raised a fist in the air at Thane.

"Understood," Thane said gravely, and I bit back a hysterical giggle that threatened to surface. What in the hell was going on? "We'll just get out of your hair."

"That's right. Run along!" Gnorman brandished his arms and Thane tugged me forward.

"We should go?" Thane asked and I realized I was still standing there, gaping at the gnomes.

A bark sounded and the gnomes froze. I gasped as they morphed from living and breathing beings to statues, as Harris ran over to greet us. Reaching down, I accepted his exuberant lick on my hand. Turning, he gave the same attention to the gnomes, swiping his slobbery tongue over both of their faces.

I was quite certain I heard a muffled shriek.

Choking on a laugh, I dove for them both when Harris lifted his leg to pee and pulled them out of the danger zone just in time.

"Bloody dog!" Gnorman shouted from my arms, coming to life so fast I almost dropped him. Gnora turned and wiped her face against my sleeve.

"Thanks, doll. That could've gotten ugly."

"Sorry about that. I wasn't sure if it was rude to pick you up, but I figured you couldn't abide the pee."

"What I can't abide is Gnorman talking to some hussy." Gnora stuck her nose up in the air, and I looked up to see Thane grinning at me.

"I asked her what mulch she was using for her roses," Gnorman said, his face thunderous.

I have no idea what to do, I mouthed over their bickering heads at Thane.

"There you two are!" Shona strode around the side of the hedge. "I'm sorry, are they bothering you?"

"Um, I have no idea how to answer that," I said. "So these are your gnomes?"

"Yup, and they're a pain in my arse. I was just dropping some supplies off for Lia and they insisted on coming. They don't get out much."

"Seems there's some drama." I handed them over to Shona and she dropped them both into the tote hanging over her shoulder. The bag muffled their argument, but didn't stop them. It looked like dumping two cats in a bag, and when a muffled giggle erupted, Shona just sighed.

"Och, they just like to create a little excitement for themselves. A bit dramatic, they are. I've gotta run, but it's nice to see you again. Thane, all good with you?"

"All's well. Good to see you, Shona." Thane gave her a nod, and Shona bustled away, taking her gnomes with her, and I just gaped after her.

"I have no idea how to respond to what just happened," I finally said, tearing my eyes away from where Shona scolded her tote bag, and looked up to Thane. "I have no frame of reference for that."

"Nor do I." Thane's grin was wide and normal, and some of the awkwardness between us eased. Or at least the tension *I'd* been feeling eased. I couldn't really speak for him.

"Hi," Orla called, stepping out in front of the distillery. She walked out and waved us to follow her around the front of the construction site. "Come with me quick to look at this old cottage. We're going to convert this as well, but I wanted to show Kaia what I found."

"How's the progress going?" I fell into step next to Orla, Thane at my side, as we rounded the converted stables that were forming the new Common Gin distillery and stopped in front of a rustic stone cottage that had seen better days.

"Good. Honestly, I couldn't be happier with it."

Orla walked over to the door and tapped a small crest on the doorframe, a diamond ring on her finger winking in the light. I hadn't realized she was engaged to Finlay, but that made me even happier. The way he looked at her made me believe in true love.

Did Thane look at me like that?

Pushing that thought aside, I leaned in to look at the small plaque.

"I think this is a hearthward. Perhaps made by your ancestor."

"Really? Do you really think so?" Excitement bloomed and I reached up to carefully remove it from the frame.

"A triskele," Thane murmured and I turned to look at him. He gestured to the plaque. "The Celtic design. Meant for balance and harmony."

"Do you feel any power with it?"

I blinked at Orla when I realized she was asking me the question.

"Um, I'm not …" I stuttered, unsure how to answer the question, and slightly embarrassed as I still wasn't sure what Thane thought of all this magick.

"The lads talked with each other, hen," Orla said.

"Just give it a moment, Kaia. See what you feel," Thane said, and I stilled, surprised he was open to this. Closing my eyes, I held it and reached inside to find that thread of magick. Though the triskele warmed slightly in my hand, I couldn't feel much power in it. Almost a memory of power, maybe, like the last residuals of paint that had faded from wood over the years.

"I feel like there are some hints of it, but no, nothing very strong."

"That tracks," Orla said, pursing her lips. "There was a very unhappy and pretty unhinged ghost living here for a while. I don't know that she would have gotten in here had the protection triskele still been charged."

My lips rounded. "Oh?" First gnomes, now an unhinged ghost?

"What do you mean charged?" Thane asked.

"Magick doesn't always hold forever. Same with protective wards. They need to be refreshed through the years. In fact, I'd like to have you make some for the distillery, and if you don't mind, a few for my crew's and my homes."

"Right." I looked down at the little plaque and then back up at Orla. The design I could do. It was the magick I was nervous about. "Do you think it will really help?"

"Can't hurt at this point. We'll take all the protection we can get."

"I'll help." Thane touched a hand lightly to my shoulder. "We can knock a bunch out later tonight. We'll make extras for the town too. As gifts."

"It will take some time. I don't want to set us back on schedule." I worried my lower lip. What if I couldn't do the protection magick?

"That's the other thing. We've had a delay. Cabinets aren't up yet because flooring isn't in. So you'll have a few days. Think you can do this in the meantime? Maybe fifty of them if you're doing the town as well? I'll pay you, of course."

"No problem, Orla. We'll get it done for you." Thane gave Orla a confident nod, and she beamed at him, while I just stood there wondering how I was going to make fifty of these in a few days. Let alone imbue them with magick.

"Great!" Orla chattered on about the construction project and I followed them in a daze, wracked with concern. I wasn't sure why Thane had promised making fifty of these plaques. Hand forging *one* would take hours.

By the time we said our goodbyes my stomach was in knots. I stopped Thane by his truck.

"Thane," I hissed, grabbing his arm. "How could you promise fifty of the triskeles? It will take far longer than a few days."

"No, it won't."

"Yes, it will." What was the man thinking?

To my utter shock, he reached out and booped a finger on my nose.

"Trust me."

"Did you just *boop* me?" My mouth fell open.

"Och, I believe that I did. But I didn't make the 'boop' sound when I did it, so I'm certain it doesn't count."

Torn between laughter and a slight meltdown, I got into the driver's seat and started my daily argument with my car. By the time I pulled into Blackwood Forge, Thane was already in his office.

"Kaia, you're looking well." Ian was just leaving the office, and his eyes searched my face with concern.

"Yup. All healed up. I promise I'll be more careful in the future."

"See that you do, lass. You had us all worried." Ian squeezed my arm before taking a folder across the room to chat with one of the men hammering a piece in front of a blazing forge. I stepped through the door to Thane's office and closed it behind me.

"Thane," I hissed, arms at my waist.

"Yes, Kaia?" Thane gave me a look as though he was speaking to Audrey, which infuriated me further.

"You can't possibly think we can get those triskeles done in time." I glanced over my shoulder and moved closer to his desk. "Not with me having to add magick to each one. It's going to take time. And I'll have to do it, you know, after hours. Away from others."

"We'll do molds," Thane said, evenly, and I stopped what I was about to say.

"Molds?" Damn it, why hadn't that occurred to me?

"Surely you're familiar with molds? Sand casting?" Thane crossed his arms over his chest and leaned back in his chair.

"Of course I am." I didn't do them much, but I was familiar. It was a process where you'd pack special sand around a pattern to create a mold, pour molten iron into the cavity, let it cool, and then break the sand away to reveal the solid metal shape. It made slightly rougher-edged designs, and the pieces would require some sanding and sealing after, but it was doable. "Even so, that requires a significant amount of time. And molds."

"Have you seen my back warehouse?" Thane asked

and I shook my head. I'd been pretty focused on my little corner of the shop. "I have about one hundred flasks, in varying sizes out there, and loads of foundry sand."

"Oh." Some of my anxiety eased, and I walked over and dropped into a chair in front of his desk. "But we'll still need to make the molds."

"Aye, but the good thing is that a triskele is a fairly common Celtic symbol. I have the mold ready, it will just be packing the sand. If we get the lads together and take the rest of the afternoon to pack them, I reckon we'll be ready to pour by late tonight or early tomorrow."

I wasn't only gobsmakced by Thane's offer to enlist his whole company in this venture, but I was learning that *this* was who he was. Thoughtful, kind, genuine. *Good.*

"So, you *have* thought about this." I gave him a tentative smile. "I hate promising something if I can't get it done."

"I never promise what I can't deliver." There was something about the way he said it, his rough voice sending shivers across my skin, which made liquid heat pour through me. I was well aware what the man could deliver.

Ian knocked and eased the door open.

"Permission to enter?"

"Aye. Ian we've got a special project for the distillery. Any chance some of the lads can spare the afternoon to help us prep some flasks?"

"No problem. I think we're at a pretty good spot for most of the projects." Ian checked his watch. "Shall we crack on with it since it's just about lunch and we can get them started after break?"

Thane glanced at me. "Good by you?"

"Yup, that works. Let's get started." Nerves made my hands tremble, and I concealed it by digging my fingers into my palms. I hadn't done a lot of magick yet, and I still needed to grow my confidence with it. Fifty molds seemed like such a massive project. Would I be able to do it? Would it help? Frankly, I didn't have any idea whether the Kelpies could leave Loch Mirren or not, but maybe they had other powers we didn't know about—like flooding or calling down lightning. Either way, if I could do anything to help—to be a true part of the team—then I was going to do my best.

Even if it meant burying every ounce of attraction I had for Thane and working side by side until this project was done.

Maybe the attraction would wear off the more we worked together and simply acted like colleagues. I was certain things would smooth over in time. They had to.

Or at least that was what I kept telling myself.

CHAPTER SEVENTEEN

Kaia

I remembered why I didn't do sand casting that often.

It was tedious work, and not all that exciting. A flask was basically a wooden box constructed of two parts, the cope and the drag, which were just fancy words for the top and the bottom. You packed special sand into one side of the flask and then pressed the shape you wanted into the sand. It kind of reminded me of making a sandcastle, albeit a metal-themed sandcastle. Essentially you pressed your pattern into packed sand, split it into two halves, and carved little tunnels for the molten iron to flow. Once the pattern is removed, you seal the mold back together and pour in the molten iron. Then, you basically wait for it to cool, and crack the flask open like a treasure chest to reveal the now solid triskele shape.

After, the triskele would require some sanding and sealing with an oil or a patina, depending on what we went with.

The men had been great, happy to chip in with the project, and the warehouse had been busy with mindless chatter, some banter about an intramural sports team some of them played on, and rock music blaring in the background. But by the time the day drew to a close, and the men readied themselves to leave, we had most of the flasks packed and ready for pouring.

"I can see if they can help pour tomorrow, but I know there were a few more things some of the lads wanted to look over on the Kinross project," Ian said, zipping up his coat as he made to leave.

"Nae bother, Ian. We'll stay late and get it poured. That way they can cool through the night," Thane said. He'd stripped to just a T-shirt that fit his body in ways that I most certainly should not be noticing.

"You're certain?" Ian's eyes darted to mine. "That's a lot of work."

"It's not a problem. I don't have any plans tonight." I smiled at Ian. "But thanks for asking."

"Aye, thanks, Ian. All good. See you tomorrow." Thane bumped Ian's shoulder with his fist and walked across the warehouse to take a slug from his water bottle. I turned away to avoid watching how his muscles rippled in his arms when he did so.

I needed a moment before we poured the metal. More than a moment, likely, since I still wasn't sure what magick to do. I'd been playing with phrasing all day in my head, but I still wasn't confident I could create my own spell. It was one thing to do that for a small pendant for Audrey. But this was a massive project, and I wanted to make sure my magick could cover the scale of it.

A flyer dropped on the table in front of me and I blinked at it.

"Pizza?" I said, picking it up and looking up at Thane.

"Pick your favorite. I'll go pick it up."

"Oh, you don't have to do—"

"Kaia. I'm starving. I'm sure *you're* starving. Let me get some food."

"Got it. Um, I'm easy. Pepperoni please."

"Really? No olives, mushrooms? Nothing else?" Thane raised an eyebrow at me.

"Green pepper and caramelized onion if they have it," I said with a small smile.

"That's better. I'll call it in. Need anything else while I'm out?"

The contents of a perfect protection spell? Instead, I just shook my head.

"Back in a bit." With that, Thane left, and I blew out a long breath. His presence dominated a room, and I didn't realize until he was gone that I'd been on edge all day working so closely with him.

Walking outside, I leaned against the front gate of Blackwood Forge. The building was situated outside town, in a slightly elevated position, and I could just see the loch spreading out behind the rooftops of Loren Brae. The sky lingered in a burnished yellow, soft but uncertain, like the world couldn't decide if the day was over yet. I, too, felt vulnerable and uncertain as a soft knocking sound caught my attention.

Of course. *Murdoch.*

"Hey buddy, is that you?"

Aye, lass.

Murdoch flew from the trees and landed on the gate next to my head. Turning, I looked up at him, threading my fingers through the iron bars of the gate.

"Can you help me with this magick? I need a protection spell for hearthwards. And I'm nervous to do it in front of Thane. What if I screw something up?"

You won't. He's a conduit for you.

"Excuse me? A what?" I leaned back in surprise.

He'll make your magick stronger. By being there, he amplifies it for you.

"A conduit doesn't amplify," I said, absentmindedly, chewing over what he said.

He'll help. Murdoch made a sharp noise as though I'd annoyed him.

"Sorry, just thinking out loud. So my magick is better with him near? Why is that?"

Murdoch threw his head backward and chortled to the sky and I glared at him.

"What's that supposed to mean?"

Och, lass. You're blind, aren't ye?

"Ugh, forget it. I can't think about that right now. Can you just help me before he comes back?"

Of course. It's always my honor to help. Murdoch bowed his head.

I tilted my head, mirroring his movement. "And I'm lucky to have you, good sir."

By iron's strength and ember's glow, no evil may come across this threshold.

"By iron's strength and ember's glow, no evil may come across this threshold." I repeated the words and squinted up at the raven. "And anything to add to the metal?"

Are you using iron?

"Yes, that's the plan."

No, then. A triskele has its own protection properties. Iron does so as well. With the spell, you should do well enough.

"Great, thank you, Murdoch." I repeated the words over and over to myself, making circles in the gravel parking lot, until Murdoch took flight.

He's coming back.

"Thank you!" I waved to him and went inside, confident that I had the spell down. But just in case, I quickly copied the words into the notebook at my worktable, and then looked up when Thane walked in the building.

My heart sighed.

Was there anything sexier than a man bringing you food?

"It's a nice enough night, want to sit out back?" Thane asked, gesturing to the back doors.

"Sure. Thanks for getting food." My stomach grumbled at the sight of it.

"Nae bother, hen." Thane followed me out into the night, and then to my surprise, flicked a switch that lit up two string lights with chunky bulbs that hung over the three picnic tables out back.

"Well, this is nice." The string lights made the back patio much more charming. A light breeze shifted the branches of the trees along the property line, and the first few stars dotted the sky.

"I put the lights up for a wee party in the spring and they've just stayed. Sometimes I sit out here and work on projects at night after everyone's gone home."

"Do you like owning your own business?" I settled onto the chair and accepted a can of Irn Bru he passed to me.

"I do." Thane flipped his pizza box open, and I mirrored his movements with my own, inhaling the spicy scent with pleasure. "At first I felt a bit like, I don't know how to say it ... I guess, unsure of myself? Like who am I to be running my own business?"

"I get that." I stabbed a finger in the air and nodded. "You felt like an impostor."

"Exactly. I remember how much I stuttered my way through my first pitch with a client." Thane laughed, wiping his mouth with a napkin. "But I got on with it. Got a few clients. Could eventually hire a team. My reputation grew, as did my expertise, and it just kind of fell into place. Ian was a godsend, and that's the truth of it. It's been brilliant having him on board. He handles all the things that I find most annoying."

"He's great. Everyone loves him."

"Including you?" Thane's gaze sharpened and I took

a bite of the pizza, a piece of gooey cheese trailing down my chin. I laughed as I wiped it off.

"As I said, he's great."

"But nothing more, right?"

"Thane." I sighed. "What would be the point of hooking up with Ian? He's still a co-worker. It would still be breaking the rules."

"But he doesn't own your lease. I do."

"Same same." I shrugged. "Plus, he's not …" I caught myself before I finished that sentence, astounded at what I had been about to say. Instead, I shoved the pizza in my mouth, taking a far bigger bite than necessary.

"He's not what?" Thane zeroed in on me and I pointed at my mouth, shaking my head. Before I had fully swallowed, I took another bite. Thane's stare was unwavering. "I've got all night, Kaia. And eventually you'll run out of pizza. He's not *what*?"

"Just forget it," I mumbled, my cheeks heating.

"Kaia." Thane's tone was gruff, rasping against my skin. Finally, I met his eyes, and the emotions that stormed in their depths.

"You," I whispered, caught.

Thane inhaled sharply through his nose, like a predator scenting his prey, and he dropped his pizza. My mouth rounded as he gripped the side of the picnic table with both hands and seemed to need time to steady himself. I waited, the night air charged around me, and my stomach dropped when Thane finally resumed eating.

"See any good movies lately?" Thane asked, changing the subject.

Sadness filled me. *I'd* done that. I'd pushed him away so much that he wouldn't admit his feelings for me. Which is exactly what I'd wanted. Asked for. This was a man respecting the boundaries that I had set. So why did it leave me feeling so bereft? Longing filled me and I hated myself for wanting what I couldn't have. Nobody liked a hypocrite.

Even me.

Which left me with a choice—did I remove the boundaries and give this a chance? Presuming that Thane even wanted to do so? Or did I just suck it up and learn to work around Thane even though we had undeniable chemistry?

"Not really. Haven't had much time for movies," I finally said. I looked past Thane to the warehouse behind him. I liked working here. I liked the men, I was slowly meeting their families, and I was beginning to become a part of the community of Loren Brae. After the Common Gin job, I might have enough money to rent a space of my own. Which would free me up to actually date Thane—if he still wanted me. But in the meantime, another woman could swoop in. And I wouldn't be able to blame her.

I huffed out a small sigh and took another bite, chewing in silence as I worked through my thoughts.

The other big thing was that I just wasn't sure I had what it took to make it on my own. Sure, my jewelry line had sustained me, barely, but sleeping on Stan's couch was not exactly screaming what a success I'd been. However, my accommodation here was paid for. If I was mindful of my money, I might just be able to go out on my own as a metalsmith—for both of my passions—jewelry and home. The very thought sent butterflies through my stomach, and I chewed more forcefully. Was I even ready? Could I trust myself to run my own business? Thane had said it himself—it took time. Was I patient enough to build something from scratch again?

"You have the most expressive face," Thane said, and I snapped back to reality, realizing he was sitting there, staring at me. "Honestly, I'm scared to ask what you're thinking about. The swing of emotions is wild."

"Best not to go there. Right, shall we get going?"

"If you tell me what had the angry look on your face."

"Ugh, does it really matter, Thane? Can't we just move on from this?"

"By this, do you mean us?" Thane's voice held a note I couldn't quite discern.

"No, just, *this* ..." I waved a hand in a circular motion above the table. "This conversation."

"We can. If I can understand why you looked so angry." Thane stood and picked up his empty pizza box, waiting for me to speak. I was beginning to find his patience annoying.

"I'm just mad. Mad because I've boxed myself in. Mad at some future woman for dating you. Mad at not knowing how to get what I want." I slapped a hand over my mouth and shook my head when Thane put the pizza box down and advanced on me.

"Kaia." Thane caged me in with his arms on either side of me and I dropped my hand from my mouth. My breath came in short puffs as I craned my neck to look up at him. I could see the string lights reflected in his eyes.

"Um, yes?"

"I'm not going anywhere." Heat flashed through my body at his words.

"Right."

"I'm not going to date anyone else."

"Uh-huh." A corner of his mouth quirked up.

"I'm here. And I *will* be right here, darling."

"Which is dumb. You shouldn't wait around for someone who can't make up their mind."

"Why don't you give us a chance then?"

"You know why." I almost stomped my foot. "And you agreed. You had the same issue."

"Maybe I don't anymore."

"Three days ago, you were begging me to leave town."

"For your own safety." Thane reached up and brushed a loose strand of hair from my face, tucking it behind my ear. I wanted to turn and press a kiss into his palm.

"What's changed then?"

"I have to trust that you know what's best for you. As much as it kills me not to be your protector at all times, I can't. Not in this case. It's not an easy pill to swallow, I'll admit."

I softened at his words. I'd seen him with Lauren and Audrey, hadn't I? Of course he was protective by nature. I couldn't blame him for being worried for my safety. Hell, *I* was worried for my safety too. The Kelpies were fiercely scary.

"So what are you saying?"

"I'm saying I want to give us a go. But you told me to back off and I'm going to respect that."

I suddenly couldn't quite remember the several good reasons I'd requested for him to back off, though I could swear that they'd just been circling in my brain. Instead I stared at him, lost, my brain quietly short-circuiting as my body screamed at me to let this man show me all the ways he knew how to heat a woman's desire.

"You look like a deer in headlights," Thane said, and eased backward. "There's no pressure, Kaia. With any of this. Why don't you take some time to think it through? In the meantime, we should probably get started on the molds." *God, his deep, rich voice was so utterly seductive.*

"Molds," I parroted, nodding, and Thane laughed.

"The molds! For Orla!"

"Uh, right, right." I stepped away, needing the space. "Just let me get my spell."

I was glad I'd written it down, as I could barely remember my own name after the conversation I'd just had with Thane.

"I'm not going anywhere. I'm not going to date anyone else. I'm here. And I will be right here, darling."

His words. His promise to me. That delectable accent. *Simply him.*

"Do you need help with, um, your spell?" Thane followed me inside and walked over to the furnace to check the iron. He was using his medium-sized furnace, as we'd be able to melt all the iron needed in one go.

"No, I don't think so. It's just words and intention." I shrugged, feeling awkward.

"No naked dancing under the moon or cutting my palm open to drain blood onto the iron?" Thane quipped and I grinned, despite my nervousness.

"As much as I'm sure you'd like the naked dancing, no, nothing like that. Just a simple protection spell."

"Then we're all sorted." Thane nodded at the three rows of flasks, ready for pouring. It would be a two-person job, lifting the crucible and helping to steady the pour, and we'd need to reheat three times as iron cooled quickly.

"Do you want to grab the crucible or me?" Thane asked, and appreciation for him bloomed. He didn't try to take over, he didn't tell me what to do, and he trusted me to make the right decision. Pouring molten metal, with a heavy crucible, sometimes took two people. One person with the shank to control the pour, and one with tongs to help steady if needed. I thought about it as I tied my leather apron and pulled on my protective gloves. I was a bit unsteady, with my emotions roiling around inside me, and I knew it would be best if he poured, while I did my spell.

"You go ahead."

"Works for me." We both pulled our face shields on, and then we switched over to business mode.

"Ready?" Thane asked.

"Yup."

"You just tell me when you need to do the spell."

"Oh, right. Hmmm. I think I need to say it quickly with each one, so I'll just say it as you pour. Does that work?"

"Fine by me, I'm focused."

"Let's go then." Once more I repeated the spell in my mind, and then we were moving. Steadily, Thane pulled the crucible from the furnace, and I was ready with the shank, making sure it was steady when he placed the crucible inside it. Once in, Thane lifted the shank, with the crucible, which basically looked like a large ceramic bucket, at the end and we moved quickly to the castings. There was no time to be wasting. Tilting the crucible, Thane began the first pour, and I reached for that glow of power inside me.

It popped up immediately, far faster than I'd ever felt it before, and much like the molten iron now pouring into the flask, my magick flowed through me. Reaching out, I touched the tongs lightly to the crucible to make a connection.

"By iron's strength and ember's glow, no evil may come across this threshold."

Thane sucked in a breath as light flashed around the flask, but there was no time to marvel at it. We were on to the next. In about six minutes or so, we'd finished the first round, and I stepped back as Thane returned the crucible to the furnace.

"I reckon two more batches and we'll be done."

Molten iron typically became too thick to use around the ten-minute mark, and Thane was stopping it before that time to decrease the time needed to reheat the metal still in the crucible. We'd have around fifteen minutes or so of down time before we went again.

I pushed my face shield back, and Thane did the same.

"Pretty incredible, Kaia." Thane gave me an admiring look.

"I've never seen the light before." Sweat dripped down my brow and I rubbed it with the back of my leather glove. "But it felt right. This is good, what we're doing here."

"Together," Thane said, his eyes on mine. And Murdoch's words came back to me.

He'll make your magick stronger. By being there, he amplifies it for you.

Did that mean I was meant to be with Thane?

It was warm in here, but honestly, I couldn't determine if that was from the work, the magick, or the tension that stretched between us. A sheen of sweat glistened on his face, and a drop ran down his neck to beneath his shirt. I swallowed.

Thane smirked. "If you keep looking at me like that, we'll never get this done."

My insides went liquid, and I pressed my thighs together, aching for his touch. Turning away, I crossed the room to my station and took a long pull from my water bottle. I just needed a moment. Because all I could think about was Thane asking me to give us a chance.

He accepted my magick.

Somewhere along the way he'd absorbed the idea of it and no longer was pushing me to leave town. He'd respected my boundaries and was *still* respecting my boundaries. And as much as I wanted him to push, because it took the decision out of my hands, in reality I needed to be an adult and be honest about what I wanted.

Which was Thane.

In all his sweaty manliness.

Taking another gulp, I pulled my face shield down again, shuttering my eyes, as the timer went off and Thane readied the crucible again. We worked steadily, and seamlessly together, getting through the rest of the molds in record time. And when we were done, and Thane had shut the furnace down, he turned to me.

"Kaia."

It could have been a question. It could have been a promise. But either way, I didn't care. Pulling my gloves off, I slapped them on the table and walked over to him. Grabbing the straps of his leather apron, I pulled him to me, my kiss a demand to be met.

Thane didn't hesitate.

In seconds he had me hoisted up around his waist and was moving. I tore my mouth away from his as cool night air hit my face, and he strode to the picnic table out back. Thane sank down on the bench, leaning back against the table, and shifted me so my knees straddled either side of him. The muscles in his shoulders bunched under my hands as I gripped him, and then we just stopped.

We stopped and held on.

Forehead to forehead.

Breath to breath.

I eased back enough to see his eyes, those stormy, gorgeous eyes of his, a shimmer of light reflecting there.

"Say it, Kaia." Thane's voice was a rasp, sending a shiver across my skin.

Where there had once been nerves, now all was quiet. The butterflies had left my stomach, and though my heart thundered in my chest, it wasn't because of anxiety or indecision. It was because I was done fighting my need for this man. Not that I'd fought it all that much, if I was being honest with myself, but I could examine that thought at another time.

"I want to give this a chance."

"*Us* a chance," Thane confirmed. He shifted, widening my thighs, and I gasped as I felt him hard against me.

"Yes, us." His teeth scraped my lower lip as he leaned in for a soft bite.

"Hold that thought." His thick arm corded around me as he leaned forward and looped the straps of his leather apron off, along with his shirt, and then to my surprise, lifted me easily to pull the apron out and toss it to the ground next to us. I marveled at the bunch and play of his muscles in his chest and reached for the necklace he wore with the chunky Celtic pendant. It had been one of the first things I'd noticed about him.

"Did you make this?" I asked, dropping it as he tugged the shirt over my head. Cool air hit my skin, and my nipples hardened when he took my bra off with one hand.

"It was one of my first pieces I made, just on my own, after I'd decided to give this business a go. It's not great, but it's mine."

"It's meaningful." I gasped as he leaned forward and took a nipple into his mouth, and I arched against him, loving the feel of his hot mouth against my skin.

"I like working on my own," Thane said, pulling his mouth away, leaving my breasts tingling and my body aching for more. He tapped a finger at my waist, and I realized he wanted me to get up so I could take my jeans off. I stood, as did he, and we both kicked off our clothes. It seemed we were always in a hurry to be with each other, and one of these days maybe we'd slow down and linger. When he dropped back down on the bench, he reached for me.

"Not yet," I said, and dropped to my knees in the grass between his legs. Leaning forward, I gave him a long, languid stroke, before kissing the tip.

"Bloody hell, Kaia." Thane's fingers threaded my hair, not pulling, but keeping me there.

"Tell me how you like it." I gave him a long lick as his hips bucked lightly.

"Whatever," Thane said, his voice cracking. "Do what you like, darling. I trust you."

I appreciated that, because I was determined to drive him crazy. Looking up, I held his eyes as I took him deep inside my mouth, gasping against the intrusion, and widening my throat to allow him to go deeper. Thane's eyes bulged, and I began to suck, holding eye contact, as I used the pressure of my mouth to suction his hard cock. I loved the feeling of this, having control over his pleasure, and liquid heat built between my legs. Moaning against him, I sucked harder, increasing my rhythm, until he gripped my head.

"Stop," Thane gasped, and I mewled in distress. I wanted the taste of him in my mouth. I wanted to know that I brought him as much pleasure as he did me.

I poked my lower lip out, and Thane hauled me up to straddle him again.

"Darling, don't give me that look. I'll do anything you want if you give me that look. But right now, I want us both to finish at the same time. And based on this"—Thane slipped a finger down my seam and found me wet and ready. Gently, he thumbed my clit and I rolled my hips against him, the shock of his touch sending waves of pleasure through me—"I'd say you want it too. Is that right, love, do you want this as badly as I do?"

"I do," I gasped, rocking my hips into his hand, needing the release that he could give me.

"Mmm, that's a good lass," Thane said. Pulling his hand away, he gripped my hips and guided me until just the tip of him hit my entrance. Wrapping one hand around my neck, he brought my head down so he could taste my lips once more. "Tell me it's just us, love. Tell me."

"It's just us," I murmured against his mouth, rolling

my hips and trying to take him deeper. Instead he brought his other hand down, his fingers digging into the soft flesh at my hips, and laughed against my mouth.

"Och, not yet, darling." He teased me, holding me so his tip dipped in and out of me, driving me crazy. Tears sprung to my eyes as desire heightened, and still he didn't let me down onto him. Instead, he increased his torture by leaning forward to suck my nipple, his teeth scraping the sensitive skin, his mouth hot and wet. I threw my head back, arching my breasts into his face, as he bounced me lightly in his lap, playing with the nerves that banded my tight entrance.

And just when I thought I was close, that I would come just from even the hint of him close to me, he reached up and pulled my mouth back to his. His tongue speared inside my mouth, then he slid deep inside of me, bottoming out, and I screamed into his mouth as my muscles clenched around him. Thane bucked upward, thrusting heavily into me as I broke apart around him, and he shouted as he came with me.

We stayed where we were, trying to catch our breath, the cool night air playing across our skin.

"Hell, Kaia, I wasn't thinking," Thane said, wrapping his arms around me, his voice rumbling into my neck. "Condom."

"I'm protected." I tried to catch my breath, but it felt like my heart was going to explode. My need for him was enormous, and it had been since the first day we'd met. I don't even know why I'd been trying to convince myself otherwise. Some things were just too monumental to ignore.

When I went to move, he pulled me closer, his arms wrapping me tightly against his chest, and I angled my head to his.

"You're beautiful," Thane said, brushing a soft kiss over my lips. "Cosmically, terrifyingly beautiful. You're magick and muscle and softness and attitude, and you've invaded my brain. You're all I can think about. I dream about you at night, I wake in the morning with your name on my lips, and I make up excuses to come out into the shop to see you. Since the moment we met, there hasn't been a day that I've stopped thinking about you, Kaia."

"I'm the same," I admitted. "I tried to push that handsome stranger in Edinburgh from my thoughts. But you're just here." I tapped a finger between my chest. "Since day one."

It was scary and freeing to admit that all at the same time.

"It's us, darling. It's us, now."

CHAPTER EIGHTEEN

KAIA

A few days later, the weekend arrived, and I had a day off to do with as I wished.

I'd passed the third challenge. It seemed charming the hearthwards had satisfied the Stone of Truth and now I was officially a member of the Order of Caledonia.

When I'd noticed the third band in the handle of my chisel, Murdoch and I had given ourselves a little dance party in the backyard. It was about as awkward a dance party as one could imagine, with Murdoch flapping his wings and hopping across the grass and me bouncing up and down as I sang myself a congratulatory song. Off-key. Nevertheless, it was still a celebration. I hadn't told the others, as I was meant to go up to the castle on Sunday. Lia had decided to start throwing family dinner nights every Sunday, and I guess that extended to me now.

When she'd called with the invitation, my heart had warmed. I was doing it. I was really doing it. I was employed, I had my own house, I had snagged a delectable Scotsman, and somehow, I'd stepped into my magick. If I thought too long or hard about all those pieces at once, I'd freeze up. It was like I'd grown so used to struggle that I couldn't quite fathom that all aspects of my life could simultaneously be running smoothly. It made me slightly nervous, if I was to be honest. Struggle was my comfort zone. I knew how to handle struggle. But contentment? Bliss, even? That was uncharted territory for me.

I'd called Marisa in a panic the night before and she'd listened with her straight face, calmly taking it all in, before leveling me with some sound advice.

"Don't fuck it up." Those were her words to be exact. When she saw the panic on my face, she'd sighed. *"You have to learn to allow yourself to enjoy the things you deserve."*

So now my new morning mantra, if I remembered to say it, was supposed to be something along the lines of how I deserved the success I'd worked so hard for. Because it *had* been work. All of it. Including learning how to navigate a workplace relationship.

Not that I'd been navigating it all that long.

I'd been worrying over how to tell the others at the workshop, but Thane had taken the matter into his own hands by walking out back while we were all having lunch at the picnic tables, brushing a kiss lightly on my forehead, and then asking if anyone needed something to drink. There'd been a small pause in the conversation, and then everything had returned to normal. A minute later, when Thane returned with his hands full of drinks, the lads had ruthlessly lit into him for never giving them kisses on *their* heads, and all was right in the world it seemed.

Though I'd been on high alert after that, nobody had said anything untoward or rude toward me, and I hoped that pattern would continue. Thane was a fair boss, I'd been told more than once, so I think the men were happy if *he* was happy.

But for now, I had the morning to myself, and Thane would stop by later with the molds, and we'd start distributing them around the village. Starting with my own wee cottage. I giggled to myself. I was starting to pick up a bit of Scots here and there. If only in my thoughts.

"All right, Murdoch, shall we see if your idea is right?"

Murdoch looked up from where he was cracking open some peanut shells that I'd given him.

I'm certain I am.

"I like that about you, Murdoch. Confidence is key." At least that's what Marisa insisted I keep telling myself. Scotland Kaia was a confident bitch. Or something along those lines. I'd figure out a mantra soon enough.

Kneeling down, I picked at the moss that had grown over one of the stepping stones that dotted the ground in my overgrown garden. I still hadn't gotten around to clearing the back garden, and the long grass and wildflowers had grown waist high and carried all the way back to the dense tree line.

I still looked out there every morning, wondering if I'd see that unicorn again.

Maybe a unicorn needed to be my new mascot. If I could believe in a unicorn, I could believe in anything. I snorted. Not that I'd be surprised by much at this point. Since coming to Loren Brae, I'd been all but run over with magickal beings. At this point, Mickey Mouse could walk out of the bushes and I'd simply wave at him and offer him a cup of tea.

It was more than a little surreal. I think that added to this disconcerting feeling that lingered with me. It felt a little like walking into a theme park and finding out that everything was real.

My phone buzzed in my pocket and I leaned back on my heels, checking a text from Willow.

> Do you have plans to go by the loch today?

> Not that I know of.

> I just had the tiniest snatch of vision. I'm not feeling great about it. Don't go down there today, okay? Just be careful.

> Understood. I'll steer clear.

> I wish I had seen more, but I got interrupted.

I SMILED. I could imagine just who had interrupted her.

> All good. I'm working in the garden today.

> K, have fun!

POCKETING MY PHONE, I turned back to the stepping stone. They were rugged, worn with age, and moss clambered over the gray stone. They also were heavily embedded into the dirt, so I didn't want to have to pry each one out. I was hoping there would be some indication on the actual stone so I knew which one to dig up.

Maureen's words drifted back to me.

"Step by step, you walk on me, beneath one tread, the treasure shall be."

It made sense, there would be something under a stepping stone, although I had first thought perhaps a floorboard. Murdoch had insisted we start with the stones, so here I was, scraping moss away from ancient stones, looking for a treasure, while my talking bird ate peanuts next to me.

As Saturdays went, it wasn't a bad one.

Humming, I used my chisel to scrape some moss away. It had become my go-to tool for anything these days, since I carried it with me at all times. Thane had even joked that he needed to disarm me before he took me to bed. The thought of him made me smile. He was gruff, funny, tender, and fiercely protective. A man of his word, and like he'd once explained to me, dedicated to keep the fires running hot both at work and at home. I would be hard-pressed to be in a bad mood after the number of times we'd made love over the last few days.

I added a nap to the day's itinerary.

Thane's here.

Murdoch flapped his wings and took to the sky, and I stood up as I heard a car door slam. I rounded the corner of the house and was surprised to find Murdoch sitting on Thane's shoulder.

"Now, listen, lad. I wasn't sure what to get, so it's

apples for you." Thane handed him an apple slice and Murdoch took it and flew away. Affection filled me. I so appreciated the constant reminders that Thane was indeed a good man.

"Are you trying to win my bird over with snacks?"

"Damn right. If you play your cards right, I'll do the same with you." Thane sauntered forward and I put the back of my hand to my head, pretending I was going to faint.

"You had me at snacks." I tilted my head up for a kiss as Thane wrapped his arms around my waist. Would I ever tire of hugging him? It felt like being engulfed by a bear, his masculine presence surrounding me, and I leaned into him, inhaling his soapy scent.

"What are you doing in the garden?" Thane leaned back and gave me a soft kiss that had my heart fluttering.

"*I'm* on a treasure hunt," I said, stepping back and grabbing his hand to tug him along with me.

"I feel like this is something Audrey would say to me."

"The girl does love her sparkles, so I can see that." I stopped in front of the row of stepping stones. All told there were around thirty of them, winding back into the yard's dense overgrowth, and I definitely wasn't keen on digging them all out. "I'm looking for something to give me some sign or indication that I need to dig up one stone." I gave him a quick rundown of what had happened with Maureen in the bookshop and the secret she'd whispered to me on her way out of the shop.

"Just one?" Thane studied the stones, a considering look on his face.

"I'd rather not dig them all up. They're quite pretty, if not a bit slippery with all the moss."

Thane glanced back at the cottage. "Do you have a garden hose? We could power-wash these quickly."

"I have no idea. But I just want to take my time with this." I almost rolled my eyes. Leave it to a man to try to immediately bring in a noisy tool. Of course it was likely much more efficient, but I wasn't looking for efficiency right now. I was looking for a quiet, easy morning with soft breezes and digging in the dirt. A power washer would just turn this into a chore.

"Got it. Slow and steady it is." Thane crouched and pulled the rest of the apple slices from his bag, laying them neatly next to the house for Murdoch, and left the bag next to it. Wiping his hands, he stood and pointed at the stone in front of the one I was working on. "Can I work on this one next?"

"Why not pick one in the middle and we'll work toward each other? Otherwise we may be bumping into each other."

"Should I start at the other end?" I looked to where the stones disappeared into the overgrowth and shook my head.

"No. Then you'll be too far away."

A grin slipped over Thane's face, shifting those sharp edges of his jaw, and he gripped my chin with one hand and gave me a searing kiss that had me rocking back on my heels before dropping my face and wandering to a stone in the middle of the path. My breath caught as I watched him crouch and gently begin to scrape at the moss with his bare hands.

I deserve this. I had to swallow against the lump that had risen in my throat, watching Thane not question or push me on what I was doing, instead just easily joining in to help. Even though my parents and Marisa had been endless champions in my life, it seemed that I'd been the one who'd been letting myself down all along. The question was, could I accept it? Would I actually be able to believe that I deserved this chance at happiness?

For the next half hour, we scraped moss and cleaned the stones, and chattered away about nothing and everything. This was nice. Being together, working on a small project, enjoying a rare morning of no rain.

"I think I found something." My breath caught and I jumped up and bounded over to where Thane crouched by a stepping stone about halfway back into the yard. I crouched next to Thane and he pointed to the worn carving in the stone.

"A trickle," I breathed, excitement filling me. "You found it!" I high-fived Thane and he laughed, clearly pleased to help me.

"Do you have a shovel?" Thane asked, pulling me to standing. Turning, I craned my neck. I hadn't seen any laying around. Thane saw me looking around and shook his head. "I'm guessing you don't. Hold on, then."

Thane trotted away and returned quickly brandishing a crowbar in one hand. In moments he had the stone pried up and flipped over. It was a thicker stone than I had anticipated and it left a hole in the dirt behind.

"Oh look!" I slapped my hands against my cheeks when I saw a small metal box in the dirt. It was copper, and well corroded, but I could make out the triskele sign on the box. Using my chisel, I dug it out of the dirt and presented it to Thane.

"No, no." Thane waved it away. "This is your treasure."

"But you found it," I pointed out.

"You open it. I'll look on." Coming behind me, he rested his chin on my shoulder.

Brushing the residual dirt from the box, I opened it carefully to reveal a small scroll of paper and an antique key.

"'I stand where sun and shadows weave, where autumn gold and ivy cleave. My walls are old, my hearth still bright, find me hidden from the light,'" I read out loud.

"Hmmm," Thane said, his voice rumbling at my ear. "This looks like a house key, not a key to a safe or something like that."

"Where autumn gold and ivy cleave," I murmured, looking back toward the forest line. "Would that mean forest?"

"It just might." Thane followed my gaze. "Makes sense, doesn't it? Shall we have a wee wander?"

"I believe we shall." Thane took my hand and a thrill of contentment shot through me. We wandered back on the stones until they stopped at where the line of trees met the overgrown yard.

"Looks like there's still a natural formed path here." Thane gestured to where large trees lined both sides of a natural walkway. Looking up, I saw the branches mingling together, a touch golden at the edges.

"I feel like Hansel and Gretel or something." I laughed, following Thane into the cool shadows of the forest. I couldn't believe that I hadn't been back here yet, but I'd been so busy with getting the house livable and work that I hadn't had much time to explore. After only a short walk, Thane drew up.

"I think we have your treasure."

My mouth dropped open when I peered around him. Maybe I was really in Hansel and Gretel, because in front of me was the cutest stone cottage that I'd ever seen, with a massive fireplace on the side, windows with the panes still intact, and a simple mahogany brown wood door.

"No way. Is this mine?" I asked, moving around Thane.

"Let's see if the key fits, shall we?"

"Should I knock first?" I asked, pausing before I brought the key to the lock. What if there was someone living in it?

"Can't hurt." Thane reached around me and rapped sharply on the door, the noise loud against the wind that shifted through the trees.

When nobody responded, I tried the key.

It turned.

"Oh my God," I gasped, turning around to look at Thane. "No way! What is this place?"

"Oh, I have an idea. But let's see."

"Did you have something to do with this?" How could he know what it is?

"No." Thane chuckled behind me as I eased the door open. "But I know the look of these buildings."

The hinges on the door stuck, and they complained loudly as I eased it open, but open it did. I leaned forward slightly, the cobwebs dripping from the ceiling in front of the door making me hesitant to pop my head all the way through.

"Here, let me." Thane brushed past me and ducked inside, waving his arms to clear the cobwebs away. He was a better person than me. Trying not to think too deeply about creepy crawlies, I followed him in.

"No way," I breathed, when my eyes adjusted to the dim light filtering through the dusty windows.

It was a small blacksmith shop.

The fireplace was wide, with dusty old blacksmith tools lined up neatly next to it, and there were two long tables on either side of the room, one with an anvil draped in cobwebs. Shelves lined the back wall that held various instruments, and a molded leather apron was hung on a peg by the wall.

I could just see it. Working here on a bright spring day, with the doors and windows thrown open to catch the breeze. Although, realistically, it would be rainy days more than sunny, it was still my own fantasy and I got to decide the weather. Either way, this was the perfect wee forge.

Just for me.

I realized it all at once too, as Thane turned to look at me. If I modernized this space, I would have an actual workspace to complete my projects. Maybe just my jewelry line and smaller pieces to start with in here, but I could do it. I could be fully independent of him if I needed to be.

If things ever went wrong between us.

Independence was a gift in so many different ways.

Murdoch landed at the door, flapping his wings, all but screaming, and I jumped about a foot in the air. Thane caught my arm and steadied me.

"Murdoch!" I laughed, slapping a hand to my chest. "You scared me."

Audrey's at the loch. You must go. Now.

"No! It's Audrey, she's at the loch." I was already running, pulling Thane with me when a Kelpie's shriek shook the sky.

CHAPTER NINETEEN

Kaia

"Go!" I shouted to Thane as he looked over his shoulder.

It was lucky my cottage was only just on the outskirts of town, but even at a dead run, I was scared we'd be too late. Thane left me in the dust, and I didn't blame him. If he could reach Audrey first, then he needed to *run*. I followed as quickly as I could, but I was built more for endurance than speed. By the time I reached the shores of Loch Mirren, my chest was heaving, and panic was clawing its way through me as two massive Kelpies raced toward where Thane was skidding to a stop by Audrey.

The skies opened up, rain pummeling down, and a lightning bolt speared the loch, thunder shattering all around us, as both Kelpies reared their heads back and shrieked.

Audrey cowered in the rocks at the beach, frozen in terror, as the Kelpies barreled across the frothing waters of Loch Mirren. Thane reached Audrey, scooping her into his arms; and I grabbed my chisel, grateful I hadn't left it on the ground by the stepping stones.

Brandishing the chisel in the air, I screamed, "Pick on someone your own size!"

As one, the Kelpies turned, their eyes glowing, and I gulped.

First of all, I was *not* the same size as a Kelpie, so I had no idea where that had come from. And second of all, just what had my plan been exactly? To throw a ten-inch chisel into a wall of enchanted water beasts?

With a new target in mind, the beasts galloped toward me, and to my astonishment, the first one left the loch, legs forming as he raced up the pavement directly toward me, a fully formed horse.

How had this happened? I'd done some internet research on the history of Kelpies, but so far I hadn't heard of an instance, at least in Loren Brae, where they'd actually left the loch before.

They were smaller on land. This was the last thought I had before the Kelpie reared and picked me up in its mouth, shaking me until my bones rattled.

My chisel fell from my hand as the massive Kelpie whipped its head around.

My heart fell.

My only weapon clattered to the ground beneath us.

So much for the idea that I'd be fearless in the face of a threat.

I was afraid, *very* afraid, and pain was like a hot knife through my leg.

Now, I *knew* these beasts were made of water. But the teeth currently sinking into my thighs certainly didn't feel like water. No, this felt very real, and I gritted my teeth against the pain. My body shook, adrenaline coursing through me, as the world whirled around me. I was hanging upside down from the Kelpie's mouth, and it reared again, the buildings of Loren Brae swirling upside down across my vision.

Thane shouted. He looked much smaller from up here, Audrey wrapped in his arms.

"Get Audrey out of here," I screamed. He needed to focus on her, not me.

I'd be fine.

Right?

A flash of black wings flew by my eyes, and the Kelpie reared, Murdoch pecking at his eyes.

"Murdoch," I gasped out, tears rolling down my cheeks from the pain. "Be careful."

The bridle, Kaia. The bridle.

With an awkward squawk, Murdoch spiraled from the sky as the Kelpie swung his head and knocked him away.

"No!" I roared, despair filling me.

The Kelpie shook me again, its shriek vibrating my entire body, its hot breath smelling of musty seaweed. In a panic, I flailed out with my arms.

My hand brushed something solid.

Leather.

I'd clamped my eyes shut when the Kelpie had shaken me again, the speed at which he was throwing me around making me dizzy, but I forced my eyes open to see what I'd touched.

The Kelpie wore a bridle.

My thoughts jumbled as the Kelpie whirled, headed back toward the loch, and more shouts sounded below us. I remembered something about a bridle, but between the excruciating pain and fear for my life, I couldn't quite land on it. Even so, I reached up and grabbed both hands around the bridle that wrapped its mouth, just to give me something to hold on to so I wasn't hanging upside down.

The Kelpie slammed to a stop so fast that I flung forward and hit my face against his head. Hot seaweed breath fanned over me, and I lost my grip. The Kelpie started moving again.

Of course! The bridle.

Once more, I grabbed it, and the Kelpie stopped in its tracks.

There was something in mythology about controlling a Kelpie if you took his bridle. This was what Murdoch had been trying to tell me. Reaching up, I tugged, and surprisingly, it came loose in my hands.

Two things happened at once.

The Kelpie shattered into a thousand drops of water, and I fell from the sky, bridle in both my hands. I had no time to cushion myself, and the only thing that saved me was that I turned mid-air and sucked in a breath.

I hit the waters of Loch Mirren fast.

But thankfully, not flat on my back.

My feet pierced the surface and then I was under, the icy water a shock against my skin, agony knifing my side where the Kelpie had bitten me. Holding my breath, I kicked toward the surface, wrapping the bridle around my arms.

It wouldn't be enough, though. I'd barely broken the surface of the loch and gulped in another breath before the other Kelpie was upon me. Water crashed over me, dragging me down, and I sunk into the iciness, trying to stop the panic that clawed at my throat.

I forced myself to hold my breath, to not gulp in water like I needed to do, when something brushed my feet. Slivering my eyes open, shock hit me.

Clyde, the ghost coo from the castle, rose between my legs and shot toward the surface. Grabbing one of his horns, I held on as he rocketed into the air and galloped toward shore.

I had no idea why I could feel him as though he was real.

Frankly, I didn't care.

A white-hot burn flared at my side, making it even more difficult to breathe, and we were just reaching the shore when the Kelpie gained on us. I screamed as he ducked his head low, his teeth near my shoulder.

Ripping the bridle from my arm, the Kelpie turned and fled just as Clyde flung me into Thane's arms, who was waist deep in the water and running toward me. I slammed into him, but he caught and held, his strong arms pinning me to his chest as he dragged me from the loch.

"Go, go, go," I choked out, panic having me scramble to turn and look at our fate.

But the Kelpie was far away, retreating to the island.

"He took his friend's bridle back," Thane bit out and I collapsed against him, closing my eyes. I needed a second. I needed to assess how hurt I was. To catch my breath. To try and calm myself down so I didn't burst into tears and lose my shit.

Because I really wanted to.

Audrey's voice cut through the voices that greeted me.

"Is Kaia okay?"

I needed to get myself together or I'd forever scar this sweet child. Taking in a few shaky breaths, I opened my eyes to see a crowd of people around me. Audrey was in Ramsay's arms, and Agnes, Sophie, and Willow were all crowded around us.

"Thane." My voice rasped, and I reached up to cup his chin, turning his eyes down toward me. "Let me down."

"I will not."

"Please. I don't want to scare Audrey more than she already is." A muscle ticked in his jaw, but he complied, holding me close for a moment. Burying his face in my neck, he took one deep inhale followed by another.

"Kaia. I thought I'd lost you."

"I'm okay, I'm here." I couldn't process the emotions that swirled inside me. I felt drugged, like I was moving through molasses, and I couldn't quite respond in a normal manner. Whatever normal would be after being tossed about by a Kelpie. *How the hell did that happen? How had he held me? Bit me? How?*

"Kaia, are you hurt?" The women crowded around me, and I stepped back from Thane. I wobbled a bit, but I could stand on my own. I took another tentative step forward to where Audrey sobbed in Ramsay's arms.

"I'll be okay." I wasn't entirely sure of that, yet, but if I kept repeating it maybe it would be enough. Thane walked over and scooped Audrey from Ramsay's arms, and the space was immediately filled by Willow whose usually sunshiny face looked drawn and worried.

"Audrey, honey, why were you down here?" I asked, gently, because I knew Thane had warned her and Lauren away from spending time on the shores of the loch just now. This was what he had feared, and next time we might not be fast enough to save someone.

"Because you told me I was magick. I thought I was strong."

Audrey's words slammed into me, far more painful than a Kelpie, and I winced as reality crashed over my head.

What had I been thinking telling a small child she had magick now?

Even if she had a small amount of magick in her pendant, it certainly wasn't enough to withstand a Kelpie. I'd been careless and she'd almost died.

How foolish. New to magick, new to this world, and an idiot for thinking I could just tra-la-la my way into an ancient Order of magick and everything would go fine.

I couldn't speak.

Turning, I shook my head at Agnes, tears welling, and Sophie jumped into action.

"Right, Thane, you take Audrey home. We'll see to Kaia."

"But—"

"Just go," Ramsay ordered, his tone brooking no disagreement.

I couldn't look at them as I limped down the shoreline, my eyes scanning the rocks, my heart trembling inside me. Agnes walked beside me, her arm looped through mine.

"We need to get you home. To look at your injuries."

"I need to look for Murdoch. My raven. He was hit during the attack." I couldn't bring myself to say it, but I was certain he was gone. I'd seen him spiral from the sky myself.

"Got it." Agnes whistled over her shoulder. "Find the raven. Now."

I'm here.

Tears did spill over then, when I heard Murdoch's shaky voice in my head.

"He's alive," I gasped. We found him shortly thereafter, hunkered in the wet rocks on the shoreline. "Can I pick you up?"

Aye, lass.

"What do I do? Can I take him to the vet?"

"We're all going to the castle. Lia's on it. Bring Murdoch," Sophie spoke into the phone as Ramsay helped lift me into his truck.

Cradling Murdoch close, I bent over and kissed his damp head.

"You're a hero, buddy. A real hero."

Glad you're safe, my friend.

"You and me both."

With that, I stared dully out the window, pain throbbing in my side, the waters of the loch now as smooth as glass as we drove away.

CHAPTER TWENTY

Kaia

"How bad is it?" Willow asked me. She'd taken a seat next to me. I cradled Murdoch who periodically made disgruntled noises as he burrowed into my arms. I could only imagine how much pain he must be in, and if it echoed mine, it was likely severe.

"I've had better days." I pressed a kiss to Murdoch's head. "I'm more worried about him."

My wing is broken.

I closed my eyes, but Willow reached out and gripped my hand.

"He thinks it's his wing?"

I'd forgotten she could communicate with animals. I had thought it was just restricted to Calvin, but it appeared her strengths went deeper. I just nodded, unable to speak. I knew next to nothing about birds, but I had to imagine that was akin to a death sentence for one.

"We'll get this sorted. I promise. Shona's on the way. Lia's already brewing something up. Between the two of them, we'll get it figured out." Willow clucked her lips. "I wish I would have looked more deeply into the vision, Kaia. I would have told you if I had any clue that Audrey was in danger."

"I know." I swiveled my head to look at her as we pulled to a stop in front of the castle. "It's not your fault."

"It's nobody's fault. But it feels pretty shitty either way."

Ramsay opened the back door and to my surprise, he just reached in and lifted me before I could say a word of protest. Willow caught my look, and she laughed.

"He does that."

"So does Thane," I admitted, and despite my pain, I smiled when Willow hooted with laughter.

"I don't doubt it."

The dogs met us at the open front door, where Hilda stood, wringing her hands.

"Straight back to the ground floor apartment. Hush up, Sir Buster. It's not about you right now." Sir Buster immediately stopped barking, and if a dog could look affronted, he did. Ramsay whisked me through a stone hallway, with lamps that were fashioned to look like old-timey torches, and portraits of ancestors lining the walls. He went into the door that Hilda held open, past a sitting room, and gently laid me against a stack of pillows on a double-sized bed.

Stepping back, he gave me a stern nod.

"You're stronger than you may think. Don't let this make you doubt yourself."

It was the most words I'd ever heard him speak, even though I'd only met him a smattering of times so far. He turned and left the room, brushing a hand down Willow's back as he did so. I blinked after him, and then up at her. She shrugged one shoulder.

"He's succinct." Willow stopped at the door. "Be back in a sec."

"Mmm." My brain still felt sludgy, and my feelings were caught in a knotted mess in my core.

"Here now. Let's get the wee lad sorted, shall we?" Hilda bustled in with a low-sided basket with what looked to be a cat bed in it. She placed it on the bed next to me. "Do you think you could put him in here? Just so we can have a look?"

"Can I move you?" I asked Murdoch, now that I knew he was really hurt.

Aye, lass.

As gently as I could, I lifted him but then winced when pain lanced up my side. Hilda quickly intercepted, cradling Murdoch, giving him a soft landing on the bed. He settled down, one wing splayed out, and closed his eyes.

"Murdoch, you're okay, right? You're just closing your eyes to rest?" Worry made my stomach turn.

Aye. It hurts, but I'm just resting.

"The girls will be here soon. I've told them we have two patients today." Hilda moved to my side. "I'd like to get you out of these clothes. They're wet and you'll catch a cold. We can wrap you up in a blanket until I sort out clothes for you."

It was such a motherly thing to be concerned about that I felt myself softening to her. I rolled, allowing her to help me stand, and she efficiently helped me undress just as Willow bustled back in with a fluffy pink robe and some comfy clothes.

"Figured you'd need something cozy. Here, let's just do the robe for now because I can already see the bruises." Willow helped me with the robe, and I took a moment to glance down at my body.

"Oh shit." I knew I was in pain, but this was bad. Bruises were already blooming all along my legs and my side. One even bubbled up, the size of my fist, almost blister-like, and I itched to pop it.

"It's not great. But let's just see what the girls can do. Or should we take her to the hospital?" Willow whirled on Hilda. "Was it stupid to bring her here? What if she has internal bleeding?"

"I think I'm okay." *I had no idea if I was okay.* But I wanted to treat Murdoch first. Just then, Lia and Shona walked in, followed by Sophie and Agnes both carrying two cardboard boxes.

"Right, let's get down to business. Bird or human first?" Lia looked up from where she paged through her leather book, her apron still on and her hair tied back in a bandanna.

"Bird." Something shifted in the corner, catching my gaze, and I froze as a pair of eyes blinked out at me from a corner.

"Something's in here," I hissed.

It's just the broonie. Murdoch gave me a look.

"Oh!" Lia looked behind her. "That's Brice. He's my familiar."

"The broonie?" I asked, and a wee man crept forward with huge eyes, a face only a mother could love, and a red beanie pulled low over his brow. He nodded at me and chattered something I couldn't understand.

"He wants to help with Murdoch. Brice has a soft spot for animals. We feed our crows out back all the time."

"Here, I found it." Lia turned to Shona while Brice crawled onto the bed and softly patted Murdoch's head. I couldn't stop looking at him. How did everyone just get used to all of this magick?

A soft moo caught my attention, and we all turned to see Clyde poke his head through a wall.

"*Moo?*" It was gentle, just a question, and not remotely attempting to scare me.

"You did good, Clyde."

"What did Clyde do?" Hilda asked from the doorframe. The room was getting crowded and Agnes sidled closer to me and squeezed my shoulder.

"He showed up. When I was sinking in the loch."

"Is that what happened?" Willow turned and beamed at Clyde. "You silly coo. I could kiss you! We thought a Kelpie just chucked you out of the water."

"Nope, it was Clyde."

"Good boy." Everyone applauded Clyde and he bowed his head a few times. If a coo could look pleased and embarrassed at the same time, he certainly did. Lia was reading out ingredients to Shona who was cutting and mixing them in a bowl from the boxes they had brought with them.

"Right, everyone. I think we've got it for the bird. Broken wing, right?" Lia looked to me and then back to Murdoch, her words coming out rapid-fire. I almost wanted to yell, "Yes, chef!" back to her, but instead just nodded.

"He says just the wing."

"By Brigid's flame and sky so wide, let broken wing in health abide. Swift as wind and strong as sea, so mote it heal, so mote it be." Lia chanted over the poultice that Shona had made, and together they put it on a small scrap of gauze and gently laid it over Murdoch's wing. Then Brice sidled forward and put his hands over the gauze.

A soft light glowed beneath his palms and then he was gone.

Just gone.

I blinked at the space where Brice had once been, my mouth dropping open.

"He does that," Lia explained.

"Murdoch, how are you feeling?" I asked, leaning forward to look at him.

That did the trick.

Murdoch stood, flapping his wings wide, and the room cheered.

"That's … that's just incredible," I breathed, looking between Lia and Shona. "Is that something you knew how to do?"

"Nope. First time for a broken bone." Lia did a little shimmy and then high-fived Shona. "We're getting better."

"What was in the poultice?" Hilda asked. She'd gone out into the sitting room and come back with a cup of tea to put on the table next to me.

"Dandelion root, sage, elderflower, and chamomile." A proud smile flitted across Shona's face. "All grown by me."

"Your turn." Lia gave me a no-nonsense look. "What are we dealing with here?"

"I think just massive bruises." I eased myself to a horizontal position on the bed and opened my robe up. All of the women gathered around the bed and leaned over to look.

"That's gnarly," Lia said, biting her lip.

"Please tell me you're talking about my bruises," I said. It wasn't like I was exceptionally comfortable with being naked in front of women I hadn't known that long.

"Definitely the bruises." Willow laughed. "Your body's banging."

"Thanks."

"Speaking of banging, I've heard you've been

enjoying Thane?" Hilda asked as she pressed her fingers into my ribs. Everyone hooted out a laugh.

"Hilda, ya gossip." Sophie poked her.

"I'm not dead you know. You young ones aren't the only ones doing all the banging." At that, we all burst into laughter again, and I crossed my hands over myself as pain ratcheted up my side.

"I'm not entirely sure if she has any bruised ribs, but she didn't react too much when I poked there," Hilda mentioned.

"Is poking a broken rib smart?" Sophie glared at Hilda. Hilda just shrugged.

"It's a quick way to find out what we're dealing with."

"Right, I got it." Lia held her finger to a page in the book, turned to Shona, and they got to work mixing. Before long, everyone was slathering something on my body and I could only hold still and blink up at the ceiling.

"This feels like a very painful and demented spa experience," I lamented.

"I am Sigrid." Willow affected a Swedish accent. "The pain, it is good for the muscles."

"Is that so?" I winced as they finished, and Lia leaned over.

"Ready for a spell?" I nodded. Honestly, I was splayed out like a piece of meat, covered in some kind of sauce, and I had just been tossed around the loch by water beasts. At this point, what did a spell among friends matter?

"Kelpie's grip, release your hold, let no curse nor pain take hold. By Rowan's shield and moon's embrace, leave no mark, leave no trace."

Nothing happened at first.

But then, I felt it. Gentle warmth seeped into my skin, like water pouring into dry cracks of sand on the floor in the desert, and with it I could feel healing tendrils unfurl in me. The power seemed to surround the pain, curling it in, and then pulling it out of me like a weed being plucked from the dirt. It was a distinctly odd feeling, not necessarily horribly painful or anything, but it did make me want to reach down and scratch my body. Digging my fingers into my palms, I willed myself to stay still.

"Do you feel anything, Kaia?" Shona whispered.

"Yeah, it's like … pulling it from me or something."

"That's good." Shona turned to Lia, worry on her face. "That's good, right?"

"I think so?" Lia gave Shona a worried look, and despite the severity of the situation, it was also absurd enough to make me laugh. Here I was, surrounded by women I hadn't known two months ago, stripped naked and covered in a magickal poultice, while they all waited in uncertainty for a spell they'd just discovered to take effect.

"Maybe best to just move around a bit? Wash it off?" I moved my limbs and from what I could tell, the pain had lessened.

"Right. How's this? Sit with this for a few minutes longer and give us a call when you're ready to be upright and get into the shower. We can clear out because you don't need us all peering at you like you're a specimen on the lab table," Hilda announced, clapping her hands together. "Kaia, what can I get for Murdoch?"

"Blueberries, nuts, and water."

I lay in bed for a while, just staring at the ceiling, trying to process everything that had just happened. I was grateful for the time alone, to pull my thoughts together, and try to understand my emotions after the attack. Because the scariest thing was?

All I wanted to do was turn tail and run.

I suppose that was a normal reaction after almost being killed by a Kelpie. But it was more than that. *I was in over my head.* What I'd thought was a harmless magickal gift for a small girl ended up leading her into the jaws of the actual beast. I was sleeping with the man who held my business lease in his hands, I didn't really know what I was doing with all this magick, and the bird who had adopted me had almost died.

Crisis of confidence, serving of one. *How I wish I could get one of my mom's warm hugs right now. Or be told I'm going to be okay by my ever-comforting dad.*

Easing myself from the bed, I tiptoed into the bathroom and found towels laid out. I didn't feel like calling for help with the shower, and I certainly didn't want to be laid out all naked and exposed anymore. I was beyond exposed.

Exposed as a fake.

I'd been so certain that I was killing this "new life" thing and instead I'd almost gotten killed. And had hurt those around me. *Had Thane been right all along? Should I leave? Go back to the States?* Even if Loren Brae had begun to feel like my place ... it might just be time for me to go home.

Stepping into the shower, I buried my head under the hot stream of water, and let the steam cloud around me, but no matter how long I stood there, it didn't seem to shake the chill from my bones. Audrey could have died because of me. Thane never would have forgiven me, hell, *I* would never have forgiven myself. Everything swirled around inside me, like the water sluicing the poultice off me, and I watched as it spiraled down the drain.

That's how I felt. Like brown muddy water spiraling down a drain. Moving to an entirely new country was already disconcerting enough on its own. I'd been working hard at finding my groove, making a name for myself, but in doing so I'd ignored all the feelings that came with embracing being uncomfortable.

I was out of my element.

Broonies, gnomes, ghost coos, new boyfriends, new jobs, new friends. It all just slammed into me, and I had to take several deep breaths to steady myself before I got out of the shower and toweled off. Looking down, I examined the skin where the Kelpie had bitten me. His teeth hadn't broken skin, and the poultice had done wonders for the bruising. I wasn't good as new, and I could still feel pain, but I was much better. It was as though they'd sped up the healing by a few days, and now my bruises were just that gross greenish gold color they became when they were starting to fade.

Pulling on the sweats that Willow had brought me, I bundled my hair in a towel and limped back into the room. What I wanted right now was to crawl under that big duvet, cuddle Murdoch close, and have myself a big old cry. Hilda had already told me I could stay as long as I needed, and I planned to do just that, if even only for the night.

I drew up short when I saw Thane sitting at the end of the bed.

"Kaia." His face looked ravaged, his eyes stormy, and I wanted to run to him. To burrow into his arms and have him tell me that everything was going to be fine. But I'd trusted someone to do that for me once before, and it had all fallen apart. I was the one who needed to tighten my bootstraps and tell myself everything was going to work out.

Pulling the blanket back, I slid beneath it and wrapped a pillow in my arms over my chest. Thane tilted his head, looking me up and down, something flashing in his eyes as he understood the barrier I was creating.

"Are you hurt?"

"They've patched me up. I'll be just fine."

Thane nodded, shifting at the foot of the bed to reach out to give Murdoch a light scratch at the back of his head.

"And my wee pal?"

"He's on the mend too. They just …" I shook my

head. "Sewed his bone right up. With magick. It's incredible."

"It is." Thane ran his hand through his hair, and it stood on end. He looked shell-shocked, and I imagined I looked much the same.

"Audrey?"

"She's having a tough time of it, but she'll be all right. She's not physically hurt."

But the emotional damage was done.

He didn't have to say that out loud, I knew it.

"I'm so sorry, Thane. I feel horrible. I had no idea that telling her she had magick now would result in this. I have … there are no words."

"Och, Kaia, it's not your fault, you ken? She's seven. Children make mistakes." Fire blazed behind Thane's eyes, and he gestured to the pillow I was holding. "Is that what this is about?"

"That. Maybe. I don't know." I shifted, trying to figure out how to articulate my thoughts.

"Are you breaking up with me?"

"You never asked me to be your girlfriend." I gave him a sad smile.

"Och, cut the crap, Kaia. I asked you to give us a chance. What do you think I meant?"

"I know what you meant," I said. "I was just being technical."

"You still didn't answer my question."

"I don't know what I'm doing," I answered him as honestly as I could. I didn't want to play games, and I wasn't being coy, I just didn't know how I felt because I was still stuck in that weird sludgy numbness that gripped me after the attack. I imagined it was how someone would feel sinking into a pit of quicksand. "I thought I did. I thought I could finally have it all. Like a real grown-up adult with their shit together. A new country. New career. New friends. New boyfriend. New little workshop. And magick. This incredible untenable thing that lives inside me now. And now I'm not so sure. Maybe I was just fooling myself into thinking I could manage this all. Because here I am, dating a man that holds my career in his hands, relying on friends to patch me up, and I almost killed your niece."

"Bloody hell." Thane leaned forward on the bed. "She's a child. She does dumb shite. They all do. That's what kids are." *How is he being so forgiving? So understanding?* I was sure Lauren wouldn't feel so accommodating. *Damn it.*

"But what am I doing, Thane? I couldn't help you out there. I dropped my weapon. My magick was useless and I almost got myself killed. I'm supposed to be an asset to this town and instead I am a liability."

"You're worried about protecting me?" Thane stood at that, his voice rising. He jabbed a finger in his chest. "How do you think I felt? There was nothing *I* could do. Nothing. I stood there, holding Audrey, and watched you almost die. And there was not a damn thing I could do about it. And I'm getting sick of not being able to protect the women I love in my life."

I stilled at that. *Love.*

A new emotion to add to that sticky mess inside me that choked me and made it difficult to breathe.

"But I—"

"You what?" Thane whirled on me. "It's your job to do it all? On your own? Because you joined an Order, didn't you? That automatically implies you understand that you have to rely on others. Or does that not apply to you? You're allowed to help and give but you can't ask for what you need? Or want?"

"Wait ... what? I don't ... I'm not ..." I was so unsure of my steps.

"Tell me what you want, Kaia. Just tell me. Say it to me straight."

"I want to know that I can handle things on my own. That I won't be ... screwing up magick and doing things that hurt others. That I can support myself on my own merits." I rushed it all out in one breath.

"And how does me loving you stop you from doing any of that?"

I froze at his words. I had no answer. But I also couldn't tell him what he wanted to hear. I was numb, locked in my head and my emotions, and I just shook my head at him, helpless, as tears filled my eyes.

"What do you need from me, Kaia?" Thane dropped to his knees by my bed and leaned in so his face was close. "I'll always give you what you need, but I can't make the decision for you."

"I don't know. Maybe I'm just scared. Maybe it's all too much at once. Maybe I just need to believe." I wished I could give him a straight answer. He deserved that. It was just that I didn't have one. Clarity didn't always arrive on demand.

"Do you want me to stay? Here with you?"

"No." I winced at the hurt that flashed in Thane's eyes. "I'm sorry. I just think I need some time. I'm really overwhelmed and scared and tired and in pain."

At that, Thane stood and called over his shoulder. "Hilda, Kaia's still in pain."

"Oh you don't have to ..."

"Aye, lass. I do. If you don't want me here, I need to know someone else is looking after you. Take care of yourself, Kaia."

I'm sorry. I wish I knew what I wanted.

I let him leave, but somehow, his goodbye kiss was the most painful thing I'd felt all day.

CHAPTER TWENTY-ONE

THANE

It took all of my power to walk away from Kaia.

I wanted to crawl into bed with her and hold her —to let her cry it all out and then help her put everything back together.

"Maybe I'm just scared. Maybe it's all too much at once. Maybe I just need to believe."

But right now, she didn't know what she wanted. My sweet Kaia. I needed to think about how I would show her what could be, with us, and with life in Loren Brae if she'd only give me the chance. But in the meantime, she needed space to think. And I respected that. It annoyed the crap out of me that I couldn't do anything, I couldn't help her, I couldn't convince her that, duh, of course her life would be best spent here and she was going to grow a great career and build a good community of people who cared about her.

Voices stopped me, and I paused. I had planned to sneak out the door and go lick my wounds in private, but an idea occurred to me.

Maybe Kaia needed to see that independence didn't also mean being alone.

I walked into the lounge and Sir Buster raced over to growl at me. I pointed a finger at him, and he dropped the act, circling once before flipping on his back. Scooping him up, I scratched his belly as he alternated between growls and grunting noises.

Orla, Finlay, Lachlan, Sophie, Willow, Ramsay, and Agnes were all sitting on couches in the lounge, while Hilda bustled about putting tea together and Archie sat in an armchair by the window tying his flies. He'd once told me that he just enjoyed making them, but I didn't think it hurt that they commanded a high price from the visiting fishermen.

"How is she?" Orla stood and walked over to me. She hesitated for a moment before reaching up to squeeze my arm.

"Bruises are better she said. She's resting now."

"Should I still bring up some nibbles for her and Murdoch?" Hilda asked, stopping where she was preparing a tray.

"I'd give it a moment." I suspected she was up there crying, or had given herself over to exhaustion, but either way it seemed she needed a wee moment to herself. "I'd like to ask all of you for help or maybe just to tell me if you think my idea is right stupid or not." I put Sir Buster back on the floor, and he raced over to Hilda to see if there were any treats from the table for him.

"My favorite pastime." Finlay patted the spot next to him on the couch. "Come to papa. I'll be more than delighted to tell you how dumb you are."

"Och, don't listen to him. He doesn't even know what you're going to say yet." Orla took the cushion that Finlay had just patted, and she leaned casually against him.

I stayed standing, too pent-up to sit. Walking farther into the lounge, I crouched by Orla's dog, Harris, when he thumped his tail at me. He was cuddled on a bed next to Lady Lola, and I dutifully gave her attention as well.

"I'm sure most of you know that Kaia and I are together." Were we though? I wasn't sure anymore. It was all so new. Maybe it was just a house built with matchsticks, ready to tumble at the slightest wind. "Or were."

"Oh no," Willow murmured, and I turned to see the sadness on her face. "What happened?"

I stood and leaned against the windowsill, looking at the group. They all had equal expressions of concern on their faces, and I weighed keeping Kaia's privacy versus opening up to them. I wasn't much for asking advice from others, or talking over my problems, so this didn't come naturally.

But growth was rarely comfortable. I couldn't ask Kaia to trust in others if I didn't do the same.

"I'm not sure. In fact, I don't think she knows either. It seems she feels overwhelmed by it all."

"Perfectly normal after a Kelpie tosses you thirty feet in the air," Archie grumbled, snipping a feather with tiny scissors.

"True enough. But it's more than that. It's the move here. Starting her life over. She was determined to go it on her own. And she's leased space at my forge, now we're working together, and dating. It's become muddled in her mind and she's worried."

"Och, I get that." Willow nodded.

"She's afraid if things go south, she'll be out of a workplace," Orla summarized.

"That's one layer of it. It's also her magick. It's new to her, she's not trusting it yet. And it's her friends. I don't think she's used to having a big group of friends."

"Now that I can fully understand." Orla glanced up at Finlay with a smile as he wrapped an arm around her shoulder. "It takes time to get used to being a part of a group."

"I'm afraid she won't give me, or all of us, that chance. I'm worried she's going to run home before she gives this an honest shot. And I think I have an idea, but I need to see what you guys think and if you'll help me."

"Give it to us," Finlay said, leaning forward, his eyes lighting up.

"Och, there goes his project manager hat." Orla laughed.

"We found an old cottage in the woods on her property. It's run-down, but it used to be an old blacksmith's shop. I'd like to shine it up enough to show her that she has a backup in case she ever needs some space from Blackwood Forge. I also want her to know it wasn't just from me. That all of her friends helped because they want her to stay."

"That's a great idea. I see no issues. Let's go." Finlay moved to stand, and Orla grabbed his arm, stopping him.

"Just give this a second. We need a list of materials required, and we need to know if this is meant to be a surprise. Since it's on her property, she'll know if we're working on it."

"Oh, right." Finlay grimaced.

"I'll keep her here," Hilda said, crossing her arms over her chest. "She'll not be allowed to leave under my watch. I think she needs some mothering, and at least two days in bed, don't you?" Hilda was formidable on a good day, terrifying on any other.

"Och, that's the lass stuck here for a couple of days. All right then, let's see what we can get done," Archie said.

"Oh, and I have the hearthwards. Can we get those delivered and put up all over Loren Brae? I think it might help her to see it."

"On it." Agnes nodded. "I can start there as I'll be no use with any renovations of the cottage."

"Willow and I will go with you," Sophie agreed, then she turned to Lachlan. "Hearthwards or cottage?"

"I can help at the cottage. Just be safe, okay? We've had enough drama today." Lachlan kissed her head.

"I'll bring my dirk. It'll be fine. My hope is the Kelpies are licking their wounds after that whole bridle situation."

"What bridle situation?" Archie barked from where he was bent over packing up his flies.

"Kaia told us she grabbed the bridle of the Kelpie. And when she did he stopped moving completely."

"He who has the bridle controls the Kelpie," Hilda murmured, looking at Archie.

"We'd forgotten," Archie admitted, thumping back in his chair.

"This is the first time I've even seen a bridle," Sophie said. "If it's any consolation, I've never seen one come on land before."

"They're getting stronger," Archie said, ominously, looking toward the window, his bushy brows drawn together in concern.

"We just keep trying," Hilda said, walking over to pat Archie's arm. "We'll get the Order sorted soon enough. Look how far we've come already."

I had more questions I wanted to ask about the Order, but for now I wanted to get working on my plan. I knew the cottage was still open since we'd run straight from it to rescue Audrey. Speaking of which ...

"Can I hitch a ride? My car is still up at Kaia's."

"Aye, lad. Let's grab some tools and maybe supplies if you can remember what was needed," Finlay said.

"Where are the hearthwards?" Agnes asked, coming to my side.

"In my lorry at Kaia's."

"We'll meet you down there. Ladies?" Willow and Sophie left the room with Agnes, and everyone else circled me.

"How bad is the property? What are we dealing with here?" Orla asked.

"Not too bad, but I didn't get to look at it for too long before we got the alert about the Kelpies. It's a rectangle cottage, a few windows that seemed to be in good shape. Wood needs sealing, lick of paint. Shelving, storage, tables. Check the safety of the fireplace."

"Electrics? Plumbing?" Finn asked.

"Didn't get that far. I reckon no, but I can't be certain."

"Let's get on with it then," Archie barked. "Standing here talking about what it may have isn't doing much for anyone."

"Thanks, guys. I know you're all busy, but I think this will mean a lot."

"She's one of ours now." Hilda came over and surprised me with a hug. She smelled of lavender and baked goods and it made me miss my own mum. They'd been on holiday in Spain when I'd gotten back to Loren Brae, but I knew they'd visit soon. They never liked to stay away from their granddaughter for too long. "And so are you."

"I appreciate that. I just hope this plan works."

"It will. It has to. We can't lose Kaia, and judging from your face, you can't either."

I shrugged, and just gave Hilda a quick nod. There wasn't much else for me to say.

It was time to show Kaia that standing on her own didn't have to mean standing alone.

CHAPTER TWENTY-TWO

Kaia

Hilda bullied me for a solid two days and nights and it was Monday morning before she was finally willing to let me go back to my house. I protested but quickly learned that there was no arguing with Hilda. Frankly, I didn't mind staying at the castle for a couple of days. It gave me some time to lick my wounds in peace, as well as time to consider what I wanted for my future. Sophie had retrieved my phone from my house for me, and I'd had a few long conversations with both my parents and Marisa, some more detailed than others.

But their advice was the same.

Stick it out.

Give Thane a chance.

Stay away from the loch.

Ride that man like you stole him. This from Marisa, not my parents, mind you.

The most surprising thing for me had been that they'd all insisted I stay in Loren Brae, even though I told them about the magick, about Audrey, and about the Kelpie attack. Though my parents weren't particularly pleased to hear of the attack, they still wanted me to stay. Even though their worry had escalated. I couldn't quite tell if they wanted me to stay with Thane because he was good for me as a partner or because he could protect me, but either way, their choice was for me to stay. With the caveat of heightening my safety skills.

But none of them saw any red flags with me working with Thane, nor did they think it mattered how I built my career here, so long as I was happy and flourishing. Maybe I was the one who had been too strict on the definition of how the success of my new life needed to unfold.

I was better now, though. My thoughts were a touch clearer, and after an exceptionally long sleep, I'd awoken the first morning to discover that I was in a better space to assess my emotions. I guess the adrenaline rush from being almost killed had basically sent me into a spiral and then a crash into exhaustion, and from what I understood, that was also normal. It was too bad that I'd kicked Thane out in the middle of that, but I still appreciated that he gave me the space.

Even though I missed him. Desperately.

Stop moping about and call the man.

"Oh suddenly you've got relationship advice?"

Murdoch was perched on my shoulder, and I was walking home from the castle, Hilda having washed and dried my clothes. I'd wanted the walk, having lain in bed for two days, and had to stop at the vet on the way home. Murdoch insisted he was fine, but I just wanted to make sure he really was.

My bruises were still gloriously yellow, but much of the pain had faded, and it felt good to stretch my legs a bit. Though my heart skipped a beat when I came to the end of the drive that spilled out in front of Loch Mirren, I straightened my shoulders. There was no way to avoid the loch in this town, nor did I really want to. It was face it or fear it, and I needed to face it.

Also, I really had no choice. The vet's office was directly across from the loch.

It was one of those misty, overcast days, not quite warm, but not too cold either. A light breeze kicked up the surface of the loch, and a few low-hanging clouds shrouded the tips of the rolling green hills in the distance. The vet's office was set in a row of terraced buildings, with a cute wooden sign with paw prints on it.

"No flying around the room or anything crazy like that, okay?" I said to Murdoch on my shoulder.

So long as a cat doesn't chase me, I'll be fine.

I hadn't thought about that.

"Got it. No cats."

"Kaia!" Shona beamed at me as she exited a door just off the little waiting room. "And Murdoch! How are you both?" Shona carried a small basket in her arms.

"Good, thanks." I glanced over to see a woman and a

man with charts in their hands behind the counter and lowered my voice. "I can't thank you enough. What you did made such an incredible difference."

"Glad I could help." Shona leaned in. "Maybe don't mention his wing was broken? They might wonder how fast he healed."

"I thought of that," I said. Looking down at the basket in her arms, I pointed to it.

"Eugene?"

"Aye, and Edith. His mate." Shona lifted the lid just a little, and two grinning hedgehog faces greeted me. They were cuddled together in a little towel.

"They look happy."

"Eugene's pretty chuffed with himself." Shona's grin widened. "Edith is pregnant."

"No way!" I laughed. "You're going to have hedgehog babies?"

"They're going to be terrors. I can't wait."

"Kaia?" The woman behind the desk called my name, and I squeezed Shona's arm and waved goodbye.

"That's me. And this is Murdoch."

"Well, isn't he handsome?" The woman behind the counter had gray-blue eyes, auburn hair pulled back in a low ponytail, and a soft Scottish accent. "Are you already a patient of the practice?"

"No, I'm new here."

"Phew." The woman blew out a breath. "Me too. I'm Faelan. Dr. Fletcher, that is. And today is my first day taking over the practice."

"Ah, welcome."

"Thank you. It's a bit ..." Faelan winced and looked over her shoulder. "He's looking to move on quite quickly, so I'll be taking over patient files on the fly. Och, I'll get it sorted soon enough."

She's magick.

I'm sure my eyes widened at Murdoch's words, but I couldn't do much other than just smile politely at the woman.

Faelan gave Murdoch an odd look.

"Right. I'm sure there are forms for you to fill out somewhere, but I don't know where the intake forms are. The secretary quit on Saturday, and the doctor is leaving as well. I wasn't meant to take over for a few more months but, well, here we are." Faelan pressed her lips together as she held the door open for me. She was a tall woman, almost matching me in height, and wore a lab coat over a pair of jeans and a simple white T-shirt. "Come on back."

I followed Dr. Fletcher into a room and lifted Murdoch off my shoulder to put him on the exam table.

This is dumb.

I smiled as Murdoch cocked his head and made the low knocking sound of his.

"He's not too pleased with me for bringing him in."

"What seems to be the problem?" Dr. Fletcher leaned forward.

"I was worried he'd strained his wing. He was holding it a bit odd for a while. And just an overall health check."

"Sounds good. Is he friendly?" Dr. Fletcher put on a pair of gloves.

"He is."

Sometimes.

Murdoch slanted me a look.

"There now. Who's just the most handsome lad?" Dr. Fletcher ran a gentle hand over Murdoch's sleek black feathers, her fingers pausing at the delicate joint of his wing. "Nothing broken," she murmured, tilting her head as Murdoch let out a soft, disgruntled croak. With practiced ease, she checked his beak, looked into his eyes, and parted his feathers. She inspected each foot before returning to gently flex both wings.

"His weight seems good. Feathers are healthy, clear eyes, no cracks in the beak. No parasites or molting with his feathers. He didn't seem to exhibit any signs of pain when I moved his wings. All in all, I'd say he's in good shape."

"Oh, good. That's all I needed to hear. I assumed he was fine, but best to check."

"Not a problem at all."

"Dr. Fletcher, I think it would be best if I left this afternoon." A man, presumably the other vet, stuck his head in the exam room and Faelan's eyes rounded.

"I'm in with a client. I'll speak to you shortly." Her words were clipped, and a line of irritation appeared between her eyes. "Sorry for that."

"No problem. What do I owe you?"

"Och, nothing." She waved it away. "Obviously it's chaos in here right now. I wouldn't even know how to charge you if I tried."

"Thanks for still seeing us. Good luck with the transition."

Faelan walked me to the waiting room, and on impulse, I stopped at the desk. Picking up a pen, I wrote down my phone number.

"I'm fairly new to town too. If you need a friend, feel free to give me a call."

"Oh." Faelan closed her eyes briefly and then gave me a small smile. "I suspect I will. Thank you."

"Good luck." With that, I left, my thoughts whirling.

"Do you really think she's magick?"

Aye, lass.

Murdoch moved to sit at my shoulder. Maybe he still felt some residual pain because usually he'd be flying over my head. Or maybe he just wanted to stay close to me after what happened on Saturday. I couldn't help but wonder if that was what had sent the vet scrambling to leave town. Their office window looked directly out onto the loch and they would have been privy to everything that had happened with the Kelpies.

"Hopefully she reaches out then."

Does that mean you're staying?

I paused as I turned up the main street of Loren Brae, the colorful shops clustering together, the sun just starting to break through the clouds.

"I think I am. It feels right."

It is right. I'd miss you.

"Oh, Murdoch." I hadn't even thought of that. My heart dropped. If I went home, he'd have to stay behind. "I'd miss you too, buddy."

Murdoch bumped his head against my cheek, and I reached up to give him a scratch as I walked down the street.

A small plaque on a doorframe caught my eye and I stopped.

My triskele. The one I'd made with Thane. It was on the frame of the door for a small pottery shop. I whirled. There was also one on the door to the small supermarket. Hurrying up Main Street, I gaped as triskele after triskele greeted me.

Thane had put them all up. He'd delivered them all to the town, and hopefully with it, another level of protection. Warmth spilled through me.

He was a good man. A great man, even. My parents and Marisa were right. I couldn't live in the past anymore. Rushing now, I turned down the lane toward my home.

My very own home.

Maybe my crisis of confidence would turn out to be less of a crisis and more of a small bump in the road. I wasn't sure yet. I needed to see Thane. We needed to have a serious conversation.

Thane walked around the corner of my cottage as though I'd summoned him.

"Whoa. Can I make people appear now?" I asked, my mouth dropping open.

Not likely.

Murdoch made a sound that was suspiciously like a laugh.

Thane walked forward until he was close, but not

touching. My breath caught in my throat, and the corners of my eyes burned. It hurt to look at him. This gorgeous steadfast somewhat grumpy man that I'd casually pushed away, once again. And yet, here he was.

Here he was. The man who told me he loved me and let me send him away. *The man I've fallen for too.*

Did his presence mean he forgave my callousness?

"Hey," Thane said, his hands in his pockets. He wore a rugged plaid shirt, rolled up to the elbows, and there was a black smudge of dirt on his forearm.

"Hey," I said.

We stared at each other for a moment until Murdoch made a croaking sound and took off from my shoulder, swooping over the roof of the cottage.

"What are you doing here?" I asked.

"I have something for you."

My heartbeat sped up. "You do?"

"Aye, lass. I do. Can I show you?"

"But ... don't you want to talk about the other day? About all this?" I flung my hands out beside me, encompassing the cottage.

"Do you?" Thane asked.

"Of course I do." I almost stomped a foot in frustration.

"Do you want to do that now?" Thane continued, furrowing his brow.

"I mean, shouldn't we? You can't just ... I can't ..." I waved a hand in a circle in the air. "Basically break up with you after I almost died and then you're just like here, chilling out and fine with everything."

"Why not?" Thane rocked back on his heels.

"Because you should be mad at me."

"Do you want me to be mad at you?"

"I'm finding you a little annoying right now." I glared at him and crossed my arms over my chest.

"Kaia. I'm not going anywhere. We have all the time in the world to talk. But first, just come with me."

"Why are you even here? How did you know I was going to be home? Shouldn't you be at work? It's Monday."

Thane sighed, and then he reached out and tugged my arm, forcing me to uncross them, and took my hand.

"Come with me, my wee tetchy one."

"I'm not tetchy."

"You seem a bit tetchy. I know one way to relieve that."

Desire flashed through me at his words. I swallowed thickly as he tugged me around the side of the cottage.

"Oh, what is that?" I looked up at the large three-sided box on a thick wood pole in the backyard.

"It's a bird box for Murdoch. He likely won't sleep in a traditional bird house, but this gives him some shelter when it's raining or cold."

"Oh, look, you painted his name on it," I cooed, walking over and admiring the large bird shelter. "This is really sweet. Thank you so much, Thane."

Murdoch swooped down from the trees and landed in the box, tilting his head down at us.

"What do you think?" Thane asked him.

I like it. Will be nice in winter.

"He says he likes it. It will be good for winter," I told Thane. I no longer felt shy about showing my magick to him. After Saturday, we were beyond that.

"Good. I'm glad. Enjoy it, mate." Thane waved up to him and pulled me along the stepping stones toward the line of trees at the back.

"Are you taking me to see the cottage again?" I asked. "Don't you think we should talk first?"

"Wheesht, Kaia."

I clamped my lips closed, annoyed, but also just ridiculously happy to see him. I wanted to tell him that I'd seen the hearthwards. That I knew I'd been an idiot and scared and in shock when I'd shoved him away. And that maybe, just maybe, this really was all going to work out.

Instead, I found myself gaping at a picture-perfect cottage in the woods.

"What?" I gasped, holding my hands up to my chest. The stones of the cottage had been cleaned of their moss and mold, the trim and front door painted a pretty Kelly green, and the windows shone without a drop of dirt to their panes. I stepped forward, my mouth hanging open, to stare at the door. Not only had Thane hung a hearthward, but there was a large iron Celtic unicorn affixed to the door.

"Did you make this?" I ran a finger over the clean lines of the unicorn and turned to look at him over my shoulder.

"Aye, stayed up through the night. I wanted you to remember the moment we had."

"As if I could ever forget it," I whispered, remembering the day the unicorn had visited us.

"Go on, go inside." Something moved behind his eyes, and I realized he was nervous.

Nudging the door open, I stepped inside, and tears instantly sprang to my eyes.

A fire burned merrily in the newly cleaned and painted fireplace, the shelves were dusted and shiny with a fresh coat of paint, and someone had done some serious decorating in the place. I turned, in a slow circle, tears streaming down my cheeks, as I realized what had been done here. He'd transformed it not only into a small-scale metalsmith's shop, but also a place for me to make my jewelry. One entire side of the cottage was lined with tiny boxes and jars and all of my jewelry tools. I walked over to the table, running my hand across the smooth surface, and looked out the window through the woods. It was a perfect spot to dream and design jewelry.

Turning, I just shook my head at him in wonder.

"How?"

"Everyone helped. Orla, Sophie, Lachlan ... all of them." Thane tucked his hands back in his pockets and cleared his throat. "We got it connected to the electrics, but plumbing is going to take a wee while to get sorted."

"But why? Why did you do all this?" I needed to hear it, even though I had an idea what he was going to say.

"Because being strong and independent doesn't mean pushing everyone away—it means knowing who to let in. And we all want in, Kaia. Let us, let me, walk this journey with you."

My cheeks felt hot, and I splashed tears away with the backs of my hands as I crossed to him. Reaching up, I pulled his head down to mine and kissed him, pouring all of my soul and love into it. By the time I broke the kiss, Thane's arms were wrapped around me, and I was back where I loved it most, in his arms.

"I'm sorry," I said, meeting his eyes. "I mean it. I was just ... confused, out of sorts, in shock. I don't know. It all hit me so hard. Thank you for not giving up on me. Thank you for this incredible gift."

Thane's face relaxed into a smile.

"I wanted you to have something that was yours. Just in case you ever felt the need to stop working at the forge, you'd always have this. And everyone loved helping. You've only been here a short time, Kaia, but you've made a big impression. You've made friends here who want you to stay. Please don't go. Please don't leave me."

I reached up to cup his face with a hand.

"I wouldn't. I can't. My heart is here, you see. With you."

Thane closed his eyes briefly and exhaled a shaky breath.

"I love you, Kaia. I know it may seem too soon, or whatever, and we have all the time in the world to figure this out, but that's what I am asking you. To give this time." Thane drew back and gestured to a box sitting on the table that I'd missed. "For you."

"What is this?" I asked, shaking my head. "Thane, you've already done so much. You don't need to get me gifts."

"I ordered this the day after we met."

I tilted my head at him in a silent question, and then quickly lifted the lid of the box.

I gasped.

"It's a clock." Gently, I pulled the clock out and set it back on the table. Crouching, I leaned in to look at the insides. It was a kinetic clock, similar to the one in the National Museum in Edinburgh, but instead of the monkeys and demons racing around inside the clock, there were two small unicorn statues.

"I wanted something to remember you, I guess. And now I'm giving it to you and asking if you'll give us time." *I have never met a better man.* How could he have done that? If anything, more than words, it was so incredibly validating. *How can I not love him?*

I wound the clock and moved the clock hands until they met at twelve. A small trill of bells sounded and the unicorns began to dance around each other. Looking up, I beamed at Thane.

"This is perfect. I can't help feeling like we were meant to be, all along. I love it, and all of this that you've done for me. And I love you, Thane. The answer is yes, I've got all the time in the world for you."

EPILOGUE

Kaia

The gold ring lay in my palm, the metal still warm, gleaming in the soft candlelight that flickered across my worktable. It had been a while since I'd worked with gold—my focus had mostly been on the distillery project, larger pieces that required brute strength and an occasional muttered curse when something didn't bend the way I wanted it to. But this? This was delicate. Precise. It demanded something different from me.

Much like the people I'd come to know here.

Orla had commissioned the ring for Finn, a man I was only just starting to get a sense of, though what I knew, I liked. Steady, solid, the kind of man who anchored people rather than set them adrift. A rarity in my experience. Orla had been very precise about the design. She wanted a lightly etched Celtic chain to mirror the one he'd given to her. And she was so excited to have it made for him, which had brought a smile to my lips while I was crafting it. The careful etching, the lines wrapping around each other in a quiet promise. Strength and fluidity. Balance.

I exhaled and turned the ring over between my fingers. There was something about finishing a piece that always left me with a strange mix of emotions. Satisfaction, pride, and—if I was being honest—a tiny, gnawing sense of restlessness. As if my hands were never quite ready to be done.

A knock sounded at my door and Thane poked his head in the door.

"Ready for dinner?" He glanced down at the ring in my hand. "Aww, you shouldn't have."

"I didn't." I laughed when he held a hand to his heart. "It's for Orla to give Finn."

"It's good." Thane held it up to the light. "He's a bit of a pretty boy, so I think he'll like this."

"I hope so." I slid the ring into the pouch and blew out the candle, checking to make sure everything else in my adorable shop was turned off. I loved this spot and worked here most afternoons if I wasn't in the forge. It gave Thane and me a level of separateness that was important for our relationship and offered me a quiet space to work.

"Ready for the baby shower?" I asked, securing the ring in my safe. I'd give it to Orla later this week when she came by to pick it up, not at a chaotic Sunday "family" dinner that Lia had insisted become a tradition. She was used to a big, busy family, cluttered around the kitchen table, and since her family was still in the States, she was instilling this tradition here in Loren Brae.

It had only been a few weeks since the Kelpie attack, but Thane and I had dutifully attended the Sunday meals, and I had to say, I loved them. It was nice to have a routine, a community, and slowly I was beginning to understand that it was possible to have a healthy relationship with someone who respected you.

"I have no idea how to answer that." Thane took the key from me and locked up, then hooked an arm through mine. "Not only have I never attended a baby shower before, but I've also never done so for a hedgehog."

Today's Sunday dinner at the castle had a theme—a celebration for the hedgehog parents to be. When I'd called Sophie, concerned over what to bring, she'd laughed.

"Yes, we all realize this is absurd. And yes, we're still having a party. Bring nothing but yourselves."

Still, I'd looked online and had discovered that a heating pad was often enjoyed by hedgies, and I'd ordered one with a cute floral print. It might be silly, but at least we weren't going empty-handed.

"Audrey's bummed she's missing it," Thane said, as we drove to the castle. She was on a long weekend away with three of her new school besties and their moms. We couldn't have been more pleased that she was making new friends and fitting in better, and it made my heart happy to know that she was doing well.

WILD SCOTTISH GOLD

Though we could have walked to the castle, everyone was still on edge from the attack, and many of us were keeping our distance from the loch if we could. My physical bruises had healed, but I still had a few hurdles to overcome with the emotional ones. For two weeks after the attack, I awoke in panic and once Thane had learned this was happening, we'd slept next to each other ever since. We were falling into a routine, and I had a few things at his house to make life easier, and he had a few things at mine. I knew at some point we'd have to decide on a living arrangement, if that was the direction we were headed, but for now I was doing exactly what he'd requested of me—giving us time.

But it was good.

We were good. Great, even. I had discovered that I actually enjoyed working alongside him and after the initial grief the men at the shop had given us, they'd accepted our relationship with the occasional banter about us. But it was different this time than before. How could I not have seen that an open, consensual, healthy relationship with shared career interests could actually thrive? I'd been comparing an entirely different situation, one where lies and a power imbalance dominated, to one where I was respected and affirmed. *Loved.* And my parents loved him. They'd only met Thane via Zoom, but they thought he was amazing.

We parked in the lot and rounded the castle to Grasshopper, Lia's restaurant. I hadn't had a meal there yet, but I'd heard amazing things. *I might even get to see her loveable broonie.* Thane took my hand as we walked toward the castle, and contentment bubbled up inside me. The castle looked lovely, all stately and lit with beautiful lights, and the walkway to the restaurant was lined by flaming torches. I was sure I'd never get over how atmospheric it was here.

Two Gnome statues flanked the door to Grasshopper. Both were dressed in black and white, a butler and a server's outfit, to be exact.

"Are those ..." I trailed off, tilting my head.

I jumped as the gnomes came to life.

"The famous Gnora and Gnorman? Why yes, it is us." Gnora patted her hair and blew Thane a kiss. "Hey, cutie."

"This one's mine," I said, pulling Thane closer to me, feeling his low rumble of laughter against my arm.

"Oh honey, I'm not trying to steal your man. Though I could, if I wanted." Gnora gave me a look that suggested she'd sized me up and found me wanting. "I'm just keeping my man on his toes."

"You drive me crazy," Gnorman growled. "But I love ye, lass."

Gnora squealed as Gnorman chased her into the bushes, and then all we could hear was giggles as the leaves of the bush shook.

"I believe we should give them some privacy." Thane's voice was warm with laughter, and he pulled me inside. Dinner would be in the restaurant, but everyone was gathered in the lounge area, where presents were piled high on a table. Munroe was behind that, mixing drinks, and Shona was on a love seat with a basket on her lap, a man I hadn't met yet at her side.

"Let's go say hello."

A blur of motion stopped me in my tracks and then I gaped down at where I was now wearing a beaded necklace with "It's a boy!" on the pendant. Thane had a similar necklace, but his was pink.

"What the hell was that?" Thane blinked at me.

"I believe that was Brice, Lia's familiar."

"And what, exactly, is Brice?"

"A broonie? A kitchen elf?" Even as I said it, I had to force a hysterical giggle down. I was getting more used to magick, but there were still moments that just stopped me in my tracks.

"Kaia!" Shona waved me over. "Come meet Owen."

"Hi, Owen," I said, bending to give Shona a quick hug and then shake his hand. "I'm Kaia, and this is my partner, Thane." Boyfriend sounded so … not as important as what we were. Thane's eyes softened around the edges when he heard how I'd addressed him. I guess we all needed reassurance at times, even my big gruff man.

"Pleased to meet you both." Owen smiled. He was an attractive man and seemed to just radiate confidence.

"Oh, another American." I smiled at him. "Quite a few of us have landed in Loren Brae."

"It's hard not to love it here—"

"Oh my God," Shona squawked, looking down at the basket she held.

"What's wrong?" Owen wrapped his arm around her shoulder.

"I think Edith's in labor."

I peered into the basket to see one of the hedgies panting and making soft squeaks.

"Is it time? It can't be time yet." Owen sprung up and began to pace.

"Should we get the vet?" I asked. Faelan had reached out to me, and I had her number, but we hadn't managed to connect yet as she was busy trying to put her new vet practice to rights. "I have her personal number."

"Yes, please, can you call her? I'm worried. I have no idea what to do."

Pulling out my phone, I called Faelan who answered on the first ring.

"Hey Kaia, how are you?"

"Hey Faelan, I'm at Grasshopper, the restaurant at the castle? We could use some help with a pregnant hedgie."

"I'm already here. Lia had invited me to dinner."

"Perfect." Crouching at Shona's feet, I patted her arm. "Faelan's here. She was coming to dinner anyway."

"Let me through," Archie barked, pushing through the people who had gathered. He bowed over the basket, and then stood, his face wreathed in concern. He wrung his hands and began to pace. "She'll be fine. She's fine. It's all going to be fine."

Was he nervous? Hilda pushed through the crowd and threaded her arm through his. "Come along, Archie. There's not much we can do for her. We just have to wait."

"Right. Of course." Archie bobbed his head and

Hilda drew him away, making soft reassuring noises and patting his back.

Aww, the old softie.

"Where's my patient?" a voice sounded, and I turned to see Faelan, her hair braided back and a medical bag in her hand. She was directed forward and she crouched by the basket.

"Hi, Shona, good to see these two again." Faelan peered in the basket. "Ah yes, she's well on her way."

"I think so. I hadn't realized she was panting until just now."

"If possible, maybe we could go to a quiet space? It might stress her to have this many people about."

Lachlan gave a soft whistle. "Everyone into the restaurant. We're clearing out the lounge. This baby shower is about to turn into a Meet the Babies instead."

"Will this take a while?" I asked Faelan as I stood and took Thane's hand.

"Could. Sometimes it happens within an hour, depending on how long she's been in labor. Sometimes much longer. We'll just see how it goes."

Lia ushered us into the restaurant. It was such a cool space inside with walls of greenery on both sides of the large hall, and candles tucked in crevices in the stone walls. Thick wood beams crisscrossed the ceilings and large windows looked out over the well-lit gardens.

"It's family-style tonight. Italian, naturally." Lia waved us over to where she'd set up a long table on one end of the restaurant. "Smoked oat and crowdie ravioli with brown butter and hazelnuts, brassica and truffle pappardelle, neeps and gorgonzola hot honey pizza, and a wild mushroom risotto."

"This looks incredible," I said. We all grabbed plates and piled them high with delicious food, while Lia went around and put carafes of wine on the tables. In moments, we were all seated, chattering about this and that, and I relaxed back into my chair, turning to Thane.

"This is good," I said.

"Delicious," Thane agreed, taking a bite of the pizza.

"No," I said, elbowing his arm and pointing around the room. All my new friends were here, along with their own loved ones. They were becoming family, and the shared secret of magick was an invisible thread that bound us all together. I missed Marisa and especially my parents, but I felt like I was home. Like I belonged here. *I still wonder if my great-aunt had known and that was why I was the benefactor of her will.* And with Thane by my side, I felt so ... complete. *Thankful.* "This. Us. All of it is good. Right."

"Aren't you glad you stayed?" Thane leaned over and brushed a soft kiss over my lips. "I am."

"I—"

"It's a boy!" Owen rushed inside, his hands in the air. "And a girl."

We all jumped up and clapped. A voice came from the lounge and Owen leaned back.

"Never mind. I'm completely wrong." Owen ducked his head back into the lounge and then came back into the restaurant, his hands in the air again. "Four! Four babies. Sex undetermined because it takes a while to show, I'm told."

"I wonder how he decided who was a girl." I laughed as we all clapped.

"Probably thought one looked cuter than another," Thane said.

"We're parents!" Shona came into the room, and Owen lifted her to twirl her around in a circle. "Mum's doing well. Everyone's happy and healthy."

Clyde burst from the wall, bellowing, and we all shrieked and laughed as he did a victory lap of the room before disappearing back through the wall. Lia glared from the back, her hand at her chest. She notoriously struggled with Clyde's sudden appearances.

Tears sprung to my eyes. Silly, really, I knew—to be crying over a hedgehog birth. But nevertheless, I was. It was just so sweet, and when I looked around, I could see that I wasn't the only one who was touched by the announcement of the new arrivals.

"If this gets you going, just wait until Murdoch has babies."

I gaped at Thane, gripping his arm.

"I'd never even thought about that. Oh my! We could have baby ravens in our future. You're going to need to build a bigger bird box."

"Don't worry, Kaia. I'll take care of it."

He would, too. His steadfast confidence was just one of the many things I loved about him. Leaning in, I kissed his cheek.

"You're going to be the best raven dad ever."

"Do you think ravens paint their talons? Inquiring minds want to know." Thane grinned when I burst out laughing.

"Oh, I'm sure of it. Murdoch is going to look fabulous in pink sparkles."

Can't get enough of Kaia & Thane? Enjoy a special bonus scene where Thane takes Kaia gold panning for a very special treasure. Join my mailing list and download the free bonus scene here: triciaomalley.com/free

Fancy a wee drink and some grub in your favorite Loren Brae pub? The Tipsy Thistle has its own line of merchandise! Shop here: triciaomalley.myshopify.com

WILD SCOTTISH CHARM

She's hiding something. He sees too much. And in Loren Brae, secrets have a way of rising to the surface.
Order Wild Scottish Charm today!

Faelan

I was no stranger to new towns.

I had unpacked my things in more villages than I cared to count—most of them quaint, slightly odd, and filled with locals who squinted at outsiders as if deciding whether they were worthy of their trust. But Loren Brae was different. Already, I'd been welcomed, and was on my way to making a few new friends. Which made me wonder just what, exactly, was going on in this town?

For one, the last vet had fled.

People in town didn't talk about it directly, but I'd overheard enough murmurs while ordering a blackberry scone from the bakery that morning to piece together the general story. Dr. McAllister barely handed the keys off to me before he'd left. Not just the practice, but the town as well. No warning, no goodbyes. And the way people talked about it—with uneasy glances and hushed voices—told me it wasn't just because of an overdue tax bill or a scandalous affair.

Something strange had sent him running.

Which was why I was standing outside the empty stone clinic, hands on my hips, wondering what exactly I had gotten myself into.

"All right, then," I muttered, fishing the keys from my pocket and pushing the door open.

The scent of old wood, herbs, and just a whisper of something sharp and metallic greeted me. The place was cozy enough—a reception desk covered in stray dog hairs, a small exam room with an oak table, and a back room filled with supplies.

And curled up on the counter, watching me with unsettling intelligence, was a fox.

I frowned. "I don't remember ordering a welcoming committee."

The fox's ears twitched, its golden eyes locking on to mine. Then, with an almost lazy motion, it lifted its head and let out a soft chuff—less a warning, more a cry for help.

A chill ran up my spine. It wasn't the first time a creature had looked at me like that.

I set my bag down and stepped closer. "You're hurt, aren't you?"

The fox shifted slightly, and that's when I saw it—its front leg, tucked awkwardly beneath its body. I didn't need an exam to tell it was broken.

But I could mend it.

I glanced at the front window, making sure no one was watching from the street. I wasn't exactly hiding what I could do, but I also didn't need an audience. Being a newcomer in a small town meant all eyes were on you, and I'd learned long ago to try and play the game.

I crouched down, reaching out a hand, slow and steady. "I won't hurt you."

The fox didn't move at first. Then, as if sensing the truth in my words, it exhaled—a small, weary sigh—and let me touch its injured leg.

I brushed my fingers over the break, inhaling deeply. The magick unfurled beneath my fingertips, warm and soft, a golden thread through the air.

Bones whispered their alignment, sinew stitched itself back together, and beneath it all, the fox's heartbeat slowed, its pain easing. I exhaled, and the world settled.

The fox stretched its leg, testing the weight. Then, just to be dramatic, it hopped onto the reception desk and flopped down, tail flicking over the paperwork like it owned the place.

I winced. "Sure, go ahead, make yourself at home."

The fox yawned, utterly unbothered, and I just shook my head as I found a bowl to fill with water and slid it in front of him on the desk. After he drank, he lifted his head and met my eyes.

Understanding passed between us.

I see you, Faelan.
Loren Brae wasn't the only one with secrets.

Wild Scottish Charm
Book 8 in the Enchanted Highlands series

AFTERWORD

I always love returning to Loren Brae. I can visualize the town so clearly in my head, and my characters have started to become like friends to me. It's a joy to continue their stories, and I am so grateful that you all have fallen in love with this world that I've created. Gold was especially fun to write, because I always go to visit the clock at the National Museum of Scotland when I'm home in Edinburgh, and it was the perfect place for a meet cute. And that wee pub in the first chapter? You'll find it on Victoria Street just up from the museum complete with the "No Bairns, Dugs Welcome" sign on the window.

A huge *"thank you"* to the Scotsman for nursing me through the pneumonia (that he gave me!) while scrambling to meet my deadline on this. Love you, germs and all!

Thank you to my lovely editors for shining the book up, and as always, to the best readers in the world. You bring me sparkles on even the rainiest of days!

ALSO BY TRICIA O'MALLEY

THE ISLE OF DESTINY SERIES

Stone Song

Sword Song

Spear Song

Sphere Song

A completed series in Kindle Unlimited.

Available in audio, e-book & paperback!

"Love this series. I will read this multiple times. Keeps you on the edge of your seat. It has action, excitement and romance all in one series."

- Amazon Review

THE ENCHANTED HIGHLANDS

Wild Scottish Knight

Wild Scottish Love

A Kilt for Christmas

Wild Scottish Rose

Wild Scottish Beauty

Wild Scottish Fortune

Wild Scottish Gold

Wild Scottish Charm

"I love everything Tricia O'Malley has ever written and Wild Scottish Knight is no exception. The new setting for this magical journey is Scotland, the home of her new husband and soulmate. Tricia's love for her husband's country shows in every word she writes. I have always wanted to visit Scotland but have never had the time and money. Having read Wild Scottish Knight I feel I have begun to to experience Scotland in a way few see it."

-Amazon Review

Available in audio, e-book, hardback, paperback and Kindle Unlimited.

THE WILDSONG SERIES

Song of the Fae

Melody of Flame

Chorus of Ashes

Lyric of Wind

"The magic of Fae is so believable. I read these books in one sitting and can't wait for the next one. These are books you will reread many times."

- Amazon Review

A completed series in Kindle Unlimited.

Available in audio, e-book & paperback!

THE SIREN ISLAND SERIES

Good Girl

Up to No Good

A Good Chance

Good Moon Rising

Too Good to Be True

A Good Soul

In Good Time

A completed series in Kindle Unlimited.
Available in audio, e-book & paperback!

"Love her books and was excited for a totally new and different one! Once again, she did NOT disappoint! Magical in multiple ways and on multiple levels. Her writing style, while similar to that of Nora Roberts, kicks it up a notch!! I want to visit that island, stay in the B&B and meet the gals who run it! The characters are THAT real!!!" - Amazon Review

THE ALTHEA ROSE SERIES

One Tequila

Tequila for Two

Tequila Will Kill Ya (Novella)

Three Tequilas

Tequila Shots & Valentine Knots (Novella)

Tequila Four

A Fifth of Tequila

A Sixer of Tequila

Seven Deadly Tequilas

Eight Ways to Tequila

Tequila for Christmas (Novella)

"Not my usual genre but couldn't resist the Florida Keys setting. I was hooked from the first page. A fun read with just the right amount of crazy! Will definitely follow this series."- Amazon Review

A completed series in Kindle Unlimited.

Available in audio, e-book & paperback!

THE MYSTIC COVE SERIES

Wild Irish Heart
Wild Irish Eyes
Wild Irish Soul
Wild Irish Rebel
Wild Irish Roots: Margaret & Sean
Wild Irish Witch
Wild Irish Grace
Wild Irish Dreamer
Wild Irish Christmas (Novella)
Wild Irish Sage
Wild Irish Renegade
Wild Irish Moon

"I have read thousands of books and a fair percentage have been romances. Until I read Wild Irish Heart, I never had a book actually make me believe in love."- Amazon Review

A completed series in Kindle Unlimited.
Available in audio, e-book & paperback!

STAND ALONE NOVELS

Love's a Witch

She's got runaway magic. He's got a town to protect. Too bad fate has other plans.

Highland Hearts Holiday Bookshop

As Christmas looms, and lonely hearts beg for love, I'm tossed into the world of magic and romance, aided by a meddling book club who seems more interested in romance than reading.

Ms. Bitch

"Ms. Bitch is sunshine in a book! An uplifting story of fighting your way through heartbreak and making your own version of happily-ever-after."

~Ann Charles, USA Today Bestselling Author

Starting Over Scottish

Grumpy. Meet Sunshine.

She's American. He's Scottish. She's looking for a fresh start. He's returning to rediscover his roots.

One Way Ticket

A funny and captivating beach read where booking a one-way ticket to paradise means starting over, letting go, and taking a chance on love...one more time

10 out of 10 - The BookLife Prize

CONTACT ME

I hope my books have added a little magick into your life. If you have a moment to add some to my day, you can help by telling your friends and leaving a review. Word-of-mouth is the most powerful way to share my stories. Thank you.

Love books? What about fun giveaways? Nope? Okay, can I entice you with underwater photos and cute dogs? Let's stay friends, receive my emails and contact me by signing up at my website

www.triciaomalley.com

Or find me on Facebook and Instagram.
@triciaomalleyauthor

Printed in Dunstable, United Kingdom